I0761896

the perfect alibi

(a jessie hunt psychological suspense—book 8)

blake pierce

Blake Pierce

Blake Pierce is the USA Today bestselling author of the RILEY PAGE mystery series, which includes seventeen books. Blake Pierce is also the author of the MACKENZIE WHITE mystery series, comprising fourteen books; of the AVERY BLACK mystery series, comprising six books; of the KERI LOCKE mystery series, comprising five books; of the MAKING OF RILEY PAIGE mystery series, comprising six books; of the KATE WISE mystery series, comprising seven books; of the CHLOE FINE psychological suspense mystery, comprising six books; of the JESSE HUNT psychological suspense thriller series, comprising eight books (and counting); of the AU PAIR psychological suspense thriller series, comprising three books; of the ZOE PRIME mystery series, comprising four books (and counting); of the new ADELE SHARP mystery series; and of the new EUROPEAN VOYAGE cozy mystery series.

An avid reader and lifelong fan of the mystery and thriller genres, Blake loves to hear from you, so please feel free to visit www.blakepierceauthor.com to learn more and stay in touch.

ISBN: 978-1-0943-8997-4

BOOKS BY BLAKE PIERCE

EUROPEAN VOYAGE COZY MYSTERY SERIES
MURDER (AND BAKLAVA) (Book #1)
DEATH (AND APPLE STRUDEL) (Book #2)
CRIME (AND LAGER) (Book #3)

ADELE SHARP MYSTERY SERIES
LEFT TO DIE (Book #1)
LEFT TO RUN (Book #2)
LEFT TO HIDE (Book #3)
LEFT TO KILL (Book #4)
LEFT TO MURDER (Book #5)
LEFT TO ENVY (Book #6)
LEFT TO LAPSE (Book #7)

THE AU PAIR SERIES
ALMOST GONE (Book#1)
ALMOST LOST (Book #2)
ALMOST DEAD (Book #3)

ZOE PRIME MYSTERY SERIES
FACE OF DEATH (Book#1)
FACE OF MURDER (Book #2)
FACE OF FEAR (Book #3)
FACE OF MADNESS (Book #4)
FACE OF FURY (Book #5)
FACE OF DARKNESS (Book #6)

A JESSIE HUNT PSYCHOLOGICAL SUSPENSE SERIES
THE PERFECT WIFE (Book #1)
THE PERFECT BLOCK (Book #2)
THE PERFECT HOUSE (Book #3)
THE PERFECT SMILE (Book #4)
THE PERFECT LIE (Book #5)
THE PERFECT LOOK (Book #6)
THE PERFECT AFFAIR (Book #7)
THE PERFECT ALIBI (Book #8)

THE PERFECT NEIGHBOR (Book #9)

CHLOE FINE PSYCHOLOGICAL SUSPENSE SERIES

NEXT DOOR (Book #1)
A NEIGHBOR'S LIE (Book #2)
CUL DE SAC (Book #3)
SILENT NEIGHBOR (Book #4)
HOMECOMING (Book #5)
TINTED WINDOWS (Book #6)

KATE WISE MYSTERY SERIES

IF SHE KNEW (Book #1)
IF SHE SAW (Book #2)
IF SHE RAN (Book #3)
IF SHE HID (Book #4)
IF SHE FLED (Book #5)
IF SHE FEARED (Book #6)
IF SHE HEARD (Book #7)

THE MAKING OF RILEY PAIGE SERIES

WATCHING (Book #1)
WAITING (Book #2)
LURING (Book #3)
TAKING (Book #4)
STALKING (Book #5)
KILLING (Book #6)

RILEY PAIGE MYSTERY SERIES

ONCE GONE (Book #1)
ONCE TAKEN (Book #2)
ONCE CRAVED (Book #3)
ONCE LURED (Book #4)
ONCE HUNTED (Book #5)
ONCE PINED (Book #6)
ONCE FORSAKEN (Book #7)
ONCE COLD (Book #8)
ONCE STALKED (Book #9)
ONCE LOST (Book #10)
ONCE BURIED (Book #11)
ONCE BOUND (Book #12)
ONCE TRAPPED (Book #13)

ONCE DORMANT (Book #14)
ONCE SHUNNED (Book #15)
ONCE MISSED (Book #16)
ONCE CHOSEN (Book #17)

MACKENZIE WHITE MYSTERY SERIES
BEFORE HE KILLS (Book #1)
BEFORE HE SEES (Book #2)
BEFORE HE COVETS (Book #3)
BEFORE HE TAKES (Book #4)
BEFORE HE NEEDS (Book #5)
BEFORE HE FEELS (Book #6)
BEFORE HE SINS (Book #7)
BEFORE HE HUNTS (Book #8)
BEFORE HE PREYS (Book #9)
BEFORE HE LONGS (Book #10)
BEFORE HE LAPSES (Book #11)
BEFORE HE ENVIES (Book #12)
BEFORE HE STALKS (Book #13)
BEFORE HE HARMS (Book #14)

AVERY BLACK MYSTERY SERIES
CAUSE TO KILL (Book #1)
CAUSE TO RUN (Book #2)
CAUSE TO HIDE (Book #3)
CAUSE TO FEAR (Book #4)
CAUSE TO SAVE (Book #5)
CAUSE TO DREAD (Book #6)

KERI LOCKE MYSTERY SERIES
A TRACE OF DEATH (Book #1)
A TRACE OF MUDER (Book #2)
A TRACE OF VICE (Book #3)
A TRACE OF CRIME (Book #4)
A TRACE OF HOPE (Book #5)

CHAPTER ONE

Caroline Gidley, crouched in a tight ball, used her inner thighs to hug herself for warmth. Even though it was late spring, it got chilly at night, especially under her circumstances.

It was crazy that she could even think of them as merely "circumstances." But after four days tied up in a dog crate, wearing only her bra and panties, with just a thin blanket to cover her, this had somehow become her new normal.

It had started so innocuously. She'd been walking to her car after leaving work when a man asked for directions to the freeway. They were in a busy public parking lot and he was so unassuming and hesitant when he approached that her initial wariness faded quickly. She started to answer, turning and pointing back east.

Before she even realized it was happening, he was on her, placing a thick cloth over her mouth and nose. As she lost consciousness, she saw him pop the trunk of the car next to hers. She had one final thought as he shoved her in and slammed the trunk door closed.

He parked right next to me. He planned this.

When she woke up, she was in the crate, in just her underclothes, with her hands bound together in front of her by tight, thin bungee cord. She had looked around her surroundings and quickly determined that she was being held in some kind of dilapidated building. Loose wires hung from the ceiling and some windows were broken. There was no interior lighting and the fading sunlight suggested that it had been several hours since she was taken.

Almost on cue, the man had walked in through a thick metal door. Her heart began to thump almost audibly. She could smell her own fear. She tried to set that aside and focus on her abductor.

As he got closer, she'd noticed several things that she'd missed in that first, brief encounter. He was clearly wearing a wig. His thick, dark hair reminded Caroline of a 1980s heavy metal rocker. His wild beard was also obviously fake. So was the large, putty nose he wore. She doubted he even needed the thick-framed, tinted glasses he had on.

When he got close, he smiled and she saw that he was wearing false teeth as well. His getup was so over the top that she suspected it was intentionally meant to be ridiculous.

"Hello, Caroline," he had said, speaking with a slight lisp that she assumed was due to the teeth. "This is the only time you'll see me. From now on, you'll be blindfolded. I haven't gagged you but I will if I have to. If you try to remove your blindfold at any time, I will bind your hands *behind* your back instead of in front. If you try to escape, I'll have to…hurt you. I don't want to do that."

"Why are you doing this?" she had asked, trying to keep her voice from betraying her terror.

"You wouldn't understand. Your type never does."

Then he'd pulled something out from behind his back. It was some kind of dart gun.

"Please," she had begged, her voice cracking. "You don't have to do this."

"Remember the rules," he had told her impassively. "Follow them and this will go much better for you."

Without another word, he'd fired the gun. Caroline felt a sharp stinging sensation in her left thigh. Then everything felt heavy. Her eyes drooped and again the world faded to black.

When she woke up the next time, she was blindfolded, as he'd promised she would be. The initial wave of panic she felt in those first hours eventually gave way to hope as she tried to gather whatever information she could. She kept track of time by when he brought her meals, by the relative warmth in the building, and by the slivers of light that peeked through the blindfold.

At regular intervals, he would return, his shoes echoing on the concrete floor of the empty space. No matter how hard she tried to fight it, the sound made hyperventilate. She heard him unlock the padlock on the crate, slide open the containment bars, open the metal dog door, and drop two bowls on the floor. Because her wrists were bound, Caroline was reduced to lapping up the food and water from them like an actual dog.

He never let her go to an actual bathroom. Instead, she would have to remove her underwear and go in a corner of the crate. He would intermittently enter the room and hose her and the floor down. Then he would leave again. After the first day, she learned her best bet was to shove her undergarments and blanket in the holes of the crate above her so they wouldn't get as wet when the spray of water hit her.

The routine became so regular that any variation in it was cause for concern. At one meal, he only brought her one bowl, explaining that since it was stew, it met all her needs. Another time, she woke up, certain it was morning, yet he didn't arrive until lunchtime, making her fear he'd abandoned her completely.

At times she found herself wondering whether others had abandoned her too. Were her friends and family aware that she was missing? If so, had they told the cops? Was anyone looking for her?

But it was on this nippy, late spring night, as she tried to keep her pathetic blanket from sliding off her back by pressing herself against the crate wall, and as she pressed the insides of her thighs against her arms to keep from shivering, that she noticed another break in the routine.

When he'd left her after collecting her dinner of water and canned black beans, she hadn't heard the familiar sound of the man padlocking the crate before he left. He'd slid the containment bars into place but got a call on his cell phone right after that. As he walked off to answer it, he left the crate door unlocked.

Caroline waited, expecting him to return and finish the job. But after what she estimated to be an hour, it became clear that he wasn't going to. She was certain that he had a camera on her, so she was extra cautious when she ever so slightly pulled down her blindfold and glanced around.

It was dark. The only light came from the half-moon peeking in through the broken windows. In the dimness, she didn't see any surveillance equipment, but that didn't mean it wasn't there.

As unobtrusively as possible, she looked over to where the padlock on the top containment bar should be. It was there, but sure enough, it hadn't been snapped into place and was dangling off the bar. As far as she could tell, all she had to do to get out of the crate was knock the lock off and slide the bar to the side.

Caroline sat quietly, debating how to proceed. If she was ever going to try to escape, this was the perfect time. If her previous nights here were any indication, the man wouldn't return until morning at least. That would give her hours to try to get far away and hopefully find help. If she was going to make a move, now was the time.

Her thoughts turned to what would happen to her if she did nothing. The man holding her clearly intended to kill her. It was only a matter of when. How many more days would he keep her in a crate, feed her out of a dog bowl, and hose her down before he got bored and moved on to something more exciting? Was she really going to stay crouched in a ball, waiting for it to happen?

Before she'd even consciously made the choice, her fingers were through the dog crate wires, straining to reach and remove the padlock. They were numb from lack of use and the bungee cords around her wrists, but she was eventually able to clasp and remove the padlock. Then she gripped the top containment bar and slid it to the right. She did the same with bottom one. Then she pushed. The door creaked open. For a second, she sat there, frozen in place, terrified. Then she scrambled out.

Standing upright for the first time in days was painful and difficult. Caroline pushed off the ground on the unfeeling palms of her hands. As she rose unsteadily to her feet, she felt the muscles in her thighs and calves seize up. It took nearly a minute before she felt confident taking a step. Once she was fairly sure she wouldn't collapse, she made her way to the door she'd seen the man enter through on that first night. She pushed hard but it was locked from the outside.

She looked around as she yanked the blindfold off completely. There were no other visible doors. Then her eyes fell on one of the broken windows. It was too high to climb out of and she was in no position to take a running leap. She searched the room for a chair but there were none. There was the crate though.

With what little strength she had, Caroline dragged it over so that it rested just under the window. There were cracked shards around the edges of the windowsill and she used her elbows to smash them out. Then she climbed on top of the crate, praying that it would support her weight. It held steady.

Unable to brace herself with her bound hands, she leaned out over the window, resting her forearms on the sill. As she pressed down, she felt a few remaining shards of glass dig into her skin. She tried to ignore them, focusing instead on how far a drop it was to the ground below. In the dull moonlight, she guessed it was about five feet.

She didn't have much choice. So she braced her forearms on the ledge and pushed off hard against the crate with her feet. It slid away as she moved and she fell, her midsection and hips slamming against the sill and the razor-sharp bits that had collected there.

Luckily, most of her weight had landed on the outside portion of the ledge and she slowly tumbled out headfirst. She landed on her right shoulder before falling onto her back with a thud. Ignoring the bone-rattling pain, she got to her feet and staggered away from the building, looking for anything approximating a road.

After several minutes of searching, she found one by accident when her bare feet moved from grass to dirt and gravel. She looked down, barely able to discern the difference in color between the two surfaces. Still, she did her best to follow the road, using her feet as a guide more than her eyes and trying not to let panic control her.

As she rounded a corner by a hillside, she wondered where he'd taken her that she couldn't see any city lights. And then, all at once they were there. As soon as she cleared the hill, the bright lights of downtown L.A. gleamed at her like a city-sized lighthouse offering her both warning and comfort.

She stepped forward, dazzled by them. Caroline lived in West Hollywood, where it was almost never dark and she rarely noticed. Now the sudden appearance of the city made her feel as if she'd been in a desert and just come across an oasis. She took another step closer, leaving the dirt and once again feeling the damp grass below her feet.

But all once, she felt her grip on the ground slipping. She realized too late that she had stepped to the edge of another hillside and that it was collapsing under her feet. She twisted around as her body dropped and tried to fling her arms out to grab a root or branch. But with the cords on her wrists, it was impossible.

Suddenly she was tumbling down, rolling and bouncing off rocks and trees. She tried to tuck herself into a ball but found it difficult to do anything other than grunt. At one point her right leg slammed against a tree trunk and bent sickeningly.

Caroline didn't know how much longer she fell but when she finally came to a stop, it was only the excruciating pain that assured her that she was still alive. She opened her eyes, realizing that they'd been clenched tight the entire time going down the hill.

It took several seconds to orient herself. She found that she was on her back, looking back up the hill. She guessed that she'd easily fallen seventy-five feet down a steep cliff covered in rocks, brush, and dead trees. She tilted her head to the left and saw something that, despite all the pain she felt, filled her with joy: headlights.

She forced herself to roll over onto her stomach. She knew there was no way she could put any weight on her right leg, much less get to her feet. So she crawled, digging her fingernails into the earth before her and pushing off with her still functional left leg. She managed to get her body halfway into the road, where she rolled onto her back and desperately waved her bound arms above her head.

The headlights stopped moving and she heard the vehicle's engine turn off. As someone got out of the driver's seat and she saw boots moving toward her, she had a sudden, horrible thought.

What if this is the man who took me?

A moment later her fears subsided when the person knelt down and she saw it was a woman wearing what looked to be a park service uniform.

"What the hell…?" the woman said, before pulling out her radio and speaking into it urgently. "Primary station, this is Ranger Kelso. I have an emergency situation on Vista Del Valley Drive in quadrant six. There is an injured woman lying in the road. Her right leg is badly broken and her wrists are bound. Call nine-one-one. I think she was abducted, just like the others."

CHAPTER TWO

"Why do I smell burning?"

Hannah asked the question calmly but Jessie could hear the accusation in her tone. There was only one reason something might be burning—because Jessie was trying to bake and once again failing miserably.

She darted from the kitchen table where they'd been playing Trivial Pursuit over to the oven and yanked the door open to discover that her cranberry-orange scones had a distinctly blackish, scorched look to them. She hurriedly put on a glove and pulled them out, dropping them unceremoniously on the stovetop. Little rivulets of smoke rose up from the most charred scone, the small one in the back.

Jessie could hear Ryan chuckling from the table. Hannah wore a disappointed expression, like she was the official guardian trying not to chastise her troubled charge. Of course, things were usually the other way around, so Hannah's expression was also mixed with a hint of satisfaction.

"Don't rub it in!" Jessie said defensively.

"I would never," Hannah replied, faux offended.

"Maybe we could use them as hockey pucks," Ryan offered.

"Or throwing triangles?" Hannah suggested far too enthusiastically. "You know, like Chinese throwing stars, but with extra carbs."

Jessie tried not to get too annoyed at her half-sister's good-natured needling. She looked down at the smoking remains of her effort and sighed.

"I guess we're going to get your last batch out of the freezer," she said in resignation.

"Feel free," Hannah said. "But hurry. I'm only two pie pieces away from winning this game."

"Give me a minute," Jessie said as she hunted through the freezer and found the container holding the scones. She tossed them in the toaster and waited as they warmed, not wanting to risk burning these too.

"I don't get it," Ryan said teasingly. "You're the second most celebrated criminal profiler in Southern California and yet you seem incapable of cooking anything that doesn't involve a microwave. How is that possible?"

"Priorities, Hernandez," she replied simply. "Somewhere amid hunting serial killers, navigating department politics, staying sexy for you…"

"Gross," Hannah interjected.

"And raising a teenage know-it-all," she continued.

"I hardly need raising, if you'd like to know," Hannah countered, smiling.

Jessie pressed on.

"Somewhere amidst all that, I forgot to take baking lessons. Sue me."

"Is that why your ex-husband tried to kill you?" Hannah asked, feigning wide-eyed innocence.

"No," Ryan cut in. "That was because of her meat loaf. It's a crime against humanity."

Jessie tried not to smile.

"I don't appreciate all this ganging up on me. And I'll have you both know that no one who has tried to kill me ever mentioned my cooking as a reason."

"They were being polite," Hannah said.

Jessie was about respond when the toaster dinged. She took out the scones and put them on plates, handing one each to the others. Then she sat down and took a bite out of hers.

"Mmm," she murmured softly, despite herself.

"Not too burn-y?" Hannah asked.

"I want to be sarcastic, but I just can't," Jessie mumbled, her mouth full. "How do you make them so good?"

Hannah smiled broadly, without any of her trademark cynicism. Jessie couldn't help but notice how lively she looked these days. Her green eyes, typically dull with disinterest, sparkled. Her sandy blonde hair somehow seemed shinier than usual. She even appeared taller these days, walking with her head held higher. At five foot nine, she was only an inch shorter than Jessie. But with her newly improved posture and her athletic frame, she could be her sister's body double.

"The secret comes down to one word: butter. Actually let's make that three words: lots of butter."

Before Jessie could take another bite, her phone rang. She looked down and realized that this was a call she'd scheduled.

Is it nine p.m. already?

She'd been having so much fun that she'd completely lost track of time.

"Who is it?" Ryan asked.

"It's the first most celebrated criminal profiler in Southern California. He wanted my take on a case," she lied. "Give me fifteen minutes."

"Okay," Hannah said, "but after that, we're skipping your turn."

"Understood," Jessie said, taking the scone and her phone into the bedroom.

She tried to keep her tone upbeat. But not even Hannah's delicious pastry could fill the nervous pit that had suddenly materialized in her stomach. She was about to pick up when she had a change of heart. She didn't want to interrupt this near-perfect evening to discuss darker matters and decided she wasn't going to. She sent the call to voicemail and texted back instead.

Having a great night with Hannah. Don't want to cut it short. Can we talk tomorrow?

After several seconds, she got a response. She could almost hear the curtness in the reply.

Meet in person. Station break room. 7 a.m. sharp.

She typed back "ok" and left it at that. She knew the guy liked to get into the office early but she couldn't help thinking he was making her meet him at that ungodly hour as a punishment for rescheduling. Still, it was worth it if she got more quality time with Hannah.

"Hey," she called out as she returned to the living room, "I decided kicking your butts was more important than any case. You better not have skipped my turn."

As she walked back over, she knew she was only delaying dealing with what was eating at her. But one more night of playing house wasn't the end of the world. At least that's what she told herself. Reality, in all its ugliness, would still be waiting for her tomorrow.

CHAPTER THREE

With one notable exception, the break room was empty.

"Thanks for making the time," Jessie said when she arrived at 6:58 a.m. Just to be safe she locked the door behind her.

"I *am* a busy man," Garland Moses said wryly, turning to face her. He was seated at a table, munching on what looked like a granola bar. She was tempted to make a crack about it cracking his false teeth but held off.

"A busy man who has been avoiding me for the last month," she noted.

"I had a big case," he protested. "And then I had that conference in Philadelphia. And then I had my vacation."

"Don't B.S. me, Garland. In our last substantive conversation at my birthday party, you hinted that you had concerns about Hannah. And then you ghosted me for a month. I've been freaking out."

That was an overstatement. Things had actually been going amazingly well with Hannah in the last four weeks. Considering everything her half-sister had been through in the last six months, the fact that she could genuinely enjoy a quiet night of board games and scones was a minor miracle. That was part of why she didn't want to cut it short last night.

"You know I'm a senior citizen, right?' Garland said. "I don't have conversations that involve the term 'ghosted.'"

"You're stalling," she said.

"No, this is me stalling," he said, slowly standing up. "Let's get some coffee."

He led the way over to the coffee machine. Jessie tried to ignore the vending machine beside it. She hadn't had breakfast yet and felt her stomach grumble at the thought of preservative-laden snack good. As Garland walked, Jessie noted that he had on an outfit that she'd come to learn was essentially his daily uniform.

He wore a tired-looking gray sport jacket over a brown sweater vest and a dull beige dress shirt. His navy slacks were wrinkled and his loafers were covered in scuffs. His white hair shot in every direction as if he was trying to win an Albert Einstein look-alike contest. The bifocals at the bridge of his nose completed the look.

But Jessie had learned that appearances could be deceiving and that the veteran profiler cultivated the disheveled look to make people underestimate him. He was always perfectly shaved with nary a stray hair in sight. His white teeth were immaculate and his fingernails were faultless. The shoelaces on his worn loafers were new and neatly tied in double bows.

In all the important ways, he was at the top of his game. She had come to not just respect the old guy, but to genuinely like him.

"Okay, Ms. Hunt..." he started, apparently ready to end the stalling.

"I think we've reached the stage where you can call me Jessie, Garland. Hell, I'm thinking of calling you Grandpa from now on."

"Please don't do that," he insisted. "Okay, Jessie. I didn't mean to freak you out. But I did have some thoughts about Hannah. I'm willing to share them with you, as long as you keep them in their proper context."

"What context is that?" Jessie asked.

"Remember, this is a seventeen-year-old girl whose adoptive parents were brutally murdered right in front of her by her biological father, a notorious serial killer."

"I'm well aware of that, Garland," Jessie said impatiently. "First of all, I was there. And secondly, that serial killer was my father too, if you'll recall."

"I'm painting a picture here," he said patiently. "May I continue?"

"Go ahead," Jessie said, deciding not to interrupt the guy she'd been trying to talk to for a month.

"Then," he continued, "only weeks later she was kidnapped by another serial killer out to mold her into a murderer like himself and her father. In the process, he made her watch as he slaughtered her foster parents."

Jessie felt the urge to point out that, as the person who rescued Hannah in both those instances, she was intimately familiar with the details. But he obviously knew all that. He was making a point. So instead, as he spoke she stared at herself in the reflection of the vending machine window, trying to smooth her furrowed brow through sheer will.

"That's true," she noted, keeping her tone neutral.

"And in the middle of all that, she learned that she had a half-sister, one who she saw tortured and who seems to court death and danger through the very nature of her job. You are her last remaining relative. And every time she says goodbye to you, she knows it might be for the last time."

Jessie hadn't considered that fact and immediately felt bad, both for Hannah and at her own lack of insight.

"Still," she finally replied, "you already knew all of this when you hung out with her."

"You mean when you asked me to babysit her so I could secretly profile her?"

"You say potato. The point is, you knew all that when you met her and, despite that, you told me you had concerns."

"Yes, I do," he finally admitted. "I won't get into the details because I don't want to betray her trust and they're not all that important anyway. But based on the things we discussed, I'm concerned about Hannah's seeming lack of empathy. I'm just not sure how concerned to be."

Jessie found it enlightening to stare at herself in the window as she absorbed this news. She was able to see her reactions in real time. Hopefully she had a better poker face when she was in public stare-downs. But in the relative privacy of the break room and with Garland focused on adding sugar to his coffee, she didn't try to hide her suddenly ashen complexion or the fear in her green eyes. She blew her brown hair out of her face and responded carefully.

"Care to elaborate?"

"Here's the thing," he answered. "Most teenagers are inherently self-involved to a certain degree. It's part of finding their own identities. Finding out who you are requires you to put the focus on yourself. That's normal, if sometimes infuriating."

"I'm following you so far."

"But she's also been through so much trauma that it wouldn't be stunning if emotionally, she just shut down completely. If everything she's feeling is just a variation on pain, why feel anything at all, not just for herself, but for anyone? So it's possible that some part of her is just calloused over as a form of self-protection. That, while troubling, wouldn't be shocking either."

"And yet…" Jessie prodded, looking over at him.

"And yet," he conceded, "it's not clear to me that her closed off nature didn't already exist before any of this happened. Some people just don't form strong bonds or attachments for whatever reason. Her mother died when she was little. She was in the foster system for a while before being adopted. Any number of things could have stymied her ability to develop connections."

"Or she could have just been born that way," Jessie offered. "It could be a function of genetics."

"That's possible too," Garland agreed, stepping aside so she could get some coffee. "The problem is that we don't have any quality studies that provide anything definitive on that front. But that's not really what you're asking, is it?"

"What am I asking, Garland?" Jessie countered.

"You're asking if she has the potential to become a killer, like your shared father was, like Bolton Crutchfield tried to make her, like you fear that you could turn into yourself. Am I correct?"

Jessie was quiet for longer than she liked.

"You are correct," she finally said softly.

Jessie's eyes were focused on pouring cream into her coffee but she could hear the careful pause before Garland replied. She imagined him internally debating how best to proceed.

"The frustrating answer is—I just don't know. We're both well aware of the FBI's behavioral science research indicating that almost every serial killer on record had some kind of trauma as a young person. That might have come in the form of abuse, bullying, or the loss of a loved one. My personal anecdotal experience reinforces those findings."

"Mine does too," Jessie agreed. "But I noticed you said 'almost' every serial killer."

"Yes. There are records of killers who seem to have had perfectly normal childhoods without suffering any clear ordeal. Some people are just…off. You know that as well as I do."

"I do," Jessie said as they walked back over to the table. "But what I want to know is if my half-sister, the girl living under my roof, is one of them. Because if she's gone through this much horror so early in life and she's missing that—for a lack of a better term—empathy gene, then we've got a problem."

"Maybe," Garland said cautiously as they sat down. "But maybe not. To the best of our knowledge, she hasn't tortured any animals or killed anyone."

"To the best of our knowledge," Jessie granted.

"And you've been through many of the same tribulations she has. Your serial killer father murdered your mother and your adoptive parents, and he tried to kill you, as did another serial killer who was obsessed with you. And don't forget the ex-husband who attempted to frame you for murdering his mistress and then tried to kill you when you found out. You've had a pretty good run of trauma yourself and you haven't gone on any killing sprees."

"No," Jessie said, pausing before revealing something she'd shared with few others. "But I've often wondered if I entered this field as a way to be up close to the violence and cruelty of these people without having to go to their lengths. I worry that I get a contact high off their crimes."

Garland was quiet for a moment and she found herself worrying that he might be wondering the same thing.

"That's what therapy's for," he finally said unhelpfully.

She was about to offer a snarky reply when her phone rang. She looked down. It was her friend Kat Gentry. She sent it to voicemail.

"So are you willing to meet with Hannah again?" she asked. "To see if you can draw any firmer conclusions?"

"I'm willing to meet with her, assuming she's open to it," he said. "But that doesn't mean I'm going to have any massive 'a-ha' moment. In the end, it's hard to discern whether she's just a moody teenager, a traumatized, emotionally stunted young adult, or some combination of both."

A text popped up on her screen from Kat: *Need your help on a case. Meet me at Downtown Grounds at 7:30 a.m.?*

Jessie looked at the time. It was 7:10. Whatever Kat needed must be pressing if she wanted to meet so soon.

"You left off one option," Jessie noted, as she typed back "ok."

"What's that?" he asked.

"A sociopath who's hiding it well."

CHAPTER FOUR

Kat was already waiting in the bustling coffee shop when Jessie arrived.

Even before she sat down, Jessie could tell her friend was anxious.

That was unusual, at least lately. Katherine "Kat" Gentry used to be far more intense. As the former head of security for a psychiatric prison and before that, an Army Ranger in Afghanistan, it kind of defined her.

But after she was fired when Bolton Crutchfield escaped from prison and she reinvented herself as a private investigator, she'd seemed much more relaxed. And especially recently, after she'd started dating Mitch Connor, a sheriff's deputy from a town in the mountains a couple of hours away, she'd seemed downright happy. He'd helped her out when she consulted on one of Jessie's cases and they'd been inseparable ever since, driving back and forth to spend weekends together.

But now, as Jessie walked over, weaving in and out of the crowd, she saw that old, familiar apprehension on Kat's face. Somehow the long scar that ran down her face vertically from her left eye, the one she'd gotten from an unspecified incident in a far off desert, seemed more prominent when she was worried.

"How's it going, Kat?" Jessie asked loudly before she took a sip of the coffee her friend had already ordered for her. "Still having lots of sex?"

She smiled mischievously as several people turned their heads and scowled. The fact that Kat's troubled expression didn't change at the teasing told Jessie this must be serious.

"I need your help," she said without preamble.

"Okay," Jessie said, turning serious herself. "What's going on?"

Kat allowed herself a sip of her coffee before diving in.

"Do you know about the recent string of abductions of local women?"

"A little," Jessie replied. "I know that three women were kidnapped in the last month or so. All of them escaped. I haven't paid super close attention since it's not my beat and none of them are Central Station cases."

Jessie and Ryan both worked out of Central Station in the downtown-area Central Bureau of the Los Angeles Police Department.

"I have a new client," Kat said. "Her name is Morgan Remar. She was the second woman taken. She was abducted about three weeks ago and got away after being held for five days. She's been working with the Missing Persons unit out of Pacific Station. But after two weeks, they've come up empty. In the last couple of days, they haven't been very responsive at all. So she hired me."

"No offense, but if the incident happened way out near Pacific Station, why did she hire you?"

"It's a fair question," Kat said. "She works in Venice but lives nearby and her husband works downtown, just a few blocks away. In fact, I met her in this very coffee house about three months ago and we became friendly. She got frustrated and asked if I could help."

"Okay, fill me in on what you know."

Kat sighed deeply, as if the thought of explaining everything she'd learned was especially daunting.

"Here's the short version," she finally said. "The first victim was Brenda Ferguson. She's a thirty-six-year-old stay-at-home mom with two kids from her second marriage. Her husband is a record executive. She was taken mid-morning, while jogging on a trail near her Brentwood home. After being held for three days in a garden shed, she managed to get away."

Jessie furiously scribbled down notes as her friend talked.

"Am I going too fast?" Kat asked.

"No. You're good. Keep going."

"Okay. The second victim was my client, Morgan. She's twenty-nine and lives in West Adams with her husband, only a few miles from this place. But she works at a homeless shelter in Venice. She was abducted on her way back from lunch on the Boardwalk. Like I said, she was held for five days before she escaped. He was holding her in an old wardrobe."

"And the third woman?"

"Her name is Jayne Castillo. She's thirty-three, married, and lives in Mid-City. She was taken from a grocery store parking lot a week and a half ago and got away after three days trapped in a dumpster."

"Have you reached out to the other two women?" Jessie asked.

"I've tried," Kat said, looking frustrated at the memory of it. "But I keep hitting brick walls. They won't talk. The cops won't talk. That's why I came to you. I'm at my wits' end here. Morgan's paranoid that this guy is still out there and I can't offer her any assurances because I'm no closer to finding him than I was the day she hired me."

Jessie took another sip before asking her next question. She knew what Kat was getting at but wanted to think about how she'd answer.

"How can I help?" she finally asked.

Kat didn't need any prompting to reply.

"Can you reach out to the detectives handling the cases? Maybe they'll be more forthcoming with you. Right now, I'm flying blind here."

Jessie sighed.

"I can try," she said. "The problem is that these guys are all from other stations. They aren't likely inclined to share details of their cases with a profiler from another station where we don't also have a victim. But it can't hurt to try. Maybe I'll find someone friendly."

"I know it's a lot to ask," Kat acknowledged. "Are you sure you have the time?"

"It's fine," Jessie assured her. "Things are actually a little slow right now. I'm wrapping up paperwork on a case from last week and waiting to testify in another. But I don't have anything active at the moment. Of course, that means Captain Decker could assign me to something new at any time. But until then, I can try to shake something loose."

"I'd really appreciate it."

"Are you kidding me?" Jessie said. "How many times have you helped me out on a case when I didn't want to go through official channels? This is the least I can do."

"Thanks, Jessie," Kat said, sounding relieved for the first time since they started talking.

"Not a problem. But let me ask you, can I talk to Morgan? It would really help me to get her firsthand perspective."

"Of course," Kat said. "She's at an out-of-town conference right now and won't be back until late tonight. But I can set something up for tomorrow."

"That sounds good. I'll see what I can find out in the interim," Jessie said before taking another big sip of coffee. "Now that we've gotten all that out of the way, I have another question."

"What's that?"

"You having lots of sex?"

Kat finally broke into the smile Jessie had been hoping for when she asked the first time. Her face also turned a deep pink.

"I'm keeping busy," she said cryptically.

"I'll bet you are," Jessie teased.

"What about you?" Kat countered, trying to apply a little pressure of her own. "How are things with Ryan?"

It was Jessie's turn to blush.

"They're good," she said. "We trade off where we spend the night, though it's usually my place because of Hannah."

"And you don't mind living in sin with an impressionable youth under your roof?" Kat asked, a teasing smile playing at her lips.

"Believe me, that girl has seen enough stuff that I don't think she's fazed by her sister's boyfriend spending the night. I think she actually finds it reassuring."

"We'll see if she's so reassured when you all fall into the pit of Hades," Kat persisted, trying not to laugh as she said it.

"You're really enjoying this, aren't you?"

"You have no idea."

Despite the teasing, Jessie allowed herself to relish the moment. For a few seconds at least, she could forget that she wasn't sure if her little sister was a sociopath or if she or her boyfriend might get gunned down at work. She could pretend she led a normal life with normal family and relationship issues.

Then the moment passed.

CHAPTER FIVE

Jessie got lucky.

As she walked into the bullpen of LAPD's downtown Central Station just after 8 a.m., trying to keep a low profile, there was a flurry of activity. Vice had just conducted a major overnight raid, busting up a large prostitution ring. The whole station was filled with hookers, pimps, and johns.

That meant that no one noticed her as she slinked to her desk. Even Ryan, who was helping a uniformed officer subdue an irate john, didn't see her walk by. She couldn't help but notice him. Even though they'd been together for a few months now and she was intimately familiar with the contours of his body, she never ceased to be impressed by his sheer attractiveness.

At six feet tall and a shade under two hundred pounds, he wasn't physically imposing. But as she knew personally, there wasn't an ounce of fat on his muscular, thirty-two-year-old frame. Despite his chiseled torso, Ryan exuded surprising humility and warmth for a veteran homicide detective. He had an easy smile and his black hair was cut short so it didn't obscure his friendly brown eyes.

When he talked, his soft-spoken tone gave no hint that he was the most celebrated detective in the department's Homicide Special Section, or HSS, which investigated cases that had high profiles or intense media scrutiny, often involving multiple victims and serial killers. Jessie sometimes thought that his ability to navigate that gig and a relationship with her should earn him a special medal of commendation.

Pushing thoughts of her boyfriend out of her head as she sat down, Jessie began pulling up the case files on the abducted women. The details were sparse, seemingly in large part because the women had all been blindfolded for much of their ordeals and couldn't offer much help.

After familiarizing herself with the incidents as much as possible, she decided to call the primary detective on Morgan Remar's case. For one thing, it was the one most relevant to Kat. In addition, the assigned detective at Pacific Station, Ray Sands, had a stellar record and a good reputation as someone who cared more about solving cases than following strict procedure. Maybe he'd be open to helping.

"Sands here," he said, picking up before the end of the first ring.

"Hi, Detective Sands," she said as casually as she could. "This is Jessie Hunt. I'm a criminal profiler based out of Central Station. How are you doing this morning?"

"I'm very busy, Ms. Hunt. What can I do for you?" he asked, polite but no-nonsense.

"I was hoping to pick your brain on a case you're working right now."

"What case is that?" Sands asked warily.

"The Morgan Remar abduction; I was hoping you could fill in a few of the blanks."

"What's your interest in the case, Ms. Hunt? I've heard of you and I thought your specialty was homicides, mostly involving serial killers."

"It is," Jessie conceded. Deciding her best hope was to just be straightforward, she told him the truth. "I'm actually looking into this for a friend, Katherine Gentry. Ms. Remar hired her as a private investigator and she's been facing some pushback in trying to get details on how the case is progressing."

"Yes. I'm familiar with Ms. Gentry," he replied with a tone of exhaustion. "She's certainly been…persistent. I'll tell you what I told her. We just don't have much in the way of quality information that we can share at this point."

Jessie got the sense that Sands was a decent guy but knew he wasn't being totally forthright.

"Detective, are you telling me that after one month and three abductions by what is clearly the same perpetrator, you don't have any useful leads?"

She couldn't hide the skepticism in her voice. Sands didn't respond for a few seconds.

"Look, Ms. Hunt," he said very slowly, punching each syllable hard as he spoke. "You're making a lot of assumptions there, first among them: that these cases are connected."

"Are you suggesting that they're not?" Jessie asked, surprised.

"We don't know definitively," he said unconvincingly. "All the abductions occurred in different jurisdictions. All the women were found in areas far from where they were taken."

"But they were all kept for about the same length of time before escaping," Jessie countered. "They were all held in contained spaces. They were all in the same general age range and the same general socioeconomic level. You're not seriously claiming these are unconnected?"

"No," he admitted. "But not every detective investigating the other abductions feels that way. And since I suspect that you're going to call them after talking to me, I want to be clear that no conclusions have been drawn."

Jessie sighed. She understood Sands's caution but it was incredibly frustrating.

"Look, Detective. I get it. This is politically sensitive. And you don't know me. But Kat Gentry is a good friend. And she's trying to help a very scared young woman. I'm just trying to get some answers that will help set her mind at ease."

"You don't think I know Morgan Remar is scared?" Sands demanded, sounding genuinely angry for the first time. "I'm the one who interviewed her in the hospital while doctors did skin grafts on her and tried to repair the ankle she destroyed kicking herself out of that wardrobe. I'm the one who had to tell her there was no useful evidence found at the location where she'd been held. I've been working on this case for two weeks straight, while my fellow detectives from the Mid-Wilshire and West L.A. stations have held back on any information-sharing. I only just got approval for a task force this morning. I'm aware of the situation, Ms. Hunt."

"I'm sorry," Jessie said, aware of just how badly she'd stepped in it. "I didn't mean to suggest you didn't care. I just, well, I'm sorry."

Sands was quiet. She could hear him breathing heavily. But she took the fact that he hadn't hung up as a good sign. Before he did, she tried another tack.

"You said you got a task force approved this morning?"

"Yes," he muttered.

"Can I ask what changed?"

"There was a fourth abduction," he said.

"What?"

"She was found late last night in Griffith Park," Sands said. "Same M.O., only this time she was held in a dog crate for four days."

"Jeez," Jessie muttered under her breath.

"Yeah," he agreed. "So that's what finally got the folks down at headquarters to override the other station captains and make us pool our resources. We hope to be up and running by this afternoon."

"Who's in charge?"

"Yours truly."

"No wonder you're so chippy," she said before realizing he might not take her comment in the joking vein it was intended.

"Are you kidding? This is me at my most charming," he said, clearly not offended.

"Okay then, as long as I've got you in what you consider a good mood, can I ask you another insulting question?"

"Fire away," he said. "I'm used to it by now."

"Four abductions. Not a single lead as to the identity of the kidnapper. And yet every woman managed to escape. Doesn't it seem odd that a perpetrator who was so adept at abducting these women is so inept at keeping them?"

"It does," Sands said, offering no further comment.

"Can I assume by your pregnant pause that you are as skeptical as I am that any of these women actually 'escaped' on their own?"

"You can," Sands said. "While not everyone agrees with me, I feel pretty strongly that this guy—and we know it's a guy—allowed his victims to get away."

"What makes you so sure?" Jessie asked.

"Apart from what you noted—that it seems exceedingly unlikely that the same man who grabbed up all these women without getting caught would be sloppy in holding them—there's something else."

"What's that?"

"We found the places where he held each woman. In each instance, there wasn't a single trace of usable DNA. There were no fingerprints. There was no incriminating evidence of any kind. That's hard to pull off under any circumstances, as you well know. But almost impossible if he returned to find these women gone and had to hurriedly clean up."

"But not if he let them go," Jessie said.

"Correct," Sands agreed. "If he allowed them to escape at a moment of his choosing, that would give him time to clean up after they left. I suspect he was cautious from the moment he brought them to the locations where he kept them, knowing it would eventually be discovered and searched thoroughly."

"Why would he do that?" Jessie asked. "Why risk letting them go when they might be able to identify him later?"

"Don't forget they were all blindfolded."

"But they wouldn't have been when he first grabbed them."

"No," he conceded. "But the first three women taken were all certain he wore an elaborate disguise."

"Still, they could estimate his height and weight, his ethnicity. They might be able to identify his voice."

"All true," Sands said.

"I feel like there's more going on here than meets the eye," Jessie mused.

"So do I," Sands agreed. "Unfortunately, I have no idea what."

CHAPTER SIX

Jessie was out on a limb.

Just because she didn't have any active cases didn't mean Captain Decker would be happy that she was off in Brentwood looking into a case she had nothing to do with. And yet, that's exactly what she was doing.

Caroline Gidley, the victim discovered last night, was unconscious and in no position to talk. Detective Sands had warned her that Jayne Castillo, the third victim, had no desire to be interviewed. And since Kat's client, Morgan Remar, was out of town, that left only one person to speak with.

When she asked Sands if it would be a mistake to try to talk to the first victim, Brenda Ferguson, he told her the detectives from West L.A. station, which handled Brentwood-based cases, would not be happy. But he also very pointedly never requested she not do so. Even in her limited experience with him, Jessie got the sense that was as close to a go-ahead as he was likely to give her.

Ryan had generously agreed to run interference for her at the station to keep her absence off Captain Decker's radar. Just before she pulled up to the Ferguson house, she checked in with him.

"How's it going back there?" she asked.

"Decker is so immersed in the aftermath of the vice raid that he hasn't even noticed you're not here."

"I don't know whether to feel relieved or insulted," she replied.

"If it's any consolation, I miss you," Ryan said.

Armed with that assurance, she got out and headed for the house. She hadn't called ahead for fear that Ferguson would check in with the case detectives. Besides, she often found she got more useful information when she surprised a witness, suspect, or even a victim. They didn't have as much time to organize their thoughts and edit out useful information.

The home was impressive, though nowhere near as ostentatious as some others on the tree-lined street. It was a two-story, Spanish-style home that extended well back on the large lot. The front lawn alone could have hosted a second house. She knocked on the door and had to wait a good sixty seconds before it was answered by a thirty-something man with a mistrustful expression.

"Can I help you?" he asked guardedly.

"I hope so. I assume you're Mrs. Ferguson's husband?"

"Yes. I'm Ty."

"Hi, Ty," Jessie said in her warmest, least intimidating voice. "I'm Jessie Hunt. I work as a criminal profiler for the LAPD. I know Brenda has been through a lot. But I was hoping to speak to her briefly. I'm trying to develop a profile of the man who abducted her and there's only so much I can glean from the case file. I've held off as long as I could out of deference to what she's been through. But speaking to her in person would be extremely helpful."

She wasn't excited to make her initial introduction with what were, at best, white lies. But she needed an "in" and this seemed the most effective route. Ty didn't slam the door in her face but he still looked reticent.

"Listen," he said quietly, glancing back over his shoulder as he spoke. "I know you're only doing your job. But Brenda's been through so much already. She's only started sleeping through the night in the last few days. I'm concerned this will reopen all those wounds again."

Jessie sensed his recalcitrance was on the verge of overwhelming his good intentions and decided now was the time to be more forthright.

"I can't promise it won't, Ty. But I'm trying to find out who this guy is so he doesn't hurt anyone else. I don't know if you're aware of this, but a fourth victim was discovered late last night."

"No," Ty said, his eyes widening.

"Yes. She's hospitalized now. She has a badly broken leg that she got escaping after four days in a dog crate. Frankly, there's no indication that this guy is going to stop any time soon. I'm hoping that with Brenda's help, we can get to him before he goes after a fifth woman."

Ty still looked torn but Jessie could tell that his inclination had now tipped toward letting her in. He looked back down the hall a second time.

"Stay here," he finally said. "Let me talk to her first. Maybe I can convince her."

"Thank you," Jessie said and stepped into the foyer as Ty disappeared into an unknown room at the end of the hall.

She could hear hushed, agitated whispers for several minutes before Ty finally poked his head out.

"Come on in," he called out. "Please close and lock the door behind you."

Jessie nodded, did as he requested, then made her way down the hall. When she rounded the corner, she found Ty walking over to sit at the breakfast table next to a plump, dark-haired woman with a haggard expression and red eyes. She didn't look happy to have a guest.

"Hi, Mrs. Ferguson," she said, her voice scratchy. "Thanks for speaking with me."

"I'm only doing it because Ty begged me to. He told me about the fourth woman. How is she?"

"She's going to survive," Jessie told her. "She was found on a dirt road in Griffith Park with a broken leg and multiple other injuries. But my understanding is that she'll be able to go home before the end of the week."

"Is she married? Have kids?"

"I don't think so," Jessie said.

"That's good. It's bad enough to go through this. But it's been almost as rough on the rest of the family. My daughter comes into our room crying most nights. My son has started wetting the bed. Ty handles all of it and I can tell he's on the verge of collapsing."

"It's okay, sweetie," Ty said, squeezing her hand. "I'm doing fine. And the kids'll get better. You just focus on you. I think this might help. If Ms. Hunt can come up with a new way to find this guy, that will help everyone sleep better at night."

"Do you think you can do that, Ms. Hunt?"

"Please call me Jessie. And with your help, I hope so."

Brenda studied her with her worn out eyes and nodded.

"Come with me, Jessie," she said. "I want to show you something."

She got up without another word and left the room. Jessie followed, glancing back at Ty, who shrugged as he stood up. Brenda led her to the hallway and stopped at a bookshelf halfway down the hall.

She reached out and tugged at a red-spined book sitting waist high on the far right end of the shelf. The book slid out slightly and then snapped back. Jessie heard a soft click. Suddenly, the bookshelf swung back like a door into open space.

A dull overhead fluorescent light flickered on to reveal a room about the size of a small study. Against one wall rested a small loveseat. Next to it were two wooden chairs. They all surrounded a mini coffee table. A tiny fridge stood in the corner.

Other than a few magazines and some coloring books and crayons, the place was devoid of entertainment. An old-style corded phone hung on one wall. On another was a large poster with the cover of Nirvana's *Nevermind* album, in which a baby is underwater reaching out for a dollar bill.

"That's cool," Jessie said, pointing at the poster, unsure how else to respond.

"I guess," Brenda said. "We used it because it's large enough to cover the opening to the tunnel we had dug under the house to the front yard."

"Okay," Jessie replied, surprised by the bland tone Brenda used to describe such an unconventional situation.

"I'm showing you this because I wanted you to get a sense of what our life is like now. I made Ty have this panic room built after I got back home. I don't know if it'll do any good in an emergency. But I couldn't sleep more than two hours at a time until it was finished."

"I get it," Jessie said quietly.

"Do you?" Brenda challenged.

"I really do," Jessie assured her. "I won't bore you with the details but I've had several stalkers. I've had my apartment redone to include multiple security measures typically employed by banks and government facilities. And even after the imminent threats to my safety were eliminated, I kept the security in place. So I understand where you're coming from."

Jessie noticed that for the first time, Brenda looked at her like she might be an ally.

"I'm sorry that happened to you," she said. "And you can call me Brenda."

Jessie smiled.

"Thanks, Brenda. Care to sit down?" she asked, nodding at the loveseat.

"In there?"

"May as well get used to it, right?" Jessie said.

Brenda looked at her husband, who hadn't said a word this whole time. He shrugged again.

"I'll wait in the kitchen so you two can have some privacy."

After he left, Brenda pushed a button on the wall and the door swung shut and clicked into place. She pointed at a small switch that seemed to approximate the spot where the red book was on the shelf outside. It was marked with the words "locked" and "unlocked."

"That's so no one can access the room once we're inside, even if they know about the book," Brenda said.

"Solid call," Jessie said. "Otherwise it's not much of a panic room, I guess."

She took the initiative, walking over to the loveseat and sitting down. Brenda joined her but sat in one of the nearby chairs.

"So," Jessie began, "I know you spoke to the police multiple times. I've read the file. So I'll try not to repeat their questions too much. I'm actually interested in some different kinds of things than they were."

"Like what?" Brenda asked as she crossed and uncrossed her legs nervously.

"I know, based on descriptions from you and the second and third women, that your abductor wore elaborate disguises, including wigs, beards, and prosthetics. I also know that each of you was blindfolded after your initial abduction. So I want to focus more on his voice right now. Do you remember it?"

"I can't get it out of my head," Brenda said, "even though he didn't talk very much at all."

"Can you describe its timbre?" Jessie asked. "Was it deep or high? Somewhere in between?"

"In between; it was a normal, medium-sounding voice."

"Okay," Jessie said. "What about an accent? Did you notice anything along those lines? Maybe a twang? Or a more flat Midwestern tone? Maybe something that reminded you of New York or New England? Did he use any words you don't normally hear out here, like 'pop' instead of 'soda' or 'y'all' instead of 'you all'?"

"I didn't notice anything unusual," Brenda said, scrunching her brow in concentration. "I'm from L.A. and he sounded normal to me so maybe he's from here too?"

"That's entirely possible," Jessie said supportively. "What about language choice? Did he use a lot of slang or was his usage more proper? Did he sound like he had a lot of education?"

Brenda took a moment to search her memory.

"I don't remember him speaking in an especially fancy way. But I don't remember a lot of slang either. It was mostly standard, straightforward language."

"Did he speak unusually fast or slow?"

Brenda's eyes lit up at that.

"Maybe a little slower than usual," she answered. "It was like he wanted to be sure he was saying exactly the right thing when he spoke. He was very measured. Does that help?"

"It could," Jessie said. "Let's explore some other areas. Did you notice a particular scent?"

Brenda was quiet and her face turned red.

"What's wrong?" Jessie asked gently.

She thought the woman wasn't going to reply but after several long seconds she finally did.

"To be honest," she almost whispered, "I don't remember a smell from him. Whatever he used to knock me out when he grabbed me had an overwhelming scent. And after that, I couldn't smell anything other than my own stench, first from the sweat and body odor, and later, from… my own excrement."

She cast her eyes downward and didn't say anything else.

"Okay, let's move on then," Jessie offered quickly. "Why don't we talk about how he behaved more generally when you were being held?"

Over the next half hour, Jessie learned that the man never got overtly angry but did get irritated whenever she talked about her husband or children. She learned not to bring them up pretty quickly. He never laughed but he did sound happier than usual when he dropped her food and water bowl in the garden shed or when he hosed her down.

"He seemed to get a kick out of my moments of degradation," Brenda told her. "He said they were part of the 'purification' process."

After that, she broke down and wasn't very helpful. Jessie ended the interview before things completely devolved. When they were done, both Fergusons walked Jessie to the door. Brenda looked slightly better than when they'd first met. As they stepped outside, she had a question of her own for Jessie.

"Do you think we could get the name of the people who did the security at your apartment?"

"Of course," Jessie said, overwhelmed with a sense of commiseration. "I'll text the info to you."

As she walked back to her car, her thoughts were swimming with alternative variations on what the abductor might be like. It wasn't until she was standing right next to her car that she realized all her tires had been slashed.

CHAPTER SEVEN

Jessie ignored the sudden pit in her stomach and scanned the area for anything suspicious.

This was a stunningly brazen act, in the middle of the day on a quiet street in a well-to-do neighborhood. Whoever did it clearly didn't have much fear of being caught.

Nothing obvious jumped out at her. About half a block down the street, there was a white van facing her. But a second later, she saw two men emerge from behind it carrying a large sofa toward a nearby house.

Moments after that, she saw a motorcycle cop turn off an adjoining street and head in the opposite direction from her. He seemed to be doing a standard patrol. Was it just bad luck that he hadn't been nearby when her tires were slashed? Or was there more to it?

She hated to draw the latter conclusion but couldn't help considering it. It was only a month ago that she'd been intimately involved in a case that uncovered a massive police corruption scandal. It helped lead to the arrest of over a dozen officers, including the head of LAPD's Force Investigation Group, and Sergeant Hank Costabile of Valley Bureau's Van Nuys Station.

During her investigation, Costabile had subtly and then later, overtly threatened both her and Hannah. Was this the act of one his cronies, getting revenge for his incarcerated buddy? If so, why wait a month and do something so random and petty?

Or was it possible that this was somehow related to the abductions? Had the kidnapper been staking out the Ferguson house? Was this his way of warning Jessie off? That seemed unlikely as she doubted he'd be hanging around. Even if he was, he'd have no way to know Jessie, dressed in civilian clothes, was looking into the case.

Whoever did it and for whatever reason, it didn't change the fact that she needed a tow truck. While she waited, she called Ryan to fill him in on both her interview and the tire slashing. She ran the particulars by him, hoping he might think of something she was missing.

"It could just be obnoxious kids," he offered, regarding the latter.

"Maybe," Jessie conceded. "But it's the middle of a school day. Even if some kids skipped out, would they drive through the neighborhood and slash all the tires of just one car? This feels more directed than that."

"You're probably right," he admitted. "Did you have more luck with the kidnapping victim?"

"A little," Jessie said. "Unfortunately, what she told me will be more useful once we have a suspect in mind. Until then, it doesn't amount to much. Have you heard anything?"

"To be honest, I've been focused on my testimony this afternoon. If it wasn't for that, I'd come pick you up."

"That's very sweet but not necessary. It would take you an hour to get here and I'm in no rush. After I get the tires replaced and come back, I just have to review the files from the Olin case."

There was silence on the other end of the line. Jessie wondered what she'd said wrong.

"What is it?" she asked anxiously.

"Nothing," he said. "I was just thinking that by the time you get your car back, there's not much point in coming in. Decker went to headquarters to update the brass on the vice raid. He won't be back for hours. And you have a rare slow day. Maybe you should take the afternoon off and hang out with Hannah without me as a third wheel."

"You're not a third wheel," she protested.

"You know what I mean. I've been around a lot lately. This could give you a chance for some girl time. And if Hannah decided to use it to share something personal, that wouldn't be the worst thing. "

Jessie was surprised at the suggestion.

"Has she seemed like she wants to do that?" she asked, wondering if she'd missed the signs.

"Don't seventeen-year-old girls always have something personal they're keeping to themselves, even if they haven't been through what she has?"

"Yes," Jessie said. "I'm just making sure you're not cryptically alluding to something specific."

"No. I just know Hannah's been seeing the therapist, Dr. Banana."

"Dr. Lemmon," Jessie corrected, trying not to laugh.

"Right, right. I knew it was in the fruit family. And you're also having Garland Moses peek into her brain."

"You knew that was him last night?"

"I'm a very good detective. Also, you assigned him a specific ring tone and have said 'Hi, Garland' when he's called. So there's that too."

"So, not so much good detecting then?" she teased.

"Anyway," he replied, not getting distracted, "I thought maybe she could just use a chat with someone who wasn't talking to her in a professional capacity. You know, like a big sister?"

Jessie realized he was right. She and Hannah had been getting along shockingly well lately. But most of their down time was with Ryan around. He was an excellent buffer. But he might also inadvertently be preventing Hannah from getting into anything too heavy. Maybe some sisterly time alone would get her to open up, assuming she even had the urge.

"Ryan Hernandez," she said, suddenly feeling unexpectedly chipper considering the state of her vehicle, "you are neither the dumbest nor the least perceptive person I've met."

"Thanks?"

"You also have a sweet ass."

She heard him cough on whatever he'd just taken a sip of. Satisfied with her work, she hung up.

*

Hannah was clearly pleasantly surprised when Jessie picked her up directly from school. That changed to extremely enthusiastic when she learned that they'd be stopping for ice cream on the way home.

"Why aren't you working?" she finally, reluctantly asked as they ordered their cones from a shop around the corner from the apartment.

"I'm not busy right now," Jessie said. "And I wanted to spend some time with you. You know, without that icky boy around."

"Icky isn't the first word that comes to mind when I think of your boyfriend," Hannah said.

"Careful," Jessie said in mock reprimand. "We don't have to share *every* feeling we have the second we feel it."

Hannah smiled, obviously amused that she'd managed to cause some embarrassment.

"I didn't know the daughters of serial killers were allowed to share feelings at all," she mused.

Jessie tried not to leap too hungrily at the opportunity presented before her.

"Technically, we're *not* allowed," she answered drily. "According to the official handbook, we're supposed to be cold, emotionless automatons who engage in perfunctory attempts to replicate normal human behavior. How are you doing at following those rules?"

"Pretty well, actually," Hannah replied, playing along. "It seems to come quite naturally to me. If there was some sort of professional league, I think I'd be a real contender."

"I do too," Jessie agreed, taking a lick of her mint chocolate chip cone. "You'd probably be a number one seed in the tournament. Not to brag but I think I'd be a strong second seed myself."

"Are you kidding?" Hannah asked, as she swallowed a healthy gob of rocky road. "You're a wildcard entry at best."

"How so?" Jessie asked.

"You express affection for others. You have genuine friendships. You are in a real relationship with a person you seem to care about. It's almost like you're a normal human being."

"Almost?"

"Well, let's be honest, Jessie," Hannah said. "You still view almost every interaction as a chance to profile the person. You throw yourself into your work to avoid painful communication in your personal life. You carry yourself like a deer afraid everyone it meets is a hunter out to shoot her. So, not completely normal."

"Wow," Jessie said, both impressed and a little disturbed by her sister's perception. "Maybe you should be the profiler. You don't miss a beat."

"Oh yeah," Hannah added. "You also try to downplay uncomfortable truths with snarky jokes."

Jessie smiled appreciatively.

"Touché," she said. "Does all this awareness of our shared stunted emotional growth mean those sessions with Dr. Lemmon are doing some good?"

Hannah gave her an eye roll that suggested she thought the attempt to redirect the conversation was especially ham-fisted.

"It means that I'm aware of my issues, not that I'm necessarily able to do anything about them. I mean, how long have you been seeing her?"

"Let's see. I'm thirty now so it's been close to a decade," Jessie said.

"And you're still a mess," Hannah pointed out. "That doesn't give me much optimism."

Jessie couldn't help but laugh.

"You should have seen me back then," she said. "Compared to the version of me from my early twenties, I'm the poster child for mental health."

Hannah seemed to consider the point as she took a bite out of her cone.

"So you're saying that ten years from now, I could have a boyfriend who's way out of my league too?" she asked.

"Now who's using snarky cracks to avoid emotional truth?" Jessie asked.

Hannah stuck her tongue out at her.

Jessie laughed again and then took another lick of her ice cream. She decided not to push any further. Hannah had opened up more than she'd expected. She didn't want this to turn into a traditional parental conversation.

Besides, she considered Hannah's willingness to admit how alienated she felt to be a good sign. Maybe the shared concerns of Garland and Dr. Lemmon were overstated. Maybe her constant fear that her half-sister might be an embryonic serial killer in the making was meritless. Maybe the girl was just a teenager who had been through hell and was trying to clumsily feel her way out.

As she watched Hannah wipe a dribble of chocolate off her chin, that's what she decided to believe.

At least for now.

CHAPTER EIGHT

Morgan Remar was wiped out.

Her flight back from the Social Services conference in Austin had gotten in late. She was so tired that she'd drifted off as her husband, Ari, drove her back from the airport. By the time they got back to their home in the West Adams district near downtown L.A, it was after 11 p.m.

She was supposed to meet with Jessie Hunt, Kat's profiler friend, tomorrow morning and wanted to get a decent night's sleep beforehand. Of course, that had been close to impossible lately.

Ever since she'd escaped, now over two weeks ago, she'd wake up at least three times a night, sometimes screaming, always sweating. She couldn't stop smelling the pine scent from the wardrobe she'd been held captive in for five days. She jumped every time a door slammed or a car horn honked. She worried that reliving her experience for Kat's friend would just exacerbate all of that.

They arrived home and Ari pulled into the driveway. Neither got out of the car until the security gate closed behind them. It had come with the house when they bought it two years ago, but like the aging mansion itself, which they had been slowly refurbishing, it was in disrepair. The day Morgan escaped, as she recovered in the hospital, she'd begged Ari to have it fixed. It was up and working smoothly when she returned home.

It shouldn't have been a surprise to her. Ari was the kindest, most generous person she'd ever met, the complete inverse of her first husband, whom she'd felt zero guilt about leaving. Even before all this happened, Ari's patience with her admitted tempestuousness was impressive. Since the abduction, he'd been a virtual saint, taking her to therapy, giving her massages, cooking every meal and just holding her close for hours on end.

"You awake?' he asked gently as she stretched in the passenger seat.

"Yup," she said through her yawn, "and surprisingly hungry. The sugar cookies they offered on the flight just didn't cut it."

"You want me to make you something?" he offered.

"No. I know you're exhausted. And I'm a big girl. I can make my own snack."

"Can you though?" he teased lightly.

She scowled playfully as she got out of the car and limped to the side door of the house, trying to balance on the large cast on her left leg. She pretended not to think about it because that also meant she'd remember why she had it. And she didn't want to remember how she'd smashed through the wooden wardrobe door her abductor had improperly locked. She didn't want to relive the memory of her left ankle cracking audibly when it bent the wrong way on that final blow, the one that opened the wardrobe door. She pushed the thought out of her head.

As Ari carried her bag into the house, she smiled to herself, perhaps for the first time all day. It was good to be home, with the one man she could trust. It was good to know that tomorrow she'd be meeting with someone that Kat was sure would move the investigation along.

Morgan was well aware of Jessie Hunt even before Kat had mentioned her. The woman had outwitted two serial killers before turning thirty. She had escaped the murderous clutches of her own husband, who sounded about a hundred times worse than Morgan's ex. And, at least in interviews, she seemed unruffled by any of it. To be honest, Morgan was a little star-struck.

But Kat had assured her that Jessie was approachable in person and that no one was more passionate about getting justice for victims. So she'd go meet with her, even if it meant worse nightmares in the short term.

But that was tomorrow. Tonight she needed that late-night snack. While she hobbled to the kitchen, Ari went to take a shower. He was a commodities broker and had a 6 a.m. meeting tomorrow with the East Coast team so he planned to just get up, get dressed, and get into the office early.

She could hear the water turn on in the master bathroom down the hall as she rifled through the fridge for something appetizing but not too heavy. There was some sliced turkey, which she decided to roll up in a tortilla with a smear of spicy mustard. That ought to tide her over until morning.

The thought of going into work tomorrow after her meeting with Jessie filled her with a complicated mix of enthusiasm and dread.

The conference had gone well and she was excited to implement some of the new programs she'd learned about.

The homeless shelter she worked at in Venice was a mainstay in the community. But it was also slow to embrace new techniques of reaching out to at-risk populations. For such a funky, avant-garde part of town, the care program they employed was surprisingly traditional.

As energized as she was by the prospect of offering something new, she was equally apprehensive about returning to the place where she'd been taken. Tomorrow would be her first day back after recovering at home for the last few weeks.

The shelter had hired an extra security officer to escort staff between the parking lot and the office. But Morgan hadn't been taken on that route. She was abducted returning to the office from lunch on the Venice Boardwalk, only steps from the famous and famously crowded Muscle Beach.

Even with all those people around, apparently no one had given much thought to the man who walked up behind her, put a chemical-doused rag over her face, and tossed her unconscious body in the back seat of a vehicle parked only yards away.

If not for the little boy who saw it happen while his mom paid for cheap T-shirts at an open-air stall across the Boardwalk, not even those details would be known. Unfortunately, the boy, only five, was so shocked that he couldn't offer much in the way of a description other than that the man was white and the car was blue.

Like the memory of the wardrobe, Morgan tried to shake this image out of her head as well. She'd gone over the plan with the shelter director repeatedly. She'd bring her lunch and eat in the office from now on. She would call security when she arrived to the parking lot and the officer would meet her at her car and walk her to the shelter's front door. He'd do the same thing in reverse at the end of the day. She would keep her phone's location function on at all times and call Ari when she arrived at work and when she was headed home.

The hope was that, with Kat and Jessie Hunt's help, the police would catch this guy and she could return to something close to a normal life. She knew three other women had been through the same ordeal as her, including one who had just escaped last night. She didn't want anyone else to have to suffer as they did. The meeting tomorrow was the next step in making it end.

As she laid the snack ingredients out on the kitchen island, she heard a loud rattling outside. Her whole body went cold with fear. She grabbed a butcher knife from the knife block on the island, turned off the kitchen light, shuffled over to the side door, and turned on the porch light.

What she saw made her sigh in relief. A raccoon was aggressively trying to squeeze into one of their locked trash bins. He managed to get a paw into the tiny open space between the can and the lid but couldn't quite squeeze through. When the light came on, his head darted in her direction and she could have sworn she saw a flash of guilt cross his face before he hopped down and darted off into the darkness.

She silently laughed at herself. If a shoplifting raccoon could cause heart palpitations, it was going to take a while to get back to something approximating a normal life. She turned the light back on and returned to the island to prep the snack.

But as she put down the knife and reached for the turkey, she noticed the tortilla was gone.

I could have sworn I got that out.

She turned back to the fridge. That's when she noticed the dirty footprints from what looked like a boot. Neither she nor Ari wore shoes in the house. The cold sensation of fear that had just subsided suddenly returned, as if a huge, frozen fist had suddenly clenched around her entire body. She picked up the butcher knife again. Glancing at the counter, she noticed something else. The small paring knife was missing from the knife block.

She started to call out to Ari when the shadow darted out from the pantry behind her, clasping his hand over her mouth just before she got the name out. She tried to struggle free but he had already jabbed the paring knife into the small of her back four times before she thought to swing the butcher knife in his direction.

Morgan gasped underneath the hand covering her mouth. She had no idea if she made contact as the pain and shock were too immersive for anything else to get through. She lost track of how many times he plunged the small knife into the soft skin above her hips. But at some point, she collapsed to the floor.

She landed hard on the kitchen tile and felt her skull bounce once before settling down again. She was on her stomach but her eyes were open so she could see him place the knife delicately on the island with his gloved hands. Then he bent over and wiped the blade of the butcher knife she was still clinging to. She couldn't see his face.

"Repent," he whispered in her ear.

Though she was quickly losing consciousness, Morgan felt a shiver of horror-stricken recognition as she realized it was the same voice as her abductor. He stood back up and looked down at her with mild interest before walking to the side door.

Just before he stepped out and closed it behind him, she saw him bring her tortilla to his mouth and take a big bite. Then he closed the door and was gone. Three minutes later, so was she.

CHAPTER NINE

Jessie was frustrated.

She knew she should probably go to bed. After all, it was almost midnight and Ryan was spending tonight at his place. But she wasn't tired. She had the case files for all four abductions laid out on the bed. As she listened to Hannah laughing in the other room as she watched an episode of *Top Chef*, she tried to connect the dots.

While these women had a lot in common, nothing jumped out that was similar enough to show an obvious pattern. All were in their late twenties to mid-thirties. All were at least middle-class, if not well-off, and lived in nice neighborhoods. But that's where the similarities ended.

None of them lived in the same area of town. None of them were found near where they were taken or near any of the other victims. Three were married, but one, the most recent victim, wasn't. Three were white but the third victim, Jayne Castillo, was Latina. One had kids. The other three didn't. Two had office jobs, one had a home business, and one was a stay-at-home mom. None had criminal records.

She wanted to have something positive to share with Morgan Remar when she met with her in the morning. But right now, there wasn't much to go on. She was hoping that maybe something Morgan would tell her might jibe what she'd learned from Brenda Ferguson today.

She was debating whether to tell Hannah it was time for lights out when her phone rang. It was Ryan.

"Miss me?" she asked.

"Always," he said. "But that's not why I'm calling. I was just assigned a case. Decker wants you with me. I'm on my way in. Can I pick you up on the way? I can be there in fifteen minutes."

"Sure," she said, already starting to put away each woman's file. "What the case?"

"I don't know much yet. Just that a man found his wife dead in their kitchen less than an hour ago. They live in West Adams. She was in her late twenties, stabbed multiple times in the back before bleeding out."

"Okay," Jessie said. "I'll meet you out front in fifteen. That'll give me just enough time to beg Hannah to go to sleep."

"Good luck with that."

"Thanks. She's watching food television so I'm going to need it."

*

They pulled up in front of the house at 12:35 a.m. The area around the home was already cordoned off and was surrounded by four black-and-whites, an ambulance, and a medical examiner's van.

Jessie and Ryan got out a half block away and walked past several hundred-year-old mansions until they reached the crime scene. This home was large and impressive too, but it was more dilapidated than the others. A tarp and a pile of lumber in the front yard suggested the owners had been trying to remedy that.

Ryan flashed his badge and a uniformed officer lifted the police tape so they could duck under and head to the front door. They were met by Officer Pete Clark, a veteran cop with a tight gray buzz cut and arms like a He-Man action figure. Known around the department for his no-guff demeanor, he didn't disappoint.

"How's it going, Pete?" Ryan asked when they met him at the stoop.

"The Dodgers were just about to bat in the bottom of the thirteenth inning when I got the call, so not great. This basically ruined the night for me."

"Sorry this pesky murder got in the way of your baseball game," Ryan replied with fake sympathy. "Mind filling us in on what happened here?"

"No problem," Clark said, clearly not taking offense at Ryan's crack as he switched into professional mode. "Follow me."

Before she entered the home, Jessie took a moment to gather her thoughts. Everything she was about to see was a potential clue into the mindset of the murderer. She pushed all thoughts of troubled half-sisters and abducted women out of her mind as she stepped inside. As Clark led them down the hallway, stepping heavily on the sagging, uneven wooden floor, he gave them a status update.

"Victim is a twenty-nine-year-old female, married, no children. Her husband had just picked her up from LAX after an out-of-town conference. He went to shower while she got a snack. When he got out, he found her dead on the kitchen floor. She'd been stabbed eleven times in the lower back. The food was still on the kitchen island, as was a paring knife covered in blood. She was clutching a butcher knife but didn't look she got a chance to use it."

They arrived at the kitchen, where another officer handed them slippers to put over their shoes. Jessie could see the victim lying face down on the floor on the other side of the island. Her head was pointed away from them toward the door. She had a huge cast on her left leg. The plaster was splattered with blood.

"We found some boot marks on the floor leading out to the driveway," Clark added. "The husband says they never wore shoes in the house so we're having them tested—no results yet. CSU also say the paring knife handle was wiped clean so they're not optimistic about finding anything on it."

"Who is the victim?" Ryan asked.

"That's the crazy thing," Clark replied. "She was one of those kidnapped women who escaped recently. Her name is Morgan Remar."

Jessie involuntarily reached out and grabbed the door frame for support. Ryan looked over at her, as shocked as she felt.

"Are you sure?" he asked Clark.

"Yeah. Her husband was talking about how she finally felt comfortable enough to go back to work tomorrow for the first time since it happened. It's a damn shame."

When she was sure she could stand on her own, Jessie walked around the island until she could get a clear look at the victim's face. Even with her face a pale blue and her glassy, empty brown eyes, Jessie recognized her from her file photos, though her light brown hair, which had been cut in the hospital, was much shorter now. Still, it was the same woman she was supposed to meet tomorrow.

"Any signs of a robbery?" she asked quietly, surprised to hear her own voice. "Anything taken? Valuables? Her purse?"

"So far, nothing," Clark said.

"Where's the husband?" Ryan asked.

"He's in the bedroom. He was pretty broken up, looked like he was in shock to me. The medics want to take him to the hospital but he won't go until they take her body away. He says he can't leave her here."

"Do we know if he has a record?" Ryan asked.

Jessie spoke up before Clark could.

"He doesn't," she said. "He was arrested during a bar fight near campus when he was an undergrad at UCLA. But the charges were later dropped."

"How do you know that, Hunt?" Clark asked, stunned.

"I was consulting on the abduction case for a private investigator friend," she said. "I actually read Morgan's file just tonight. I know all about both Remars' education, how they met, when they got married, how long they've been at their jobs. I even knew they lived in West Adams. I just hadn't made the connection."

"Why would you?" Ryan asked. "I mean, what were the chances that it would be the same victim?"

"That's a question we should pursue," Jessie muttered, almost to herself.

"What are you saying?" Clark asked skeptically. "That the same guy who kidnapped her came back to finish the job? That doesn't seem to be his M.O. from what I've seen."

"You're right," Jessie admitted. "It doesn't. It could just be a coincidence, terrible luck."

"Or maybe," Ryan added, "it could be that Mr. Remar decided to take advantage of the situation to get rid of his wife. With her abduction, he'd have the perfect way to throw suspicion elsewhere. We should talk to him before too much time passes."

"Have at it," Clark said. "The body won't be removed for at least another twenty minutes. Since he's not going anywhere until that happens, you've got the perfect opportunity."

He led them toward the master bedroom, where Ari Remar sat on the side of his bed, hunched over with his head in his hands. He was balding and had decided not to hide it but simply shave it so that there was a thin bit of stubble on top and at the back of his head. He looked frail and pathetic in his white T-shirt and shorts, the clothes he'd apparently put on after the shower.

Jessie imagined him walking out to the kitchen, hoping to coax his wife to bed after a long day, trying to set her mind at ease before returning to work for the first time. But then another image entered her mind, one she couldn't ignore. She turned to Clark.

"Has anyone checked the shower yet?" she asked.

“What do you mean?” he asked.

“Has CSU checked to see if there’s any blood residue on the shower floor, in the grate or the piping underneath?”

“I’ll double check,” Clark said.

“Please,” she insisted. “I assume they’re also checking the trash to see if there are any soiled clothes in there.”

“On it,” Clark said and disappeared to check with the on-scene deputy medical examiner.

Jessie looked over at Ryan, who nodded. After working so many cases together, he knew what she wanted to do next. They walked over to Ari Remar, who hadn’t spoken or even moved since they entered. The medic sitting beside him, a young woman with a blonde ponytail, looked up at them and shook her head. Ryan ignored her and bent down in front of the man.

“Hi, Mr. Remar,” he said soothingly. “I’m Detective Hernandez with the LAPD. I was hoping to ask you a few questions about tonight.”

Remar slowly lifted his head. It was immediately apparent to Jessie that he’d been medicated in some way. His eyes were cloudy and he had a thin stream of saliva drooling slowly down his chin.

“You sedated him?” Jessie asked the medic tersely.

“He was in bad shape,” she replied. “When we tried to get him out of the house, he started having a panic attack. He wouldn’t leave. He was slamming himself into the wall. We were worried he might hurt himself or someone else. So we gave him something. It should wear off in a few hours.”

“That doesn’t do us much good,” Ryan said, frustrated. “How are Ms. Hunt and I supposed to question him when he’s nearly catatonic?”

The medic started to reply when Remar mumbled something incoherent.

“What was that?” Ryan asked.

Remar repeated himself, much more slowly this time.

“Hunt? Morgan meeting Hunt tomorrow.”

“That’s right,” Jessie said, tensing. “Did Morgan say anything about that?”

He looked at her vaguely for several seconds before responding.

“Hunt helping tomorrow. Morgan said.”

The statement seemed to have drained all his energy. His headed lolled forward again and the medic had to grab him and hold him steady so he didn't fall off the bed completely. She eased him back so that he was lying down.

"I'm sorry," she said. "I didn't mean to screw up your interrogation. I was just trying to keep him from self-harm."

Jessie nodded and stood up. What was done was done. There was no point in making her feel worse. She and Ryan walked out of the bedroom and back down the hall. When they were back outside, Ryan blew off some steam.

"There's no way Remar's going to be alert in a few hours," he growled. "He won't be able to talk until the morning. And by then he'll be lawyered up, innocent or guilty."

"If CSU finds anything suspicious, we can take another run at him," Jessie promised. "But I'm worried that we're not looking at the other possibilities."

"Which are those?"

"Clark's probably right. This doesn't fit the abductor's history. But I wonder if we shouldn't put some officers on the other kidnapping victims as a precaution."

"I suspect Captain Decker will consider that a leap," Ryan warned. "But I'll call him and run it up the flagpole. Can't hurt to try."

"While you do that, I've got a call of my own to make."

"To who?" Ryan asked.

"Kat," Jessie said, sighing heavily. "I have to tell her that her client's been murdered."

CHAPTER TEN

The call went badly from the start.

Even before Jessie made it, Ryan warned her that giving a private detective a heads-up on the case wasn't protocol.

"I can't *not* tell her," Jessie said. "She's the whole reason I already know so much about the victim. If she finds out about Morgan's death on the news and learns that I'm working her case, she'll be livid."

"Fine," Ryan said. "But remember, it's one thing to let her know what happened. Letting her get involved is something else entirely. This is a police matter now. Keep those boundaries clear."

Kat had clearly been asleep when Jessie called. That made sense. It was 1:15 a.m.

"I have some bad news," she said once she was sure her friend was awake and coherent.

"Okay."

"Morgan Remar is dead."

"What?" Kat demanded, disbelieving.

After Jessie walked her through the basics of what she knew, Kat was quiet for several seconds before responding.

"I can be there in twenty minutes," she finally said.

"No, you can't," Jessie replied, surprised by the firmness in her own voice.

"What do you mean?"

"It's a crime scene, Kat. They won't let you in."

"*You* can get me in," Kat insisted.

"Not during a homicide investigation. It's a violation of protocol. Technically, I shouldn't even be calling you now. But I thought you deserved to know."

"Okay," Kat said, though Jessie could tell from her voice that it wasn't. "At least tell me what you have on the suspect front, because this seems awfully coincidental. What are the chances that the same woman is randomly abducted, gets away, and is then murdered less than three weeks later?"

"We're looking into all the options," Jessie assured her. "Husband, random robbery gone bad, and yes, the abductor too."

"That's all you can tell me?" Kat asked, her voice getting harder.

"That's all I know," Jessie insisted.

"Would you tell me if it wasn't?" Kat wanted to know.

"I'll tell you everything I reasonably can. But please, don't make unreasonable demands that put me in an awkward position."

"Unreasonable demands?" Kat repeated, her voice thick with emotion. "Jessie, Morgan Remar came to me for help. I promised to do everything I could to find the guy who took her so that she could resume some kind of normal life. I gave her my word that I, and *you*, would help her. And now she's dead. So don't talk to me about unreasonable demands. We both owe this woman."

Jessie forced herself to take a breath before responding.

"I know," she said in slow, measured words. "And I'm going to do everything in my power to get justice for her. This isn't just a favor anymore. It's my case now and I'm committed to it. But you have to respect the boundaries here."

"That sounds like something Ryan would say," Kat spat back.

Before Jessie could reply, she realized the line was dead. It occurred to her that it was just as well. She didn't have a comeback.

*

Jessie managed to get an hour of sleep on the couch in the break room. But other than that, she and Ryan worked straight through the night, coordinating with CSU, the medical examiner's office, and the tech unit. None of them had much new to offer.

The paring knife handle had been wiped clean and was devoid of prints or DNA. The butcher knife blade had also been wiped down, which made Jessie wonder if Morgan had gotten in a successful swipe at her killer and he'd removed the evidence.

The house had a security system with cameras, which Ari had installed right after Jessie's escape from her kidnapper. But somehow the battery hadn't properly charged yesterday and there was no usable footage. Ari was supposed to review an inventory of items from the house to see if anything had been stolen but Jessie was already skeptical about the usefulness of that. There was a laptop sitting on the breakfast table, which hadn't been touched. A garden variety thief would have considered it easy pickings.

They were still waiting for results from the samples collected from the shower. But the CSU tech Ryan spoke to didn't sound hopeful. As to Ari Remar himself, Ryan had been right. When they showed up at the hospital to question him at 4:30 a.m., his attorney was already at his bedside.

Other than repeating his description of the events earlier that evening, including the discovery of Morgan's body, Remar was instructed not to answer any questions. He didn't seem personally reluctant, but followed the advice of his lawyer, who was adamant.

After calling Hannah to make sure she was up and getting ready for school, Jessie waited until what she considered a reasonable hour, 7 a.m., to reach out to Detective Sands from Pacific Station. His cell phone was answered by an annoyed-sounding woman Jessie gathered was his wife.

"This better be work-related," the woman said irritably. "Because if this is some secret girlfriend, you're doing a terrible job of being clandestine."

"I'm sorry, ma'am," Jessie said, impressed at the early morning snark. "This *is* work. I'm trying to reach Detective Sands about a case we discussed yesterday. Could you ask him to call Jessie Hunt from Central Station when he gets a chance?"

"He's in the shower now. But I'll give him the message."

The woman hung up. Jessie doubted Sands would have gotten the abduction task force up and running since they last talked but figured it was worth a shot. With so little to go on, any scrap of information might prove useful.

When she was done with her calls, she headed to the break room for either her fourth of fifth cup of coffee—she'd lost track. Ryan was waiting there with a sour expression.

"What is it?"

"I just ran into Decker," he said.

"Why do I not like the sound of this?"

"He said he had an update on our protection request and that he'd talk to us about it at eight, once he's settled in."

Jessie looked at the clock on the wall. It read 7:06.

"Screw that. I'm not waiting an hour for him to give us the run-around and blather on about departmental resources," she said, turning on her heel to head for the captain's office.

To her surprise, Captain Roy Decker, who had just entered the room, was standing right in front of her.

"Blather, do I?" he said, more amused than angry.

To look at him, one would think he'd pulled an all-nighter too. His sixty-year-old body was sunken and beaten down after years of stress. He had more wrinkles than strands of hair remaining on his head and his weathered suit jacket hung off his skinny frame. Only his hawk-like eyes, beady and penetrating above his long, sharp nose, suggested he was more than just a senior citizen in waiting.

"I hope not," Jessie replied without a beat. "I assume you're here to tell us that we got approval for protective orders on all the other recent abductees?"

The only other people in the room besides Jessie, Ryan, and Decker, two uniformed officers perusing the vending machine, quickly scurried out without a word.

"Good morning to you, Hunt," Decker said, resignation and frustration fighting a battle in his voice. "I'm afraid it's not as simple as that."

"It never is," Jessie retorted.

"Very rarely," he admitted. "In this case, Deputy Chief Sklar felt it was premature to approve security when there is no evidence that this murder has anything to do with the abductions."

"What kind of evidence does Sklar need? Another body? Would that be a solid enough clue that there's a connection?"

"I imagine that would do the trick," Decker said wryly. "Listen, Hunt. I'm not saying the idea that the abductor might have done this is outrageous. In fact, it seems as valid a theory as any other. And if all the women who were taken were in our jurisdiction, I'd give them protection, despite the costs. But the other three women live in Brentwood, the Mid-Wilshire District, and West Hollywood. That last one is currently in a hospital in Beverly Hills. We are talking about multiple stations across various commands. The only way to get approval for all of that comes from headquarters. And they're just not willing to authorize it right now."

"Maybe I should have a chat with Chief Laird and see what he says," Jessie offered.

No one spoke for a second. All three of them knew that was a not-so-veiled reference to how only a month ago, the LAPD chief of police had personally threatened to have her fired for insubordination only hours before thanking her for helping nail a ring of corrupt cops, including the sixth highest ranking member of the whole department.

"You could have that chat," Decker said. "But remember, you can only pull that lever once. The chief owes you. And you can definitely collect. But once you've used that chit, it's gone forever. So you have to ask yourself—if this what you want to spend it on?"

"I shouldn't have to use it, Captain," she insisted. "This should be done because it's the smart thing to do."

"And yet, here we are," Decker replied. "So you can go to the mat for this. Or you can pursue the leads you have and see where they take you."

Before Jessie could respond, her cell phone rang. Worried that it was Hannah with some problem, she glanced at it. Her heart sank immediately. It was Brenda Ferguson.

"I have to take this," she said bitterly. "It's one of the other abductees. I'm sure she's calling just to have a friendly catch-up session."

Neither Decker nor Ryan replied as she walked out of the room.

CHAPTER ELEVEN

"Hi, Brenda," she said, bracing for the inevitable as she walked back to her desk.

"Did you hear that one of the other abductees was killed?" the panicked woman immediately asked.

"I did," Jessie said, trying to sound calm. "I'm actually working the case. But it's not public knowledge. How did you find out?"

"A private detective who was working for her called to warn me. She suggested I reach out to you. I told her we'd already spoken."

Jessie felt a tide of frustration rise in her chest. She knew Kat was upset but the idea that her friend would use an abductee like this filled her with a sense of fury she found it difficult to contain.

"Was the detective's name Katherine Gentry?" she asked slowly, making sure not to reveal her state of mind.

"Yes. She said you know each other."

Jessie sighed silently, not wanting to take her frustration out on Brenda.

"That's true. In fact, I'm planning to call her right now, as soon as we hang up, in fact."

"So, if you're handling this," Brenda began, asking the question Jessie knew was coming, "does that mean you'll be assigning officers to keep me and the other women safe, in case the person who killed Morgan Remar is the same man who took us?"

"Brenda, I've looked into that," Jessie said apologetically. "Unfortunately, I was just a consultant on the abductions. I only have input on the murder case and I can't make the department give you protection. Trust me, I've tried. But I haven't given up. I'm going to keep pushing for it. In the meantime, my recommendations aren't going to make you feel super secure but I'm going to recommend them anyway."

"Okay," Brenda said, desperate for any help she could get.

"Keep your doors locked at all times. Don't leave your home alone. If your husband can continue to work from home, have him do so. Only go out on essential trips. If you have to go and Ty can't go with you, see if there are friends who can accompany you. Use the contact info for the security company I gave you. They're good. They can get something solid set up for you in the next forty-eight hours. Mention my name. God knows I've spent enough money with them. Otherwise just keep busy. Spend time with your kids. Work out at home. Anything that keeps your mind off this is a good thing."

"I appreciate the help," Brenda said, clearly disappointed. "But you'll have to forgive me for not being impressed when the best the police can recommend is for me to keep busy."

"I'm sorry I can't offer you more right now. All I can say is that I'm investigating the case. I'm going to catch this murderer. If it's the same man who abducted you, then your nightmare is over. If it's not, then maybe you can feel better knowing the guy who took you isn't interested in coming after you again. Either way, you'll be better off than you are now."

"Thank you," Brenda said half-heartedly.

"Thank me when I catch him," Jessie said.

She'd barely hung up before she was dialing Kat's number. It went straight to voicemail.

"I know you're pissed," Jessie said the second she heard the beep. "And I get it. You have every right to be. But calling Brenda Ferguson to scare the crap out of her and tell her to call me? How does that help anything, Kat? You know I'm working non-stop on this thing. I don't need the peanut gallery throwing stuff at me too. Please call me back when you get this. I think we should meet when I get a ten-minute break, assuming I ever do."

She hung up, dropped the phone on her desk, and leaned back in her chair. Closing her eyes, she tried to shut out the noise of the station bullpen. She needed a few seconds to let her brain process everything that had happened in the last eight hours.

But she only got about twenty seconds of solitude before she heard her phone ring again. Despite her deep desire not to, she glanced at it. It was Ray Sands. Apparently his wife had accepted that he wasn't having an affair and given him the message. She picked up.

"Hi, Detective Sands," she said, faking cool professionalism. "Thanks for getting back to me."

"I'm sorry," he told her, sounding genuinely rueful. "I know you were just helping out a friend on these cases. Now you've been dragged in. It must suck."

"Thanks, Detective," she said, appreciative of the sentiment. "It does truly suck. But this is where we are now. So I'm just diving in. I was hoping you could help me with that."

"Of course," he said. "I'm happy to do whatever I can. Just so you know, I've already sent over some material to you and Detective Hernandez. I heard he's working the case with you."

"He is."

"He's a good detective," Sands said. "At least that's what I hear. I've never worked with him."

"He'll do," Jessie said, deciding not to expound on that. "What material did you send?"

"It's everything from the task force files, not just related to Morgan Remar, but the other abduction victims too. I'm assuming you're looking into any possible connections."

"We are. Thanks," Jessie replied. "But are you telling me you already got the task force up and running since we spoke yesterday?'

Sands chuckled softly.

"I'm a pretty persuasive guy when I want to be, Ms. Hunt, kind of bullheaded too."

"That's one of my favorite qualities in people," Jessie said, smiling. "Is there anything specific I should be looking at?"

"Well, you could probably stand to look at some of the folks we originally interviewed as potential suspects in Morgan Remar's abduction. Before we realized it was a serial kidnapper, we were looking at lots of folks. After the third abduction, we basically stopped looking at all of them. Maybe she was unlucky enough to have two different people after her."

"But none of them jumped out at you?" Jessie asked.

"No one I felt strongly about," Sands admitted. "But like I said, I was checking alibis for when she was taken. Maybe everything changes now that you're looking for a killer."

"Thanks, Sands."

"Not a problem," he said warmly. "And like I said, I also sent details on the other abductions, way more than you could have accessed otherwise. I'm not sure it will matter for your purposes, especially if we're looking at a different perp. But I figured it couldn't hurt."

"I appreciate all of it. We're dealing with slim pickings here. So I'd rather have too much to sift through rather than nothing at all."

"You bet," he said. "Let me know if there's anything else I can do. And I'll keep you apprised on anything worthwhile we uncover."

Jessie hung up and clicked on the task force file he'd sent her and Ryan. It was massive, with detailed subheads for each victim. How Sands had managed to pull all this together since yesterday was beyond her.

Ryan walked over hesitantly. She knew he'd been avoiding her until she finished all her phone calls. It was the wise move. He'd learned to steer clear until she was done letting off steam.

"How's it going?" he asked, audibly wincing.

Jessie smiled, letting him know he was safe for now.

"I'll skip the bad news. The good news is that Sands from Pacific Station sent us a treasure trove of files on all the abductions, including their interview notes with all the suspects in Morgan Remar's original abduction. That should help us find a place to start."

"Great," Ryan said. "How many interviews are we talking about?"

"It looks like they targeted four credible suspects. Want to split them up?"

"Sounds like a plan," he agreed.

CHAPTER TWELVE

Two hours later, they had nothing.

All four suspects had credible alibis for the time of the murder. Jessie was reduced to checking the manifest of Morgan's flight back from Austin last night to see if anyone on board had a record. Two folks did but a quick check indicated that both of them had alibis as well.

In desperation, she turned to photos of the location of Morgan Remar's abduction to see if there was anything about it that reminded her of the murder scene. Nothing jumped out. She was just about to get up for another cup of coffee in the hopes that it might soothe her developing headache, when she noticed something she hadn't paid attention to before—a sign on a fence at the site.

The sign read "Coast Construction." Morgan had been held in a still-under-construction warehouse on an isolated hill in Playa Vista. The construction had been stopped because of a dispute between the company having it built and the lender.

Detective Sands had already looked into the employees of both companies, as well as the construction firm workers, as most of them would have known the warehouse would be unoccupied for several weeks. That made it an ideal spot to hold someone without fear of discovery. While several of the employees at the various companies had records, none of those people had trouble accounting for their time.

But that wasn't what Jessie found so interesting. Rather, it was something that wasn't in the files Sands had sent.

"Check this out," she said to Ryan. "The construction company listed in their records is Coast Construction. But in Kat's files on Morgan's abduction, the construction company is listed as Construction Associates."

"Could Kat have made a mistake?' he asked.

"That's what I assumed at first," Jessie said. "But when I looked more closely, I saw that both of them were right. Coast Construction is a subsidiary of Construction Associates. Since Kat wasn't able to access the crime scene or get interviews with the construction company, she had to go with the name listed in public records."

"Right," Ryan agreed, catching on. "But Sands and his team at Pacific Station were able to access the crime scene and saw the actual signs that indicated the company on the project was Coast Construction. He had no reason to pursue the matter beyond that because the information he needed was right in front of him. And Kat didn't have the time or resources to investigate what company did the construction work at the locations where the other abductees were found."

"No," Jessie said. "But I do."

She resumed poring over the paperwork, following a hunch that she kept to herself. If Coast Construction was a subsidiary of Construction Associates, she couldn't help but wonder if the larger company had other ancillary firms as well. It took less than five minutes of working with the tech team to discover that Construction Associates had seemingly intentionally created an untraceable web of ownership, possibly to hide the fact that many of their workers were undocumented.

So she called the company directly. But while she hit a brick wall asking for their financials, it only took one call on her behalf from an assistant district attorney to get the breakdown sent to her. When she reviewed the data, she found that Construction Associates had seven subsidiary companies under their banner. When she cross-checked them, she found something that by now seemed almost inevitable.

Every abduction site was at a location owned by a subsidiary of Construction Associates. In addition to the warehouse in Playa Vista where Morgan Remar was held, all three other women were held in various abandoned or under-construction commercial properties in isolated areas, each owned by C.A.

There was no reason for Sands to have noticed this, although Jessie was sure he would have soon, now that all the case files had been compiled. And there was no way that Kat, operating solo, could have made the connections in the time she had.

Of course, finding a connection among the places where the women were taken didn't necessarily mean any of them were connected to Morgan Remar's murder. But it was something to go on at least. In fact, it was the only thing.

She looked up at Ryan and smiled.

“What is it?” he asked.

She enjoyed a brief moment of satisfaction before responding, knowing how rare they could be.

“We have a lead.”

CHAPTER THIRTEEN

Jessie thought she might throw up.

The dirt road out to their intended location was bumpy and the police car's suspension left a lot to be desired. As she tried to take deep, calming breaths and fight the urge to tell Ryan to pull over, she wondered if this was even the right call.

But then she remembered that it was by far their best option. After having the tech team run some calculations, they discovered that there was only one person associated with all four job sites, the parent company's client representative, Scott Fellows.

As the Construction Associates rep, he was obligated to keep in touch with the clients, the lenders, and the subsidiary builder. He was the one person best positioned to know where all the sites were and whether work was in progress or had been stopped for some reason.

Unfortunately for Jessie and Ryan, he was also the representative for one additional subsidiary construction firm, Valley Builders. And according to his office, he was currently on site at their job in Sylmar, deep in the mountains of the San Fernando Valley at the edge of the Angeles National Forest.

On the way up, Jessie texted Detective Sands what she'd learned and where she and Ryan were headed. She wanted a head start in talking to Fellows but didn't want to alienate the head of the task force that had given her the lead.

It was about fifteen degrees hotter in Sylmar than downtown, close to ninety, and Jessie could feel it. With the dirt road so dusty, they had to keep the car windows up and the air conditioning blasting. By the time they'd arrived at the under-construction stables in a small orchard on an otherwise barren hillside, she was ready for a Dramamine and a nap.

They pulled into the small parking lot for the stables next to a red BMW that looked like it had seen its fair share of dusty roads. Jessie got out and hurried over to a thick-trunked tree. She knelt behind it, hoping she was out of sight, and waited for her breakfast to come back up.

But after about a minute, her stomach settled and she stood up again. Ryan was leaning against the hood of the car, trying not to laugh.

"How ya doin', slugger?" he asked teasingly.

She scowled at him and walked back over slowly.

"I blame your driving," she said, only half-seriously. "It was like you were *trying* to make me puke."

"You see dead bodies all the time," he said incredulously. "And a dirt road is your undoing? I thought you were tougher than that, Jessie Hunt."

"And I think you may want to zip it if you ever want to spend the night again, Ryan Hernandez."

Ryan raised his hands above his head in surrender, though his smirk suggested he wasn't entirely chastened.

"Can I help you?" someone called out from behind them.

Jessie turned around to find a man walking toward them in black loafers, khakis, and a button-down shirt.

"Maybe," Ryan said. "Are you Scott Fellows?"

"Who wants to know?" the man asked with a snide tone that made Jessie half-wish she still felt bad enough to vomit on him.

His look matched his tone. In addition to the seemingly inappropriate attire for checking on a stable, he wore aviator sunglasses and had his black hair slicked back within a Brylcreem pinch of its life.

"The LAPD wants to know," Ryan said with a sharpness that let the guy know his bullying style wasn't going to play with them.

Fellows stopped walking briefly before regaining his composure.

"I swear I was about to pay those tickets, Officer," he said, trying and failing to sound jokey.

"It's Detective, Mr. Fellows," Ryan said, not amused. "We'd like to ask you a few questions."

"Yeah, okay," Fellows said less confidently. "What's this about?"

"Is there somewhere we can go with a little shade?" Jessie asked.

"There are some benches in the stable," he replied and motioned for them to follow him. "Should I be asking for badge numbers or something?"

"We can show you those if you like, Mr. Fellows," Ryan said, really hitting the bad cop vibe hard. "I'm Detective Ryan Hernandez. I work Homicide out of one of our downtown stations. This is Jessie Hunt. She's a criminal profiler for the department."

They entered the comparative shade of the empty structure. Jessie found something disconcerting about being in a stable devoid of horses, straw, or any hint of manure.

"Profiler?" Fellows repeated as they sat down on benches directly across from each other right outside the stalls. "I thought that was just something out of serial killer movies."

"No," Jessie said. "We're real. So do you know why we're here, Mr. Fellows?"

Fellows looked briefly like he might try to work them, then seemed to give up on the idea.

"I could think of a lot of reasons people might be pissed at me but none of them would require a criminal profiler to get involved."

"What kind of reasons?" Jessie asked. "And can you please take off your sunglasses?"

"You want me to incriminate myself?" he asked disbelievingly as he did what she asked. His light blue eyes flickered with apprehension.

Jessie had reviewed everything she could find on Fellows on the way up north so she was already well aware of the kind of activities that might make him unpopular. But she wanted to make him feel vulnerable so she pressed.

"We investigate homicides, Mr. Fellows," she told him. "Unless you're about to confess to one, we don't really care that much about the improprieties you're involved in. But being deceptive about them will certainly engender suspicion from us. Do you want us to be suspicious of you, Mr. Fellows?"

"No."

"Then you're probably better off being straight with us, even if your misdeeds involve hiring workers without legitimate paperwork, manipulating property owners into selling for less than market value, or working with unscrupulous brokers who might pay you off for your assistance."

Fellows stared at her in disbelief.

"So if you already know everything," he demanded, "why are you asking me?"

Jessie smiled at him, though there was no warmth to it.

"Because you coming clean is a sign of good will. Detective Hernandez and I are big fans of establishing good will, isn't that right, Detective?"

"I'm getting impatient with the run-around, that's for sure," Ryan said, continuing to project the aura of a cop whose fuse was dangerously short.

Jessie raised her eyebrows at Fellows, as if to hint that there wasn't much she could do once her partner's patience ran out completely.

"Okay, fine," Fellows said. "So I can't guarantee that every construction worker on every site has every document they need to work legally. And I have, on rare occasions, worked with a broker to get the best possible deal on a property and then flip it when the values in the area increase."

Jessie again smiled. Ryan grunted impressively.

"Just to be clear," she said, her voice saccharine sweet, "your broker friend pressures locals, usually folks on the verge of bankruptcy, to sell their distressed properties on the cheap. Then he sits on them while you convince your firm's clients to buy, offering them sweet deals. After a few sign up, the broker jacks up the price on the remaining, now valuable properties. And on every transaction, he gives you a generous commission for steering them his way. Is that about right?"

"It's not illegal," Fellows said obstinately.

"You know, that's debatable," Jessie replied. "A motivated prosecutor can often find crimes that others miss. The question I guess you should probably be asking is whether the detective or I know any motivated prosecutors."

Fellows looked back and forth between them. As he did, Jessie studied him, trying to determine if he was truly just concerned about getting busted for kickbacks or if there was something bigger he was worried about. She couldn't tell.

"What exactly do you want?" Fellows asked.

Ryan dived in the next second.

"Where were you last night, Mr. Fellows?"

"What?"

"I want to know where you were last night," Ryan repeated forcefully.

"I was…last night I was…" He stumbled nervously for words for several seconds before seeming to recall his whereabouts. "Oh yeah, I was at my girlfriend's. She made us dinner. Then we binged a couple of episodes of *The Crown*."

Ryan and Jessie exchanged dubious looks.

"You don't strike me as *The Crown* type," Ryan said.

"You have a girlfriend?" Jessie added skeptically, more to throw Fellows off than because she doubted him.

Before he could answer her, Ryan tossed another question at him.

"When did you leave her place?" he wanted to know.

Fellows seemed uncertain who to answer first, but apparently chose Ryan since he appeared angrier.

"I spent the night. I left early this morning, around six, to go home so I could shower and change clothes."

"You were at her place all night?" Ryan pressed.

Fellows nodded.

"How long have you been dating your girlfriend?" Jessie asked, putting an extra dollop of suspicion on the last word.

"About a year," he said, impressively not taking the bait. "Why? Can you please tell me what this is about?"

Jessie's developing profile of Morgan's killer didn't include the likelihood that he was in a long-term relationship. She envisioned him as someone who had trouble forming romantic attachments. She had drawn the same conclusion about the abductor. If Scott Fellows was legitimately in a romantic relationship that had been going on for a year, the probability that he was the culprit in either crime dropped dramatically.

"We'll need her contact information," Ryan said. "And consent to check your phone records and GPS data without a court order."

"Fine," Fellows said. "Just tell me what's going on. This can't possibly be about some shady property deals."

"Do you know the name Morgan Remar?" Jessie asked.

Fellows's forehead creased as he thought about it.

"It sounds vaguely familiar. I'm not sure why."

"What about Brenda Ferguson?" Ryan followed up.

Fellows's furrowed brow softened and his eyes filled with recognition.

"Oh," he said slowly. "I get it now. This is about the women, right?"

"Yes, Scott," Jessie confirmed. "This is about the women."

“I know about them, of course,” he said. “I recognize the Brenda name. The other one was taken too, right?”

“These women escaped from days of captivity on properties your construction company handles and you only have a passing awareness of it?” Jessie said.

Fellows’s expression suggested he was more peeved than worried.

“Ms. Hunt, I deal with client coordination for five construction subsidiaries, all under the banner of a large company. At any one time, I’m dealing with between fifteen and twenty job sites. I admit that finding out that three women were held on ones operated by Construction Associates was freaky. But no one talked to me about it until now so I figured it was just a coincidence.”

“Four women,” Jessie corrected.

“I’m sorry?”

“There were four women taken. The most recent was at the abandoned wood shop property your company owns near the old zoo in Griffith Park.”

“I didn’t know about that,” Fellows said, looking credibly surprised.

“She escaped two nights ago,” Ryan said.

Fellows didn’t have a response to that.

“We need your help,” Jessie prompted. “Assuming you have nothing to hide in relation to these crimes, what we need shouldn’t be hard for you to do.”

“What do you need?” he asked, trying to sound reticent, though Jessie sensed that he would give them anything that would get them off his case.

“We need a list of everyone who knew those sites would be unoccupied, not just at the construction firms but among the clients, lenders, and everyone else. I don’t just mean people officially in the loop but everyone who would logically know. The person who kidnapped these women had to know those locations wouldn’t be disturbed. We need to know who that list includes. Can you do that?”

Fellows mentally calculated what was required to make the request happen. Eventually he answered.

“I can’t promise that I can come up with everyone. There’s always casual conversation, you know. But I can create a list of everyone who would reasonably have access to property statuses. It'll be pretty long though."

"When can you have it to us?" Jessie asked.

"Tomorrow morning?"

"Let's shoot for today," Ryan said definitively. "I think mid-afternoon should be enough time. Sound good?"

Fellows nodded, as if he had a choice. Ryan and Jessie gave him their contact info and got up to leave. They were just exiting the stable when Fellows called after them.

"Wait, you never explained why a homicide detective and a profiler are handling this. I thought you said all the women got away."

Jessie had already largely dismissed him as a suspect, pending confirmation of his alibi. But it couldn't hurt to get a real-time response from him. So she spun around.

"The second abductee, Morgan Remar, was murdered last night, stabbed multiple times in her own kitchen. You know anything about that, Scott?"

The color drained from his face and he reached out for the stable's wall to steady himself. The arrogant jerk of a few minutes ago had been replaced by a shell-shocked schmo. Jessie found it somehow heartening that the guy was so stricken. Despite his cocky smarminess, he hadn't completely lost his humanity.

Of course, it also meant that they'd lost their best suspect.

CHAPTER FOURTEEN

Hannah looked surreptitiously at her phone.

At the therapeutic high school she attended, specially designed for students "facing extreme emotional and psychological challenges," they weren't officially supposed to access phones or other non-approved technology while on campus.

But unofficially the teachers and administrators were pretty lax over the lunch break. As long as students didn't congregate or draw attention to themselves, staffers let it slide.

As usual, Hannah sat alone. She had yet to meet a kid at this school she felt any connection to. Besides, she was hoping to transfer to the "normal" high school in the next few weeks and figured it wasn't worth the effort to get to know anyone well. So she sat by herself at the courtyard picnic table, nibbling at her sandwich and scrolling through her feeds.

Thankfully, Jessie had stopped asking her if she'd made any new friends. Her older half-sister was making a real effort to be interested and supportive without hovering over her every second. Luckily, the woman had eventually figured out without being told that peppering her with questions about whether she liked her classmates didn't jibe with that goal.

Just then, a Facebook post alert popped up from Jessie, an event so rare that Hannah couldn't recall ever seeing one before. Curious, she clicked on it. As she read, she didn't notice that she'd stopped chewing completely. Her fingers tingled slightly and she felt her face flush red. After taking a few breaths, she reread the post, certain she must have misunderstood it.

So tired of the teenager grind. Didn't know when I signed on to be a substitute parent that every waking second would be about trying to keep a selfish know-it-all happy. Can't decide if the proper title is "brat" or "bitch." No good deed goes unpunished I guess. Who's with me?

Hannah read it a third time, still having trouble processing that Jessie actually sent this out into the world. But it was right there, just above her last post from almost six months ago sharing pictures of her most recent round of criminal-inflicted body scars.

No longer hungry and feeling mildly nauseated, she shoved her phone in her pocket and tossed the last of her sandwich in the trash. Then she walked quickly to the nearest bathroom, where she hid in a stall, waiting for class to start and hoping the tears that stained her eyes would be gone by then.

*

Jessie and Ryan had only just returned to the station after their outing to the stable when her phone rang. She assumed it would be Detective Sands. He'd texted her while she was in Sylmar asking for any worthwhile updates from her interview with Scott Fellows. She'd gotten voicemail when she called back and assumed this would be the end of their game of phone tag. But the call was from Kat.

"Hi," Jessie said.

"Hey," Kat replied. "I'm outside the station. Do you have five minutes?"

"Sure. I'll be right out. You want some bad coffee?"

"I'm good," Kat said.

When Jessie stepped outside, she saw Kat leaning against a light post, looking very detective-like in blue jeans, a leather jacket, and sunglasses. She walked over and waited for her friend to speak first. It didn't take long.

"So," Kat began. "I shouldn't have called Brenda Ferguson. I was pissed and I used her to make you feel guilty about shutting me out of the investigation. It was thoughtless and unprofessional."

"Thank you," Jessie said.

After an uncomfortable silence, Kat spoke.

"Your turn."

"My turn for what?" Jessie asked.

"Your turn to apologize," she said intensely.

"What exactly am I supposed to be apologizing for?" Jessie asked indignantly, though she had a pretty good feeling she knew where Kat was headed.

"For freezing me out of a case I brought you into in the first place," Kat accused.

"I thought I explained this last night. I called you to tell you what was going on but I was prohibited from letting you come to the crime scene. It wasn't personal. You should know that."

"It felt personal, Jessie," she said, pushing off from the light post. "It felt like I was good enough to pass information along to you. But once the varsity squad stepped in, you didn't want the JV around anymore. I was on this thing first. Doesn't that count for anything?"

Jessie could feel the frustration rising in her chest and tried to force it back down.

"Of course it does. And the information in the files you gave me has actually been really helpful. It gave us at least one new lead. But this isn't just a private investigation anymore. It's a murder case. You can't just go traipsing around in the middle of it."

"So what are you saying?" Kat challenged. "That I'm out of my depth?"

"I didn't say that," Jessie insisted.

"What then?"

Jessie stared at her friend, wondering if there was anything she could say that would lessen her anger and if she even had an obligation to. She was getting pretty irked herself.

"Look, I get that you're put out. But I've told you repeatedly, I didn't have a choice here. And I know you don't want to hear this but the person who hired you is dead. You don't *have* a case anymore."

Kat looked wounded. Jessie immediately realized she'd gone too far. Before she could fix it, Kat replied, her voice cold.

"I guess I'm doing it pro bono now."

She started to walk away.

"Kat, wait," Jessie said, hoping to patch things over.

But her friend didn't turn around as she walked away, saying one last thing.

"I'm seeing this through, with or without your help."

CHAPTER FIFTEEN

The True Avenger moved down the hall with careful stealth.

He loved to refer to himself by that title, even if he couldn't say it out loud. After all, unlike some comic book heroes, he was doing the hard, real-life work of righting wrongs, of rebuking faithlessness. It wasn't glamorous. He didn't wear a costume. But at the end of the day, he was making a real difference in the world. He was eliminating the perpetrators, the ones who had aggrieved the innocent.

As he walked along the dimly lit hall of his office building, he carried his documents, the ones essential to his work, rolled up tightly so no one could catch a glimpse if they walked past. He had a switchblade in his right pocket, ready to pull it out if necessary. He'd practiced snapping it open many times in the privacy of his home. He had it down to a science.

He'd even bought several department store dummies at auctions to use for practice. He took them into his spare room, where he would wrap towels around the necks and waists of the mannequins and put a black "X" on spots representing vulnerable organs. Then he would rehearse pulling out his knife and jabbing it into the marked spot, imagining it was soft human flesh. One time, he'd get the carotid artery. The next it would be the small of the back where a kidney rested. He'd gotten very proficient.

He'd never had to use the knife at work. But he kept it close because he sometimes liked to review his plans while sitting on the toilet. It was an inherently risky move but one he was willing to take. No one he'd ever encountered in the restroom or the hall had given him a suspicious look or taken an interest in the rolled up documents he carried to or from the restroom. But that didn't mean he shouldn't stay vigilant.

It wasn't easy to complete his mission. In the middle of his efforts to cleanse the world, he was still subject to the vagaries of everyday life. There were clients who constantly demanded his attention. And because of the nature of his work, he couldn't put them off too long without putting his livelihood at risk.

He had just listened to a voicemail from an irate man yelling that there could be potential legal consequences resulting from a delay he blamed on the Avenger. Some small part of him did feel guilty about it. Any time a good man suffered in this unfair system, it was cause for upset. And he hated to think that he was partly responsible for that. But in order to expedite the deliverance, sometimes the innocent suffered.

The first three of the four stages of The Deliverance had ended. They couldn't have gone more perfectly. All four women had been assembled without complication. He called that first stage of the plan The Collection.

After being taken to isolated locations, they had all been held for the required length of time. He called that second stage The Purification, in which they were humbled for their sins, forced to exist in tight quarters, eat like the fallen animals they were, and wallow in their own filth.

Stage Three, The Unraveling, had only recently come to a close. Counterintuitively, it was perhaps his favorite stage. In it, the women "escaped" and managed to return to their previous lives. Of course those escapes had been permitted and carefully stage-managed. And the escapes were far from complete, as each of the sinners still suffered from grievous physical and, more importantly, psychological wounds.

That wasn't quite true. Not all of them still suffered. One of them had already completed Stage Four, The Reckoning. But as satisfying as beginning Stage Four had been, he knew he had to be careful. The authorities would be on to him now.

That was why he constantly reviewed his plan of action notes. On this day, once he had safely exited the hallway and returned to his desk, he resumed studying them. Now that The Reckoning had begun, he had to be more careful. No one had anticipated him returning to visit a woman who had been abducted and "escaped." But that would surely change now.

If the authorities hadn't already connected the abduction to the murder, they soon would. That meant he would have to be more careful in his movements, more wily in his methods of subterfuge. Of course, he'd planned for all this, had contingencies for every move they would make. But that was all theory. Getting it right in the real world was much more complicated, much more difficult.

But, he reminded himself, all worthwhile endeavors were difficult. That was what made them worthwhile. If it was easy to accomplish this task, then anyone could do it. It would not require the True Avenger. But it *did* require him. Only he truly understood the nature of what had to be done.

It was simple: only when the remaining sinners had also faced The Reckoning would The Deliverance be complete for them, and for him. Steps couldn't be skipped. There were no shortcuts. But it gave him enormous satisfaction to know that the end was in sight. Soon The Deliverance would be upon them.

CHAPTER SIXTEEN

After her dust-up with Kat, Jessie decided to make a brief pit stop at home. She hadn't been there since last night and craved a quick shower and a change of clothes. Maybe the shower could also ease the unpleasant aftertaste of their argument.

When she walked through the door, she knew instantly that something was wrong. Hannah was nowhere in sight but music was blasting from her bedroom. Empty bowls and food containers were sitting out on the kitchen counter and shoes and a jacket lay on the hardwood floor.

That was a common occurrence in Hannah's first few weeks living here. But more recently, she'd made a concerted effort to clean up after herself. Jessie couldn't explain why, but she sensed that the situation was not just a matter of thoughtlessness. It seemed to be by design.

She put her things down and wandered over to Hannah's room. The door was slightly ajar but she knocked anyway. After waiting several seconds without a response she knocked again loudly before pushing the door open. Hannah was on her bed, lying on her stomach, scrolling through her phone. She didn't speak or look up.

"How's it going?" Jessie asked.

Without giving her a glance, Hannah shrugged.

"Is everything okay?" Jessie asked, unsure how hard to push. "Did something happen at school today?"

Hannah finally made eye contact. She pushed a button on her phone and the music stopped.

"You could say that," she answered acidly.

"What?" Jessie asked, sensing an ambush in the making.

"Someone wrote an awful comment about me on Facebook."

"Who?" Jessie pressed. "What did they say?"

"You don't want to take a guess?" Hannah retorted with bile.

"How could I possibly…what's going on, Hannah? What aren't you telling me?"

Hannah sat up, glaring at her angrily, though her eyes were damp.

"Funny that you would say that. That's the question I should be asking—what aren't *you* telling *me*? Or maybe why didn't you tell me?"

"I truly have no idea what you're talking about," Jessie said, completely lost.

"No?" Hannah said as she tossed her phone at Jessie. "How do you explain this?"

Jessie caught the phone and looked at the screen. As she read, she felt nauseated for the second time today. Before she could speak, Hannah plowed ahead.

"Why couldn't you just talk to me if you felt this way? Instead you had to share it with the whole world!"

"Hannah," she said slowly, trying to stay under control. "I didn't write this."

Hannah shook her head in disbelief.

"Don't take the coward's way out," she hissed quietly. "You can't just wash this away."

"I swear to you, I didn't write this. It's not how I feel. Even if it was, I'd never post it to social media. I barely use Facebook at all."

"Really?" Hannah challenged. "Because it seems like you've been pretty busy today."

Jessie looked at the screen again, scrolling up from the post about Hannah. There were two others. The first was an attack on Captain Decker, calling him an out-of-touch dinosaur. The other was a rant about the LAPD more generally, calling it an organization defined by corruption and ineptitude.

Those posts, along with the one about Hannah, were all thoughtfully composed and well-written. Each seemed specifically designed to alienate people central to Jessie's world. And each was completely bogus. She looked up at Hannah, who was staring at her expectantly.

"I know you're upset," she said carefully. "But think about this for a second. Do you really think that after having posted on here about a half dozen times in the last year, I would suddenly go on a tear, writing terrible things about you, my boss, and the place I work, all in one afternoon?"

"How am I supposed to know what's going on in your head? I know you were out all night. Maybe you just reached some breaking point and started spewing out what you really think."

"I've been hacked, Hannah. I don't know by whom. But it's clearly someone who wants to make every relationship in my life fall apart. Please don't help them."

Hannah shook her head.

"Here's the problem, Jessie," she said, apparently unconvinced. "I don't know if I can trust you. You held back the fact that we were sisters for months. I know from your hush-hush conversations with Dr. Lemmon and Garland Moses that there's some other big secret that you're keeping from me. I don't know if what you said in that post is how you really feel about me. But it *feels* true to me. Almost as bad, everyone can read it and they'll believe it's true. It's out there. It can't be taken back. So whether you meant it or not, it's my life now."

Jessie was at a loss as to how to respond to that. Before she could even try, her phone rang. It was Ryan. She knew she shouldn't but she picked up, if only to break the tension.

"I'm kind of busy right now," she said. "Can I call you back?"

"We've got a new potential suspect. Decker wants us to run him down ASAP. He's waiting in his office right now for me to brief you both together."

Jessie sighed, wondering what else could come here way.

"Give me twenty minutes," she pleaded.

"I'll try to stall," he replied. "But he's antsy. Try to make it ten if you can."

He hung up and Jessie looked back at Hannah, who wasn't making eye contact. She walked over and handed her the phone back.

"Listen…" she started to say.

Hannah cut her off.

"I know that's where you want to be, not here, not with me. Which am I right now, a brat or a bitch? Maybe both, I guess?"

"Please believe me…" Jessie pleaded before being cut off again.

"Just go," Hannah said.

She pushed a button on her phone and the music resumed. She rolled over on the bed, facing away.

After several helpless seconds, Jessie left.

CHAPTER SEVENTEEN

It was hard to concentrate.

Jessie had managed to get back to the station in fifteen minutes and was now sitting on the battered old loveseat in Captain Decker's office as Ryan walked them through the lead he'd uncovered.

Thoughts of her arguments with both Kat and Hannah were still swirling in her head when he began and it took all her effort to force her brain to focus exclusively on his words. Whatever he'd discovered, he seemed excited.

"So I was catching up on all the kidnapping cases, looking for potential connections between them and the Morgan Remar murder."

"I thought we were looking at all possibilities," Decker interrupted, "not just the kidnapping connections. You're still looking at exes, a robbery gone wrong, and people who did construction work on the house, correct?"

"Yes, Captain," Ryan answered impatiently. "We've largely eliminated her old flames. Even her ex-husband, who clearly still resents how she ended things with him, has an airtight alibi. He was at a bar with friends after a Lakers game. The robbery angle looks like a dead end. Detective Trembley is looking into the criminal history of people working on their home but hasn't found anything yet. Jessie and I have been focused on the kidnapping connection."

"Okay, go on," Decker said, seemingly satisfied for now.

"So as I was looking through the abductions, I noticed a parallel to an older case from six years ago. It had actually been flagged by Detective Sands from Pacific Station, who's been helping us out. Back then, a woman from Santa Monica was abducted and held for two days in a warehouse in Commerce before getting away. A few weeks later she found herself being stalked. She informed the police and told them she was sure it was the same guy."

"Was it?" Jessie asked.

"They could never prove that," Ryan said. "She'd been drugged and blindfolded so she never got a good look at the man who took her. But she said that when she was trying to fight him off, she felt thick scars on his forearms. The guy who stalked her had multiple burn scars on his arms. They were never able to make a definitive connection. But it turned out this guy had also stalked several other women, at least two of whom he wrote threatening letters to. They were able to nail him as a serial stalker and he was sentenced to nine years in Lompoc."

"But Sands looked into this already?" Decker noted.

"He did," Ryan confirmed. "When he checked the guy's current status, the database showed that he had three months left on his sentence. But I noticed that Lompoc has been having issues lately. You might remember that case I worked three weeks ago with the guy who was turned in by his boss for stealing burgers from the fast food place where he worked."

"I remember," Decker said. "He went back after he was released and gunned down the restaurant owner and his wife."

"Right," Ryan confirmed. "But when I was first looking into suspects, the records from Lompoc indicated the shooter was still inside and would be for at least two additional weeks. The screw-up set back the investigation a couple of days. They've got a backlog problem with updating data on folks released early for good behavior. So I checked on our stalker—his name is Bryce Laterno. Turns out he was released six weeks ago, before the first victim—Brenda Ferguson—was taken."

"And you think he's back at it?" Decker said.

"I don't know that he's into murder or even serial abductions," Ryan conceded. "But it seems worth checking out, especially since those written threats he made six years ago involved stabbing the women he was stalking. And did I mention that he's missed his last two meetings with his parole officer?"

"Maybe you should hand this over to Sands," Decker suggested. "This sounds more promising to their abduction case than to our murder."

"I already let him know about it," Ryan said. "I thought he'd be pissed about us horning in on talking to Scott Fellows. But he wasn't. He said he's got more leads than he knows what to do with and he'll take all the help he can get. If we can justify it as part of our investigation, he's cool with us checking it out. All we need is your sign-off, Captain."

Jessie looked over at Decker. She thought Ryan had made an airtight case for pursuing the lead and didn't want to say anything to change his mind. The captain, whose expression rarely veered beyond mildly annoyed to mildly satisfied, looked to be leaning more to the latter.

"Okay," he said. "But don't lose track of the other leads. I don't want them to dry up because we're so focused on the kidnapping connection."

"No, sir," Ryan said, starting toward the door.

"One more thing," Jessie said now that the decision had been made. Out of the corner of her eye she saw Ryan get a panicked look, worried that she was going to screw it up.

"Yes, Hunt?" Captain Decker said, cringing slightly.

She had been about to explain the Facebook posts and her certainty that she'd been hacked. But it was clear from his uneasy expression that he was worried she was going to make some unwanted request regarding the case. She decided in that moment to hold off on the posts and pivot into his vulnerable spot.

"I really think we need to reconsider asking for protection for the other abductees. If this killer is the same guy and we left these women vulnerable, it's going to blow back hard on the department."

"I know where you stand on this," he said, clearly having expected her comment. "And anticipating it, I put in another request with Deputy Chief Sklar. It was shot down immediately. In addition to the cost and the logistical headaches, he's worried that if we did it, it would get out publicly and every woman in the city whose abductor is still out there would demand ongoing protection, bankrupting the department."

"But Captain, not every victim was abducted by a serial kidnapper who may go back and murder them."

"A point I made, Hunt. That was around the time Sklar told me that if I had proof the kidnapper and the killer are the same person, he was all ears. When I said that I didn't, he suggested I shut up and leave him alone until I did. That's where we left it. And that's where you and I will leave it."

"Yes, Captain," she said.

She walked out of his office right behind Ryan, frustrated by the decision but unable to justify fighting the losing battle.

"Good try," Ryan told her once they were outside. "But it sounds like he went to the mat already."

"Yeah," she agreed. "But I wanted to give it one more shot, especially considering that Decker likely won't be interested in my opinions starting real soon."

"What does that mean?" Ryan asked.

"I'll explain in the car."

CHAPTER EIGHTEEN

When the call came in, it was Jessie's turn to wince.

They were on their way to the last known address for Bryce Laterno and she had just finished telling Ryan about the Facebook posts and Hannah's reaction to the one about her when Decker's distinctive ring tone came up on her phone.

"Hi, Captain," she said hesitantly.

"Hunt," he said in that quiet voice that freaked her out more than when he yelled, "it seems you forgot to mention something to me earlier."

"Yes sir," she said. "I assume you're referring to the posts. You have to believe I didn't write them."

"Of course you didn't," he said dismissively. "But that's not really the point, is it? You should have told me so we could have dealt with it right away. Now we've got to do damage control with the media."

"The media? Is it really that bad, Captain? I thought it would just be an internal personnel issue."

"Are you kidding?" he asked incredulously. "There are going to be multiple minority rights organizations calling for your head in a few hours."

"For what? What do those groups care about some fake posts with a random criminal profiler attacking the department?"

"When's the last time you looked at your page, Hunt?" Decker asked. "Because it's a lot more than that."

"What?" she asked, feeling the pit in her stomach grow exponentially as she pulled up the relevant screen.

"Just look," he said flatly.

"Oh god," she said as she scrolled through.

"What is it?" Ryan asked anxiously from the driver's seat.

Jessie put the call on speaker.

"There are three more posts since I last checked," she said. "They get progressively worse."

"How bad?" Ryan asked.

"Bad," she said, reading them silently.

Decker answered for her.

"They're a series of screeds with various racist and anti-Semitic epithets," he said. "There's basically no minority group that they don't attack. It's impressively all-encompassing."

Jessie groaned, barely able to process everything. Ryan glanced at the screen.

"One of those messages was posted while we were in the meeting with you, Captain," he said. "It shouldn't be hard to prove Jessie couldn't have written them."

"We've already got Camille Guadino from the tech unit prepping to back trace the source. You need to give her all your social media accounts so she can delete them. It's only a matter of time before whoever did this starts posting on the others too. In the meantime, I'm having media relations craft a statement on your behalf. It should be ready for your sign-off within the hour. Stay close to the phone, all right?"

"Yes, sir," she said, before adding, "Can I ask, how likely is Camille's back trace to find the culprit?"

"Don't hold your breath," he warned. "She's not optimistic. The people who can do this are usually pretty good at covering their tracks. We're more likely to have success the old-fashioned way, by determining who would want to do this to you."

"That list is endless, Captain," she said dejectedly.

"Maybe not," Ryan reminded her. "Did you tell him about the tires?"

"What's this?" Decker asked.

"Oh yeah," Jessie remembered. "Yesterday I discovered all four of my tires had been slashed. It happened in the middle of the day on a quiet street in a nice neighborhood. It felt like a message of some kind."

"Don't forget the cop," Ryan prompted.

"Right," Jessie said. "Around the time I noticed the tires, I saw a motorcycle cop riding away in the other direction."

"You think it's connected?" Decker asked.

"I don't know, Captain," she admitted. "But Sergeant Costabile made it pretty clear that he has it in for me. He threatened both me and Hannah. And that was *before* he got busted on corruption charges. We all know that he has lots of friends left in the department. Is it crazy to think that he might get them to do the dirty work as part of his vendetta against me?"

"It makes sense," Ryan added. "First the physical damage to a possession, followed by attempts to undermine her at work and home. Captain, I don't know if you saw the first hacked post about Hannah Dorsey. She's pretty torn up, thinking her big sister wrote it. Costabile's definitely not above these kinds of dirty tricks."

"I don't dispute that," Decker acknowledged. "We'll have someone review all his recent calls and visitors. If it's him, he's probably too smart to make such an obvious mistake. But who knows, maybe something will shake loose. The bigger problem is if it's not him."

"What do you mean?" Jessie asked.

"Right now I'm scrolling through all your closed cases since you started with us. In the last two years alone, you've been responsible for putting away seventeen murderers, including several who made personal threats to you after their convictions. I count at least three of those."

"I can't keep track," Jessie said. "Remind me again."

"There's Eliza Longworth, the woman who killed her best friend after discovering she was having an affair with her husband. She blames you for separating her from her children."

"In my defense," Jessie answered wryly, "I warned her about that possibility and her response was to try to kill me."

"Don't forget the plastic surgeon, Dr. Richard Kallas," Ryan added. "His trial for killing his porn actress crush hasn't even begun yet. You know he's feeling raw about it. Plus he's definitely proven himself to be the obsessive type."

"And then there's Andrea Robinson," Decker piled on. "She was the first case you worked for the department, if I recall. Didn't she almost frame her lover's maid for killing him?"

"That's right," Ryan added. "And you two were starting to become besties. You even went to her house for a girls' night of drinking and movies. Isn't that when she tried to poison you?"

"I was new to the job," Jessie said defensively. "And looking for friends. I may have made some poor decisions as I settled in."

"She was a real sociopath," Decker recollected. "We'll have to double-check but I think she was sent to a psych unit."

"Speaking of sociopaths, we haven't even mentioned your ex-husband," Ryan reminded her. "He doesn't seem like the type to let things go either. You really know how to pick 'em, Jessie."

She gave him a glare that he understood to mean, "I'm with *you* now so what does that say?" but she kept her actual verbal reply more restrained.

"Okay, I get it," Jessie said, overwhelmed. "There are lots of people who might have a grudge against me. Once we get back to the office, we can go through every likely suspect and see who they've been communicating with. Maybe we'll find that one of them recently got a visit from their hacker cousin or something."

"That's too many suspects for you guys to handle on your own. I count five credible ones. I'll farm some of that out now to other members of the unit," Decker said. "Then you'll have less legwork to do when you return. Besides, we don't know for sure that the tire incident and the hacks are even related. I need you two focused on the case at hand. Got it?"

"Yes sir," Ryan said.

"And don't forget, Hunt," Decker added. "Keep that phone close. Media Relations will be reaching out to you soon."

"I can't wait," she replied, unable to hide the sarcasm.

CHAPTER NINETEEN

The drive to Bryce Laterno's last known address was long. He lived in a run-down apartment complex in San Pedro, within sight of the massive Port of Los Angeles and the associated hazy, smog-choked air.

They parked a half block away and made their way down Laterno's street, which was a mix of industrial buildings, cheap motels, and cheap motels that had been converted into apartment buildings.

"Lots of big warehouses, "Ryan noted. "I could see a guy looking at those and getting the idea that large, empty buildings under construction might be the ideal place to keep his captives."

"Good point," Jessie agreed. "But I'm not sure how Laterno would know all those sites were unoccupied. I looked at his file. He has no connection to Construction Associates. According to his parole officer, his only gig since getting out of prison was as a part-time welder at a metal shop in Long Beach."

"So you're saying we should be on the lookout for the guy to answer the door with a blowtorch?" Ryan asked jokingly.

Jessie looked at him, unamused.

"Considering how this day has gone, it wouldn't stun me."

They arrived at Laterno's building. It too was a converted two-story motel. They walked up the rickety stairwell to the second-story unit and listened quietly. They could hear sounds inside but couldn't discern what they were.

Ryan motioned for Jessie to stand behind him as he stood to the side of the door and knocked. He unsnapped the holster of his gun and rested his hand there.

"Who is it?" came a gruff voice.

"LAPD," Ryan announced loudly and firmly. "Your P.O. asked us to check on you to make sure you're okay."

There was a second of silence before they got a response.

"You can tell him I'm fine," Laterno said.

"You know that's not going to cut it, Mr. Laterno," Ryan replied. "We need to visually verify that you're not under duress. And if you are all right, you need to explain why you've missed your last two appointments. Please open the door."

They waited a good fifteen seconds before there was any reaction.

"Show me your badge and I'll open the door," Laterno finally said.

Ryan held it up to the peephole and a few moments later the door opened to reveal a thirty-something guy in sweatpants and a long flannel shirt that seemed way too warm for the weather. His long black hair, greasy and unwashed, hung in his face. He had about a week's worth of stubble. His eyes were red and the room smelled strongly of pot. His hands were shoved in the pockets of the sweatpants and he swayed slightly, though he seemed unaware of it.

"Can you please remove your hands from your pockets?" Ryan asked. "Very slowly."

Laterno followed the instruction. Ryan used the moment to step over the threshold of the door, making it impossible to close it without hitting him. Jessie stepped into view as well. Laterno gave her a half-glance before returning his attention to Ryan.

"You can see I'm fine," he said, full of surliness. "Can you go now?"

"I'm afraid it's not that simple. Your P.O. needs a formal statement explaining why you missed your last two visits."

"Aw, man, come on," Laterno squawked. "I just forgot, okay. I got a little high. It happens."

Jessie and Ryan exchanged looks. Either Laterno was too stupid to have possibly kidnapped four women and gotten away with it or he was one of the most convincing performers they'd ever encountered.

"You know that missing a scheduled meeting with your parole officer is cause for re-arrest," Ryan said. "As is taking drugs, which you just admitted to. We could haul you in right now."

Laterno slouched pathetically.

"But," Ryan continued, "we might cut you a break if you can answer a few questions. Mind if we come in?"

"No, man. You need a warrant for that," Laterno whined.

Jessie glanced at Ryan, wondering how he wanted to handle this. They were investigating a murder and could reasonably claim this was an exigent circumstance that would allow them to enter his place without a warrant. But she could sense Ryan wanted to avoid playing that card for as long as he could.

"That's fine," Ryan said. "Then we'll just take you in now."

"What?"

"Those are your options, buddy. You can either welcome us in for a friendly chat and let us take a look around or we can take you to the station, where you'll definitely spend the night and maybe a lot longer. It's your call."

Laterno, looking defeated, waved them in. They entered and Ryan motioned for the man to join him at the small kitchen table. Jessie didn't follow them, instead choosing to take a look around the apartment.

"Where were you last night?" Ryan asked.

As Laterno fumbled for an answer, searching the inner regions of his apparently bong-resin-addled brain, Jessie scanned the living room, which was a collection of strewn-about socks, half-empty bowls of cereal, and fast food wrappers. If Laterno was faking being a stoner, he had really committed to the bit.

"I was here, man," Laterno insisted after several uncertain seconds. "I was right on that couch watching some shows."

"Was anyone with you?" Ryan asked.

"Nah, man. I was alone."

"What did you watch?" Ryan pressed.

"I don't remember, man. Reruns?"

You can do better than that," Ryan prodded.

As they went back and forth, Jessie opened the door to what she assumed was the bedroom. It was a sad excuse for a room, basically a large walk-in closet separated from the rest of the apartment by some thin drywall. There was a futon bed against the far wall with a tiny end table. A half dresser was shoved in the corner.

As wretched and depressing as the room was, that's not what drew Jessie's attention. Taped to the other wall were a series of papers and what looked to be photos. She turned on the bedroom light and moved over to get a better look.

What she saw made her blood curdle.

"Ryan," she called out to the other room. "Cuff him!"

*

When Laterno was safely tied to the floor heater in the living room, Jessie showed Ryan what she'd found. The wall was a detailed compilation of the movements of Janey Mills, the woman who had accused Laterno of kidnapping her before he was later arrested for stalking.

There were photos of her leaving her home in Carson, only seven miles from here, as well as shots of her entering work, at a Starbucks, and multiple other locations. He had a piece of ripped, spiral notebook paper with her daily schedule scrawled on it.

Finally there were the drawings in the form of comic book panels. They were crude but it was clear what was going on. In the first one, a woman who looked like Janey was naked, getting out of a bathtub. In the next, she was lying in bed, still naked, in an embrace with a long-haired man who looked like Laterno. In the third, she was still lying in bed, but this time she was bloody with a knife sticking out of her chest. The Laterno figure sat on the bed beside her dead body, a smile on her face.

Ryan called Harbor Station's CSU and they returned to the living room. While they waited for the unit to arrive, Ryan read Laterno his rights.

"Now that I've read these rights to you," he concluded, "would you agree to answer some questions?"

"What's in it for me?" Laterno demanded belligerently.

"You're in a tough spot, Bryce," Ryan said simply. "If you can give me an explanation for what we just saw in your bedroom, maybe there's a way you don't go right back behind bars. I want to help you if I can."

"Hard pass," Laterno said, looking away petulantly.

Ryan looked over at Jessie and shrugged as if that was what he'd expected. When the locals arrived to take custody of Laterno, Ryan and Jessie asked them to check the GPS data on his phone to see if he'd gone anywhere last night. Then they headed back downtown.

"I don't think it's him," Jessie said after several silent minutes in the car.

"Why not?" Ryan asked, though he didn't sound like he needed much convincing.

"He's fixated on Janey. I think we potentially stopped something terrible from happening to her, though I'm not even sure of that. He could have set up that wall as a fantasy plan. I wouldn't be surprised if he never intended to act on it."

"We don't know that," Ryan countered.

"No we don't," she agreed. "And of course it's better to be safe than sorry. But there was nothing in that place about any of the other victims. And I read his notes. It was basic stuff. I just don't think he had the capacity for the elaborate planning that was required to abduct four women and hold them for multiple days. Whoever did that was meticulous. Bryce Laterno is not that. He can barely organize two consecutive thoughts. He's not going to be our guy."

"Assuming you're right," Ryan said, sounding crestfallen, "we're back to the drawing board."

"I'm not even sure we have a drawing board to go back to," Jessie replied dejectedly.

CHAPTER TWENTY

Caroline Gidley had to pee.

Normally that would not be a big deal. But trying to get from her hospital bed to the bathroom with a broken leg was no easy undertaking. Still, she was sick of bedpans and didn't want to call the nurse again. Besides, she told herself, she'd recover faster if she made a conscious effort to be self-sufficient.

Caroline was trying hard not to let what happened to her in Griffith Park incapacitate her. She kept reminding herself that she was a survivor, not a victim. She'd escaped the clutches of a woman-hating psycho. She'd rescued herself.

Now if I can just stop flinching at every unexpected sound and breaking down in tears every few hours, I'll be well on my way to reclaiming my life.

Going to the bathroom alone was a literal and figurative step in that direction. It took a good two minutes, but eventually she was able to swing her legs off the bed and stand up. The massive cast encased her right leg from hip to toe and navigating her way the twelve feet to the toilet took both energy and balance, each of which she was sorely lacking these days.

She was just about to begin the journey when her phone buzzed. It was her fiancé, Shane. He was running late to visit her because one of the dogs had dug up part of the small backyard garden. He suspected that it was because of anxiety over her having been gone for so long. Caroline tended to think he was just after the carrots embedded in the dirt. Either way, his lateness would give her more time to finish the adventure she was about to undertake.

She was almost to the open door of the bathroom, ignoring the effort-induced sweat coming down her forehead, when she heard something inside. She couldn't identify it. It might have been heavy breathing or a repeating, low grunt. Suddenly her whole body seized up with the fear she'd managed to keep at bay for the last few hours. She froze in place, trying not to breathe.

Caroline glanced back at the hospital room door. It was only five feet away. But there was no way she could reach it before someone hiding in the bathroom got to her. She looked around for something to defend herself with but there was nothing.

From where she stood, she could see an extra bedpan resting on the bathroom counter. It was only two steps away. If she could grab it, maybe she could hit the intruder with it and get out. And if she turned on the bathroom light, maybe she could temporarily blind the attacker to get in that swing. It was a sad plan but the only one she had.

She took one more small step, trying to stay as quiet as possible, and prepared to take the last, large one that would get her to the bedpan. When she was in position, she stood still for a moment, girding herself for what was to come. Then, when she couldn't stall any longer, she moved.

Grabbing the door handle with her left hand, she swung it open hard and fast as she stepped forward and flicked on the light switch. Then she grabbed the bedpan and lifted it high over her head.

She saw no one. The bathroom was empty. Even with the frosted glass, it was obvious there was no one in the shower stall. She stood there, breathing heavily, dumbfounded. And then she heard it again, the repeating sound from earlier.

Only now it became clear that it wasn't grunting or heavy breathing. It was a drip from the shower head. Every two seconds, there was a small plop which echoed in the stall. To an active imagination it could be mistaken for a soft grunt.

Caroline breathed a massive sigh of relief and leaned back, resting her exhausted body on the bathroom counter. After a moment, she bent over, turned on the faucet, and splashed water on her face. She was so relieved that she almost forgot her original reason for entering in the first place.

After taking care of that issue, she made the long trek back to the bed, deciding that next time she wouldn't be too proud to ask for help. She was halfway across the room when the nurse came in.

"What are you doing?" he asked in dismay, his high, squeaky voice sounding slightly panicked as he hurried over to help her.

"I tried to be a hero," she admitted sheepishly, allowing him to wrap his arm around her waist and ease her back to the bed.

"Don't do that anymore," he insisted as he guided her back to a prone position.

"I've learned my lesson," she said, smiling. "Don't tell the other nurses. Where is Ella, by the way?"

"She's on break," he said, lifting her legs back onto the bed. "I'm just helping out, doing the dirty work. You can call me Joe. Some folks call me Average Joe."

Something about the phrase jogged something unpleasant in her memory. It took her a second to realize that it was just that the nurse had inadvertently said the same word her abductor had used so often: dirty.

He had constantly described her as unclean, sinful, debased, and yes, dirty. If she never heard the word again it would be too soon.

"Is everything okay?" Joe asked. "Your face just turned white."

She shook her head as she rested her head back on the pillow.

"It's nothing. You just said something that brought back a bad memory."

"Oh, I'm sorry," he said as he pulled the top sheet up to cover her legs. "What did I say so I don't make the same mistake again?"

"Don't even worry about it," Caroline said. "It's no big deal."

"Was it the word 'dirty,' Caroline?"

She looked up at him. The tenor of his voice had changed. The high squeak was gone, replaced by something deeper, more familiar.

"What did you say?" she asked.

Her chest was suddenly gripped by a panicky tightness. All her extremities began tingling at once as if she'd been injected with a shot of adrenaline.

The nurse smiled down at her, revealing his discolored teeth.

"I was asking if the word that bothered you was 'dirty.' Would you prefer I said something else? Impure? Polluted? Because those describe you equally well."

Caroline, though she couldn't catch her breath, opened her mouth to scream, but his hand clamped down before she could get anything out.

"Do you recognize my voice now, Caroline?" he whispered. "It's your old friend Average Joe, though I prefer Avenging Joe. Have you been using your brief stretch of freedom productively, Caroline? I hope so, since it's coming to an end."

Caroline watched in helpless horror as he pulled a pair of long shears out of his scrub pants pocket. Again she tried to scream, but it only came out as a muffled moan. She tried to wriggle free, but with his size advantage and her immobility, it was impossible.

As he gripped the handle of the shears, she had another idea. Her hand darted out and she tried to push the emergency call button. But he grabbed her wrist before she could push down. He bent it back until she felt it snap.

Caroline gasped in pain but barely had time to process it before she watched him slowly puncture the side of her waist with the shears. He pushed them in slowly, patiently. She closed her eyes, trying to push away the screaming anguish she felt as the metal went deeper and deeper. Then there was new pain as he pulled them back out again.

"You shouldn't have committed your sins, Caroline," he whispered, his lips brushing against her ear. "Now it's time for your reckoning."

She felt the shears again, this time quicker and harder than before. At some point she lost track of how often they entered. At some point she lost track of everything.

CHAPTER TWENTY ONE

Jessie awaited the storm.

In the car on the way back to the station, she'd signed off on the carefully phrased statement the LAPD Media Relations rep had sent her. But the rep had also warned her that even with the statement, things were about to get ugly. She should expect protests outside the station, calls for her dismissal, and vitriol directed at her throughout the broadcast and online world.

She was sitting at her desk, still absorbing that news, when the call came in from Harbor Station CSU. Ryan put it on speaker.

"Bryce Laterno's GPS data shows that he was home all night," the technician on the line said.

"Could have left his phone at his apartment while he went out?" Ryan asked hopefully.

"Afraid not," the tech said, sounding disappointed himself. "Bryce Laterno doesn't have a car. He's used rideshares exclusively to get around since being released from prison. There's no indication that he used one last night."

"That doesn't necessarily mean he didn't use some other kind of transportation," Jessie pointed out.

"No," the tech acknowledged. "But his data also showed that he ordered a pizza with his phone last night. The delivery guy confirmed seeing him at ten thirty-five. There was simply no way he could have gotten to Morgan Remar's West Adams home in that amount of time."

"Maybe you should have led with that," Jessie said, annoyed.

After Ryan hung up, he looked over at Jessie. She must have had a hangdog expression because he flashed her one of his "we'll get through this" smiles.

"Well, we had pretty much ruled him out anyway," he said, trying to put the best spin on things.

Decker walked over. Jessie could tell from his expression that he wasn't the bearer of good news.

"I heard your guy in San Pedro was a bust," he said.

"Yes sir," Ryan confirmed. "Though it looks like he had ill intent toward the woman he was stalking before. He's probably going back behind bars for another spell."

"That's one good thing at least," he said before turning to Jessie. "How did it go with Media Relations?"

"As well as could be expected," she said. "I tweaked some of the language in the statement to personalize it a bit. But it was pretty solid. I was told not to expect it to help much."

"We'll just try to ride it out," he said. "In the meantime, Detectives Trembley and Reid have been reviewing the files for everyone we discussed who might have a vendetta against you. They should have some updates by later this afternoon."

"That's good news," Jessie said, though it didn't really feel that way.

"Mostly," he agreed. "They did hit a few brick walls though. You may have to pursue them directly. Your ex-husband's file is sealed, apparently by the FBI."

"I know what that's about," she said. "You know I'm friendly with Agent Jack Dolan. He told me that Kyle's been getting cozy with a drug cartel gang in the prison. I think the Bureau is hoping they can use him to get at those guys. I'll talk to Jack. What are the other brick walls?"

"Just one. Andrea Robinson is in the psych ward but they wouldn't give up any details. Maybe your therapist friend, Dr. Lemmon, could wrangle some info. I know she's got connections."

"I'll reach out to her."

"Great," Decker said. "Maybe we can get a handle on this thing before the end of the day."

"It would be nice to have something go our way," Jessie agreed.

Decker nodded and was turning to leave when Ryan's phone rang. Jessie could tell something was wrong when he looked at the screen.

"What?" she said.

"It's the hospital," he answered, picking up. "This Detective Hernandez."

He listened, his face turning more ashen with each passing second. When he looked up, he seemed stunned.

"Caroline Gidley has been murdered."

*

Jessie stared at the body in silent fury.

Caroline Gidley looked so helpless lying in her small bed, wearing only a bloody hospital gown. The massive cast on her right leg seemed to make her sink even further into the thin mattress. Her eyes were closed and Jessie could tell that they'd been squeezed tight in pain when the attack happened.

This was preventable. As Jessie looked at this woman, who had escaped one horror only to be undone by another, she felt the urge to yell. She'd already done it at the station, though it was in the relative privacy of Captain Decker's office.

It had taken Ryan gently putting his hand on her forearm to remind her that she couldn't ream out her boss interminably without consequence. To his credit, Decker had quietly taken it as she called out the entire department for the inaction that left the woman in front of them dead.

Decker had responded by quietly instructing them to go to the hospital and investigate the case. He assured Jessie that by the time they arrived at Cedars-Sinai Medical Center, the other two abductees would have protective details assigned to them.

Jessie tried not to linger on her anger as she looked around the hospital room. Instead, she focused on the state of the room. Nothing seemed strewn about. The person who did this came in and managed to complete his task without much fuss.

Other than the look of anguish on Caroline's face, there was no real indication of a struggle. Nothing had been knocked over. The bed sheet didn't even seem disturbed. Had he slipped in while she was asleep? If so, how had he managed to enter and leave without drawing any attention from the multiple medical staffers on the floor?

She got her answer to that question quickly. The two Beverly Hills PD detectives assigned to the case, Van Nielsen and Ken Oxford, were deferring to the HSS unit since this case seemed to be part of a pattern. But in the brief time that they'd been involved, they'd done good work.

"We've looked through the hospital surveillance footage from around the time of the crime," Detective Nielsen said. "We had it sent to your CSU folks already but I can show you on my phone now. The guy was dressed as a nurse."

Jessie looked at the footage. It showed a man dressed in nurse scrubs enter Caroline's room. He was clearly wearing a wig to go with his gold wire-rimmed glasses and kept his head facing downward the entire time so no camera ever got a clear look at his face. She did notice a bandage on his right forearm and wondered if perhaps Morgan Remar had gotten him with the scrupulously wiped down butcher knife that they'd found in her kitchen.

"If he didn't work there, how come no one challenged him?" Ryan asked.

Here's why," Detective Oxford said, pulling up footage from about five minutes earlier.

They watched the screen as what was clearly the same man exited the elevator onto the ward. He was wearing a long trench coat that covered up his outfit below. Different shots showed him walking by multiple rooms and looking in before walking into one on the other side of the ward.

"He's in there for about three minutes," Oxford narrated as he fast-forwarded the footage. "When he comes out, he's in the scrubs. He'd stuffed the coat in the medical waste bin in the room."

The man walked out at that moment and confidently moved across the hall. Moments later, multiple medical personnel ran to the room he'd just left. There was no audio so it was unclear what was going on.

"What happened?" Jessie asked.

"He cut a hole in oxygen tube of the man whose room he left," Oxford said. "Alarms started going off. Staff rushed to help. No one noticed him going the other way and entering Ms. Gidley's room."

"The hole he cut in the tube was well-hidden," Nielsen added. "By the time personnel figured out the problem and how to solve it, he was already leaving Gidley's room. He was in the elevator again before the oxygen emergency was resolved."

"Find any prints yet?" Ryan asked without much optimism.

Nielsen shook his head.

"He wore gloves every second he was on the floor," he said. "We're having exterior cameras checked now. But if his caution at avoiding detection inside the hospital is any indication, we shouldn't hold out much hope of getting a break outside either."

Jessie looked more closely at Caroline Gidley's wounds. They didn't look like they came from a knife.

"Do we know what he used to stab her?" she asked.

"CSU thinks it was medical shears," Nielsen said. "It makes sense. In that uniform, no one would be too suspicious if he was found with them on his person."

"One more thing," Oxford added. "Before we knew about the connection to your other case, we started checking into her romantic life. We were looking hard at her ex; name is Gregg Dozier."

"Why is that?" Ryan asked.

"Apparently the relationship ended badly," Oxford said. "She was cheating on him and it all blew up about a week before the wedding. That was about a year ago. She subsequently got engaged to the guy she was having the affair with. Apparently her former fiancé didn't take it very well."

"What does that mean?" Jessie asked.

"Threats against the new guy, threats against her, and her car was keyed. She got a restraining order and it seemed to stop after that. But until we got the call that you guys were coming over because it fit your pattern, we were going to look into it."

Jessie glanced over at Ryan and could tell they were thinking the same thing.

"It'd be a real help if you'd still pursue it," she told them. "We're slammed trying to find connections between the victims. If there's any way to definitively rule Dozier in or out, it would help us out a lot."

"Not a problem," Oxford said.

"Thanks, guys," Ryan added. "And if you do find anything that ties him to the other abductees, please let us know right away."

"Will do," Nielsen promised.

Jessie and Ryan left the hospital room and headed back to the elevator. As they walked down the hall, Ryan mused aloud.

"You think there's any chance that Gregg Dozier planned all of these abductions and Morgan Remar's murder as a cover so that he could get revenge on his cheating fiancée without drawing suspicion?"

"We've seen crazier," Jessie acknowledged as the elevator headed down. "But Oxford and Nielsen seem pretty on the ball. If Dozier has any kind of suspicious history, I'm confident they'll suss it out. But even if he did all that himself, he'd still need to be sure the place each woman was kept at wouldn't be discovered while they were kept there. That feels like the key to solving this to me."

Ryan nodded in agreement. The elevator doors opened and they stepped out into the lobby where they were greeted by Kat Gentry. She looked like she wanted to take a swing at Jessie.

"We need to talk," she snarled.

CHAPTER TWENTY TWO

Ryan waited in the car.

Kat did Jessie the courtesy of waiting until the two of them were out of earshot of anyone before tearing into her.

"You feel good about yourself?" Kat spat when they finally found a stretch of unoccupied sidewalk outside the hospital.

"What do you mean?" Jessie asked, trying not to sound defensive in the face of her friend's vitriol.

"You froze me out of the case. Your department wouldn't give these women protection and now two of them are dead."

Jessie forced herself to remember that, while Kat might be pissed at her, much of this was undirected anger about what happened. She tried not to take it personally.

"I understand how upset you are," she replied calmly. "I am too. I begged Decker to make sure each woman had protection. He tried but was overruled. I read him the riot act earlier and he promised me he'd make sure Jayne Castillo and Brenda Ferguson got it right away. I was actually about to check in with him to make sure it was done."

Kat shook her head vigorously, clearly unsatisfied.

"But it should have happened earlier, Jessie. There's a dead woman up there who shouldn't be. You could have prevented it."

"How?" Jessie demanded, feeling her blood pressure rise. "How am I supposed to authorize uniformed officers to stand guard? Do you think I have that kind of authority?"

"You could have asked me to do it," Kat countered. "You ask me for work-related favors all the time. You think I would have said no to this? Or would it have been a violation of department policy?"

It was impossible to miss the sarcasm in her tone.

"To be honest it didn't occur to me," Jessie said. "And even if it had, I wouldn't have figured you to be in much of a favor-giving mode."

"I would have set aside how I feel to help these women. I can't believe you would even think of doubting that."

"I don't," Jessie conceded. "Look, I just didn't think of it. I haven't slept in about thirty hours. I've been burning the candle at both ends. Someone is apparently secretly trying to destroy my career and reputation. It didn't occur to me."

Kat stared at her for several seconds before responding.

"And because of that, Caroline Gidley is dead," she replied quietly. "You've got blood on your hands."

Jessie felt like she'd been punched in the gut. Kat didn't wait for her to respond, instead turning and walking away without another word.

As Jessie watched her go, she fought the urge to defend herself. As bad as she felt about Caroline's death, she knew it wasn't her fault. She had fought for protection for her. She'd been grinding away at this case non-stop since she got it.

Even if she'd thought to ask Kat to stand guard at the hospital, there was no guarantee it would have worked. The guy was clever and methodical. If he'd found someone in Caroline's room, he might have killed them too.

If she was honest with herself, she wasn't confident the protection the other women were now supposed to be getting would be enough either. This killer had clearly planned the murders well in advance, just as he had done with the kidnappings. She had a strong suspicion that he'd already anticipated that the remaining victims would get protection and planned for that contingency. She suspected he'd view getting to them anyway as some kind of sick challenge.

She was walking back to the car to meet Ryan, imagining how he might do that, when her phone rang. It was Hannah. She picked up immediately. Before she could say anything, her sister spoke.

"You need to come home right now."

*

The Social Services investigator was waiting in the living room with Hannah when Jessie arrived.

Hannah got up quickly to greet her, giving her a hug. As she leaned in, she whispered.

"She's got it in for you," she muttered. "Don't take the bait."

Behind her, the woman stood up and smoothed out the creases in her long, gray dress with a muted floral pattern. The woman looked to be in her mid- to late forties with graying hair tied up in a bun. She wore no makeup and had thin, wire-framed glasses.

"Hello, Ms. Hunt," she said, nodding but not extending her hand as she spoke in a clipped, overly polite manner. "I'm Delia Armbruster. I work with Los Angeles County's Department of Public Social Services. The reason I'm here is because DPSS received an anonymous call in regard to you and your half-sister. I've already spoken to Hannah about the allegation but I wanted to get your input."

"You spoke to a minor outside the presence of her guardian?" Jessie asked, already on guard.

"Under certain circumstances, that is permitted," Armbruster said, offering a thin, unconvincing smile. "These circumstances fit the exception. Would you like to chat privately?"

Jessie could sense that despite the woman's prim bearing, there was something predatory lurking just beneath the surface.

"No, that's not necessary," she said carefully. "Anything you want to ask me, you can do in Hannah's presence. I don't have anything to hide."

"Very well," Armbruster said. "Shall we sit down?"

She did so without waiting for a reply, taking one half of the love seat. Jessie sat in the easy chair. Hannah, in an apparent show of solidarity, took a chair from the breakfast table and sat down beside Jessie.

"As I mentioned," Armbruster continued as she pulled a thin file out of her bag, "we received an anonymous call. It came in last night. According to the transcript, the caller claimed that on multiple occasions, they've heard abusive language directed at Hannah, coming from you in this apartment. They also heard what sounded like physical abuse and crying."

Even as the woman spoke, Jessie started putting the pieces together. This had to be another attempt by the person trying to ruin her life to undermine her reputation. Reminding herself that, as Hannah had warned, Armbruster wanted to bait her into getting upset and making the allegation seem more credible, she stayed cool.

"Let me be clear. I firmly deny that charge or anything like it. I've never been abusive to Hannah, unless you consider asking her to pick up her clothes or turn down the TV to be abusive."

Armbruster didn't smile. After a moment, she glanced down at her report and then back up again.

"There is another claim that a student overheard Hannah sobbing in the bathroom at school and murmuring softly about the indignities she suffered at your hands."

"I told her that's not true," Hannah interrupted.

"But Hannah," Armbruster replied mildly, "you admitted that Ms. Hunt had you dragged out of a classroom in humiliating fashion just last month."

"No," Hannah corrected, clearly not for the first time. "I said that the campus security officer dragged me out. He was doing it to protect me because someone had threatened me and Jessie wanted to make sure I was safe. It was humiliating, yes. But that isn't why she did it."

Armbruster gave her a pitying look.

"In my experience, it's not uncommon for young people to justify the actions of the people whom they place their trust in, often misguidedly."

"May I ask you a question, Ms. Armbruster?" Jessie jumped in.

"Of course."

"How did you get to our apartment?"

"Why, Hannah met me in the lobby and brought me up," she said, looking mildly perplexed.

"So you saw our elaborate security procedures," Jessie confirmed. "The unmarked floor, the hidden stairwell access and such."

"Very elaborate indeed," Armbruster replied.

"Indeed," Jessie agreed. "We've had some issues in the past. But the funny thing is that, including us, this floor only has four units, whose residents' identities I won't compromise for their privacy. But it just so happens that I know each of them has been out of town for at least the last week. So I'm wondering who it was that heard this alleged abusive language and more. You know, considering we're alone on the floor."

"A good subject for the pending investigation, Ms. Hunt," Armbruster said, untroubled.

"Don't you verify allegations before taking action?" Jessie asked, unable to keep the tartness out of her voice completely.

"Before taking action? Of course. But how can we possibly verify or dismiss allegations without investigating, Ms. Hunt? I would have thought you'd know that. Aren't you a detective of some sort?"

"I'm a criminal profiler," Jessie said.

"Very exciting," Armbruster replied insincerely. "In any case, we follow procedure at the DPSS. And I regret to inform you that there seems to be enough merit to the allegations to proceed to the next stage of the investigation."

"On what basis are you claiming there's 'merit'?"

"My years of experience, Ms. Hunt," she answered icily.

"You're not taking me away?" Hannah asked, though it sounded more like a statement than a question.

Armbruster gave her another smile, full of faux sympathy.

"Not at this time, dear," she said, then turned to Jessie. "Sadly, the wheels of justice move slowly. But I assure you, I'll be in touch about next steps. In the interim, here's my card. I've already given one to Hannah and told her to call me anytime, for any reason. I trust you won't interfere if she were to try to avail herself of my services."

"I couldn't stop Hannah from doing what she sets her mind to, even if I wanted to," Jessie said.

"Then I'll see myself out," Armbruster replied, getting up and walking to the door.

"Are you sure you don't need an escort?" Jessie asked, "What with the confusing building layout and no one else on the floor to guide you."

"I'll get by," Armbruster said crisply.

When she was gone, Jessie locked the door and turned back to Hannah, who had an oddly guilty look on her face.

"You okay?" she asked.

"Yeah," Hannah said. "I just feel bad. I can't believe the thing with the security officer at school led to this. And I've never dealt with such an awful DPSS person. Most of them are pretty nice, all things considered."

"Don't feel bad," Jessie said. "I'm not sure that any of this is just bad luck."

"What do you mean?"

Jessie debated how forthright to be. Hannah had already been through so much. She didn't want to pile more weight on a girl who was clearly struggling with what she was already carrying. But it might be better to let her know what was going on so she could better deal with it. In her limited semi-parenting experience, she'd usually (with one big exception) found being honest more effective than hiding things.

"Okay, here's the deal," she finally answered. "In the last few days, I've been dealing with some unusual events that seem to be connected. It looks like someone is actively trying to mess with my life. First, all of my tires were slashed. Then, as you well know, my social media was hacked. And now there's this out-of-the-blue visit from Social Services suggesting abuse. It's possible that they're all connected. We're investigating who might want to do me harm."

"Have you looked at the cop, Costabile?' Hannah suggested. "He's already threatened us both. I doubt being in jail would stop him from doing more."

"We're definitely looking at him, as well as some other folks I've pissed off in the past. It turns out there are quite a few. That's why I need to ask you a question."

"Okay," Hannah said, sounding wary.

"I don't want you to take offense. But before I officially add this visit to the list of incidents we investigate, I need to know: is there any chance you were so upset about those posts you thought I wrote that you called DPSS to get back at me?"

Hannah looked at her like she'd just said Santa Claus wasn't real.

"How can you even ask me that?" she asked.

"I don't want to," Jessie said. "But if I'm going to ask LAPD detectives to try to see who made those anonymous calls, that's a delicate request. I have to be sure they're not going to uncover an embarrassing surprise."

Looking at her sister, Jessie was already regretting her decision to ask. She'd never seen Hannah looked so wounded, not even after learning her father was the serial killer who murdered her adoptive parents.

"No," she said slowly and plainly. "I didn't make the call. Good night."

Then she walked to her room and closed the door. It was only 6:30 p.m. but Hannah never left her room. Jessie knocked several times, asking to come in, but got no response. She decided not to push. Instead, other than making a grilled cheese sandwich which she left outside the door, she didn't bother the girl again that night.

Before she crashed for the night herself at the shockingly early hour of 8:45 p.m., one bitter thought passed through her mind as she recalled her interactions with both Kat and Hannah.

Someone may be trying to destroy my life. But I seem to be doing a pretty good job of it all by myself.

CHAPTER TWENTY THREE

Breakfast was a silent affair.

Hannah wasn't speaking and Jessie didn't want to pretend everything was all right by being overly chipper. In fact, when they both left for their respective destinations and Jessie said to have a good day, she realized it was the first time she'd spoken. Hannah nodded but didn't say a word.

At the office, she discovered that while she'd been home dealing with allegations of abuse and emotional blowouts, the rest of the HSS team had been hard at work. Ryan had exchanged updates with Detective Sands from Pacific Division, though neither had much to offer the other.

"That's a bummer," Jessie said.

"There is some good news," Ryan offered.

"What's that?" she asked.

"Captain Decker was successful in getting protective orders for both Jayne Castillo and Brenda Ferguson."

"What exactly do they entail?" she wanted to know, still tentative in her enthusiasm.

"They entail the following," someone behind her said, startling her and making her spin her chair around quickly.

It was Decker, who stood with his arms crossed defensively. He continued.

"There are now two uniformed officers camped outside each of their homes who will also accompany them on any outings."

Jessie decided not to revisit her outburst yesterday. Instead she merely nodded in acknowledgment. Decker had apparently made the same choice as he simply went on.

"Though no more leads have been uncovered regarding the murders, the HSS detective squad has made some progress in checking out folks who might want to undermine your reputation. Why don't we go somewhere a little more private for that conversation."

The whole team went to a secluded conference room to avoid prying ears in order to review what they'd uncovered. Before they started, Jessie told them about her visit from Delia Armbruster at DPSS and suggested they add it to the list of harassment. With that in mind, they told her what they'd found.

Detective Alan Trembley started. As the junior detective on the team at just twenty-eight, he was anxious to make a good impression and his nervousness was obvious. His glasses were smudged and his curly blond hair was, as usual, a mess. He'd been tasked with looking into Sergeant Hank Costabile, the corrupt Valley Division officer who'd tried to protect a police commander from being discovered as a client of a murdered porn actress who escorted on the side.

Even though the commander wasn't ultimately implicated in the murder, Costabile had gone to extreme lengths to cover up his former boss's indiscretion, including threatening both Jessie and Hannah and even having one of his minions try to hit Jessie and Ryan with an unmarked car.

"In order to protect him from the general population," Trembley started, "Costabile is being held in a special wing of the Men's Central Jail while he awaits trial. There is a long record of his calls and visits. With the exception of his lawyers, we have video and audio recordings of them. None of them is incriminating in terms of threats against you."

"I feel like there's a 'but' in there, Trembley," Decker said.

"Yes, Captain," Trembley conceded. "Normally I'd be reluctant to go there, but not with this guy. I did find a few records of folks from his station in Van Nuys going to the jail but not signing in as visitors. I can't confirm that they were seeing Costabile on those trips and there is no record of meetings. But that doesn't mean they didn't happen. If they did, it could have been an ideal time for Costabile to give his minions instructions on how to ruin Jessie's life."

"Were any of the guys who stopped by but didn't sign in tech types?" Ryan asked.

"No," Trembley answered. "They were all street officers. But that doesn't mean they couldn't pass the request along."

"Okay," Decker said. "We're not there yet. But the next step would be to see if our tech team can somehow link anyone at Van Nuys station to the social media hacks or to these anonymous calls to DPSS. I'm reluctant to pull the trigger on that until I have to since it will require a warrant. If it gets out that a captain from one station is requesting warrants on the staff at another station, that could get ugly fast. So we'll hold on that for now. What did you find, Reid?"

Everyone turned to Detective Callum Reid, the forty-something veteran of the team. He slid on his bifocals and stared at the sheet of paper in front of him. He'd been assigned to investigate Eliza Longworth. The wife of a wealthy Pacific Palisades real estate broker, she'd been convicted of murdering her best friend, whom she'd learned was having an affair with her husband.

Jessie had confronted Longworth when she learned the truth and told her that she might get a reduced sentence if she confessed, which would allow her to get out of prison before her young children were adults. But Eliza had gone a different way, trying to stab Jessie with a butcher knife.

Reid glanced at his notes one last time before looking up at everyone.

"Unless she's the most devious wronged wife in history, I think we may be able to rule Longworth out," he said.

"I'd love to believe it," Jessie said, still remembering how Eliza had come at her with murder in her eyes. "Set my mind at ease."

"From what I learned, things were bumpy for her in prison the first few months," Reid said. "But at some point, she seemed to make peace with her situation. She recorded an apology video to the children of Penelope Wooten, the friend she killed. They'll see it when their dad thinks they're old enough. She's apparently made one for you too, Jessie, though I'm told she doesn't feel ready to send it yet. She started a support group for incarcerated mothers. In general, she's been a model prisoner."

"Just the kind of façade that could come in handy if she had ulterior motives," Ryan noted.

"Possible," Reid acknowledged. "But she hasn't been visited by anyone out of the ordinary who might be able to organize a complicated effort to damage Jessie. Other than her lawyer, her only visitors have been her kids. I doubt she's passing them coded instructions."

"Fair enough," Decker said, sounding convinced. "What about our other most likely suspects?"

Reid continued.

"I also checked on Dr. Richard Kallas, the plastic surgeon you guys just nailed for murdering that teenage porn actress he was fixated on. We've got good news on that one too."

"What's that?" Jessie asked.

"He's been in isolation since he was arrested. Apparently he hasn't been playing well with others. Other than a couple of visits from his lawyer, he hasn't had a single visitor or call. I think we can rule him out."

"Oh happy day," Jessie said more cynically than she'd intended.

Ryan raised his hand. Decker nodded at him to go ahead.

"I did preliminary checks on both Jessie's ex-husband, Kyle Voss, and Andrea Robinson," he said. "But it looks like Jessie is going to have to do the follow-up conversations. My call to the prison where Voss is being held, the Theo Lacy Facility in Orange County, was referred to the FBI. I know you said Agent Jack Dolan might be able to fill you in. I'm hoping so because I got nothing."

"I texted him this morning," Jessie replied. "He's available so I'm going to call him after we're done here. All I know is that Kyle was worming his way in with a gang associated with a cartel. Dolan thought it was to get protection but he wasn't sure. I'll see if he has anything new."

"Okay," Decker said. "Then what about Andrea Robinson?"

Andrea "Andy" Robinson was Jessie's first case for the LAPD. Andy was a bored, rich society girl with a biting wit, a sharp tongue, and an apparent willingness to help Jessie navigate the cutthroat world of country club secrets. Jessie was drawn to her immediately and, after the case was seemingly solved, decided to hang out with her new friend.

Unfortunately, Andy turned out to be a sociopath who had poisoned her married lover's wife and framed an innocent maid for the crime. When Andy sensed the profiler was on to her, she poisoned her too. Only Jessie's quick thinking saved her from meeting the same fate as the murdered woman. She still beat herself up for allowing Andy's charm to blind her to the woman's true nature.

"Now that one was interesting," Ryan said, pulling Jessie out of the unpleasant memory. "As I feared, since Robinson's being held in the Forensic In-Patient Unit at the women's unit of the Twin Towers Correctional Facility, they wouldn't give me any information on her visitors, or anything else for that matter. So I decided to call your friend Dr. Lemmon."

"Who's that?" Trembley asked.

"Jeez, Trembley, sometimes I forget just how green you still are," Decker said with mild annoyance. "Dr. Janice Lemmon is one of the most preeminent behavioral therapists in the country. She's consulted on tons of cases for us, as well as for the FBI. I heard she even worked for the CIA for a while. She's like Garland Moses without a badge."

"And she's your friend?" Trembley asked Jessie.

"Among other things," she said. "She's also my therapist, has been for years. When your father kills your mother when you're six years old, then slices you open along your collarbone from your neck to your shoulder, and leaves you alone with her body in a freezing, abandoned cabin in the woods, you find that you need some top-notch therapy. She's the best, so I went to her."

"But what does she have to do with Andrea Robinson?" Trembley asked.

"In addition to the work the captain mentioned," Ryan said, "she also consults for multiple psychiatric hospitals in Southern California. I thought she might be able to grease the wheels and get us the information we needed."

"Any luck?" Reid wondered.

"Not in getting access to records," Ryan replied. "Even Lemmon would have to jump through more bureaucratic hoops than we're probably willing to take on right now. But she was able to get one concession."

The way he said that last line made the hairs on the back of Jessie's neck prickle. Whatever the concession was, she doubted it was going to be without a price.

"What is it?" she asked cautiously.

"Dr. Lemmon told me that Andrea Robinson is willing to talk. But only to you."

CHAPTER TWENTY FOUR

Jessie couldn't decide which was worse.

Did she want to talk to an FBI agent about what the sociopathic ex-husband who tried to murder her was up to? Or did she prefer to talk to the sociopathic psychiatric prison resident who tried to kill her after inviting her over for a girls' night?

Ultimately she decided to start with the conversation *about* a killer and work her way up to the chat directly *with* a killer. So she called FBI Special Agent Jack Dolan.

She and Dolan had worked together on a case last year and kept in touch since. He was the one who'd told her that an informant in prison had reported that Kyle had expressed a desire to "gut her like a pig and bathe in her warm blood." If anyone could find out if her ex had been somehow messing with her life, it was him.

"Hope I didn't catch you at the beach," Jessie teased when he picked up. Dolan was notorious for showing up to meetings with wet hair and salty skin after sneaking in a few weekday waves.

"Nah," he answered chuckling. "I get my time in early. That gives me a chance to shower the sand out of my crotch before hitting the office."

"Still staying classy, I see," she jibed good-naturedly. "So the surfing's good. How about the sobriety?"

"Just got my seven-month chip," he said proudly. "I thought I'd get a cash prize too but no luck. Speaking of, I hear your luck hasn't been great lately."

"Are you referring to the social media hacks that make me look like a racist, anti-Semitic xenophobe? Or the visit from Social Services investigating whether I beat the sister I only discovered I had a few months ago?"

"I didn't even know about the second one," Dolan said. "At least there aren't any serial killers out to get you."

"The day is young," Jessie countered. "But I'm hoping you can turn it around for me."

"I'll do my best. How can I help?"

Jessie wasn't sure he could but launched in all the same.

"I have a strong suspicion that my recent run of bad luck isn't pure chance," she said. "It's looking increasingly likely that someone has it in for me and is trying to make my life hell in all kinds of ways, both big and little. There are lots of contenders. We're looking at all of them. But right near the top is my dear ex-husband. I was hoping you could help me determine if he's the mastermind behind this whole thing."

There was long silence on the other end of the line that didn't fill Jessie with confidence.

"Why do I suddenly have a sinking feeling?" she asked.

"Am I that obvious?" he wondered.

"You are," she told him. "Whatever it is, just tell me. I'm starting to become numb to bad news so there's no better time."

"The truth is I haven't heard anything about him secretly plotting to ruin your life. But I do have bad news. I was actually planning to call you but was holding out hope I wouldn't need to."

"What is it?" she demanded.

"Your ex-husband may be getting released," he said reluctantly.

"What! How is that possible?" Jessie said, feeling her heart pounding against her chest.

"It's not a sure thing," Dolan said. "Right now it's not confirmed. But I'm hearing rumors that the prosecutor in his case may be about to file paperwork admitting improper prosecutorial conduct."

"What the hell does that mean?"

"It's all hazy right now. But supposedly he's planning to confess to withholding evidence or something along those lines."

Jessie was silent for a few seconds as she tried to regroup.

"Are you okay, Jessie?" Dolan asked when she didn't speak.

"I don't get it," she finally said. "Even if that were true—and color me skeptical—I'm a direct eyewitness to his attempt to, you know, murder me. Shouldn't that be enough, regardless of anything else related to evidentiary issues?"

"One would hope," Dolan said. "But criminals have been released on technicalities before, even when the evidence was overwhelming."

"Dolan, he killed his mistress, framed me for it, and then tried to kill me when I found out. None of that is in doubt."

"I'm not saying it is," he said, sounding as frustrated as she felt. "But he still might get out. It's not a done deal though. Nothing has been filed with the court yet."

Jessie thought for a moment, circling an idea that had just occurred to her.

"What about your informant, the one who heard Kyle threaten me in prison?" she asked. "That's a separate crime that happened independent of the prosecutor. Charge him on that."

"We can't."

"Why not?" she asked, trying to prevent her voice from filling the entire station bullpen.

"Because he's dead," Dolan said quietly. "His body was found in his cell yesterday."

Again Jessie needed a few seconds before responding.

"How convenient is that?" she said bitterly. "The one guy who can attest to my ex-husband's ongoing malice toward me dies in prison."

"It *is* suspicious," Dolan acknowledged. "But there's no way to prove it had anything to do with what your ex said to him. That was just a lucky, unexpected moment of revelation. The informant was already in deep, trying to get details on the Monzon cartel and how the leadership at their headquarters in Monterrey, Mexico, communicates north of the border. It's entirely possible he was taken out by them because they learned what he was doing."

"Okay," Jessie said, her mind racing. "You can still submit an affidavit attesting to what the informant told you about Kyle's threat. A formal declaration from an FBI agent should hold some weight with the court, right?"

More silence on the other end of the line. Jessie waited for the inevitable bad news.

"It's not as simple as that," Dolan finally said. "First, the judge in the case has longstanding animosity toward the Bureau. It's very likely that he'll throw my statement out as hearsay and claim it's a desperate attempt to manipulate the system. It wouldn't be the first time he's said something like that."

"Can you at least try?" Jessie pleaded.

"I would. You know I would, even if there was only a one percent chance of it working. But I can't."

"Why not?"

"Because we have another informant in the gang," Dolan said. "And acknowledging the first one puts the second one at risk. I can't do that."

Jessie was tempted to press the issue but knew it was out of Dolan's hands. The Bureau wasn't going to put a major investigation of a drug cartel at risk to, possibly futilely, keep her ex-husband in prison. She tried another tack.

"Is it possible that the prosecutor was threatened to confess to misconduct? Maybe the cartel got to him on Kyle's behalf."

"It's certainly possible," Dolan said. "We don't have any proof of it and the prosecutor denies any pressure, of course. But that may be why Voss cozied up to them in the first place. He was in finance before prison, right? Maybe he offered to help them if they could get him out. Does that sound like something he would do?"

"Frankly, knowing Kyle, I'm surprised he didn't come up with this idea months ago," Jessie said.

She heard Dolan sigh through the phone.

"Listen, Jessie," he said, sounding beleaguered, "whether or not your ex-husband has been trying to screw up your life from behind bars or not, I don't know. But the reality is that he is almost certainly going to be a free man in a matter of days. That means that if he wasn't already a threat to you, he's about to be. You need to prepare yourself for that, fast."

CHAPTER TWENTY FIVE

Jessie was nervous.

Despite the litany of disturbing news she'd already gotten today, the idea of having a video discussion with Andrea Robinson filled her with dread. She hadn't seen the woman since her trial. The whole time Jessie testified, Robinson stared at her with a half-smile, as if she was secretly amused that her old gal pal would accuse her of such atrocities.

Camille Guadino, the rookie from the tech unit who had quickly become Jessie's go-to expert on all things beyond her technological knowledge set, was helping her set up the meeting in a private interrogation room. She apparently sensed Jessie's apprehension.

"You okay?" she asked.

"Great," Jessie said sarcastically. "Just having a challenging day. I guess I was being selfish, thinking I'd get more than a few months without having to look over my shoulder to see if a psycho who'd already tried to kill me was about to make another go at it."

"But I thought Andrea Robinson was convicted to a life sentence," Camille said, confused.

Jessie realized the tech had no idea what she was talking about. Though she'd informed Ryan and Decker about Kyle's potential release, no one else knew.

"She is," Jessie said. "I'm just being dramatic. Are we good to go?"

"Yep," Camille said. "Your conference starts at ten. She should already be waiting. Just hit the green button when you're ready. Remember, she'll be able to see you so, you know…"

"Don't look freaked out?" Jessie finished for her.

"Something like that," Camille said. "I'll give you some privacy."

She left and Jessie looked at the clock on the wall. It read 9:59 a.m. She tried to clear her head of all the muddled and conflicting concerns. A corrupt cop might be trying to destroy her life. Or her ex-husband might be. Even if he wasn't, he was on the verge of walking the streets again.

And even though Eliza Longworth and Richard Kallas seemed to have been eliminated as likely culprits in this campaign against her, that still left two strong contenders, not including Andrea Robinson or others Jessie might not even be considering.

Meanwhile, this entire pursuit was taking valuable time away from the actual murder investigation she'd been assigned to, one in which two women's lives were still very much at risk. Finally, she was apparently not on speaking terms with either her sister or her best friend.

So a pretty crap day all around.

The clock struck ten and she closed her eyes, aggressively shaking her head as if her troubles were cobwebs that could be physically dislodged. She couldn't go into an interrogation of someone as wily as Andrea Robinson without a clear head. Her goal was to find out if Andy was behind the campaign to undermine her credibility and she'd need all her faculties working to make that assessment.

Deciding punctuality was secondary to clarity, she allowed herself a minute to just breathe, doing her best to, if not relax, and least unclench. When she opened her eyes again, it was 10:01. She hit "call" and waited.

After several seconds, an image popped on the screen. It was of what looked to be an empty visiting room. After a moment, a voice spoke, though no one appeared on camera.

"This is Assistant Warden Kimberly Stephens at the Twin Towers Correctional Facility. To whom am I speaking?"

"This is Jessie Hunt, forensic profiler with the LAPD, Central Station."

"Hello, Ms. Hunt," Stephens said. "We've coordinated this video on your behalf at the request of Dr. Janice Lemmon. I have to admit that it's highly unusual. Were it not for Dr. Lemmon's personal entreaty, we wouldn't be doing this."

"I appreciate the consideration," Jessie said. "I don't anticipate this taking too long. And if Ms. Robinson is uncooperative we can just shut it down. Is there anything special I should be aware of before I speak with her?"

"Yes. Andrea has a regimented schedule, as do all our residents. This break in the pattern of the day has her very excited, even though she doesn't know why she's here. She's currently in the adjoining room and I can see her grinning enthusiastically. I know of your history interviewing mentally ill offenders and your reputation, which until recently was quite stellar. So I'm sure I don't need to go over all our procedures. They're standard in a facility like this."

Jessie tried to push past the reference to her sullied reputation, almost certainly related to the news about her faked social media posts.

"Understood," she said, leaving that topic untouched. "Is she currently medicated?"

"No. We're holding off on her first daily dose until she talks to you," Stephens said. "I'll bring her in now."

A few seconds later Jessie was greeted by the giddy face of Andrea Robinson. Despite being incarcerated, without any access to makeup or her hairdresser, she still cut a stylish figure.

She looked much as Jessie remembered her. Her blonde hair was cut shorter than it had been before. But Andy had never gone in for heavy makeup in her country club days, so the total lack of it now didn't make much difference. In fact, the fresh-faced look made her appear even younger than her thirty-three years.

She was still attractive in that nondescript way that had made her seem so unthreatening when they'd first met. The only features that jumped out now, as they had back then, were her eyes. Bright blue, they twinkled with what Jessie had originally misjudged as amiable playfulness. In truth, that gleam suggested darker mischief.

At first glance at least, Andy seemed to have adjusted to life behind bars. Even in her assigned yellow uniform, she looked more like a gal enjoying a lazy stay-at-home weekend than a woman behind bars for murder.

"Is that Jessie Hunt?" she asked, sounding genuinely enthused at the sight of the woman she'd tried to poison. "Of all the people I thought I might see on that screen, you were definitely not at the top of the list. How's it going, girlfriend?"

"Hi, Andy," Jessie said evenly. "You're looking well."

Andy grinned broadly.

"Well, I've found that if I look at this place less as a prison and more as a spa with really good security, it helps me keep a positive attitude."

“That’s great to hear,” Jessie said, not entirely sure how to broach the subject she’d called about.

Andy sensed that her enthusiasm for their chat wasn’t mutual and reined in her zeal a fraction.

“Enough about me though. How are you doing? I hear you’ve really made a name for yourself since…our time together.”

“How did you hear that?” Jessie asked, wondering if this was an admission that she’d been tracking her.

“You’re kidding, right?” Andy asked incredulously. “We *are* allowed to watch TV in here, assuming we behave. And you’ve been on the news a lot. If you’re not catching serial killers, you’re taking down corrupt cops or catching killer hookers. Kudos.”

“Thanks,” Jessie said, trying not to look surprised that residents were allowed to watch the news. That was a no-no at most other facilities she’d visited.

“Of course,” Andy continued, “it sounds like it’s not all peaches and cream. I saw a report just last night suggesting that you’d posted some really awful things, the sort of comments I’d only hear people mutter under their breaths back in my country club days. I have to say I was shocked. It didn’t sound like the Jessie Hunt I know.”

“It’s not,” Jessie assured her, deciding this was her best chance to get a real reaction. “It turns out someone hacked my social media accounts. You wouldn’t know anything about that, would you?”

Andy kept grinning, giving no indication that she found the question accusatory.

“No. I was lucky enough never to have that happen to me,” she said without any obvious hint of deception. “And of course, it’s not an issue for me in here. It’s not like they let me scroll through my Insta during yard time. But I’m glad to hear it wasn’t you. Otherwise my perception of you would have really taken a hit. Did they catch the bastards yet?”

“Not yet,” Jessie said, deciding not to press too hard. She wasn’t certain whether Andy really misunderstood the question or was being purposefully dense. Her gut told her it was the latter but since she couldn’t be sure, she didn’t want to tip her hand.

“You get many visitors these days, Andy?” she asked.

Robinson’s face darkened and she looked at the screen curiously.

“I thought that kind of information was confidential,” she said coolly.

"It is," Jessie answered. "That's why I'm asking—because I don't know."

"Are you trying to make me feel bad, Jessie?"

"Why do you ask that?"

"Because other than this 'visit' with you, no one has come to see me but psychiatrists and lawyers. It's actually been very hurtful."

"To be fair, you are a murderer and a sociopath," Jessie reminded her. "You're not exactly a fun hang."

"But you know that's not true. I *am* a fun hang. I was already a murderer and a sociopath when you met me and we had a great time together. If it hadn't been for the messiness at the end, I think we'd be thick as thieves right now."

"By the messiness," Jessie noted, "I assume you're referring to your attempt to poison and then stab me?"

"You really hold a grudge, don't you?"

"That's actually what I was wondering about you," Jessie replied. "Is there any chance you're nursing a secret resentment toward me, one that you'd like to act on?"

Andy stared at her silently for several seconds as the grin on her face slowly disappeared, replaced by a cold, tight-lipped grimace. Jessie thought she might end the interview right then. But eventually she answered.

"Jessie, sweetie, I'd be lying if I said I didn't think of you every day and wonder what my life would be like if things had gone differently that night at my house. And I can't honestly say that I've never had a sour feeling toward you in the time since. But if you're suggesting that little old me, trapped in a psychiatric prison under constant surveillance, would somehow be capable of doing you harm out there in the real world, maybe you're the one who needs the straitjacket."

The smile had returned but not the warmth.

"That's not a denial," Jessie pointed out.

"Isn't it?" Andy asked before looking off-camera and speaking to someone out of sight. "I think we're done here."

Two seconds later the connection ended and Andy disappeared from the screen, if not from Jessie's mind.

CHAPTER TWENTY SIX

"Can I talk to you?"

Jessie was just returning to her desk when Ryan approached her with the question. Something about his tone made her nervous but she nodded and followed him to the station's courtyard. They sat on a bench next to a thick-trunked tree.

"How did the call with Andrea Robinson go?" he asked.

"Hard to say," Jessie admitted. "She was very chatty but when it was over, I had no more clarity on whether she could have done all this to me. She said she didn't have any visitors other than doctors and lawyers. And without access to her records, I have no way of knowing if that's true."

"You don't think Dr. Lemmon could get a peek?"

"She probably could. But I'm not sure she would. And I don't want to put her in the position of asking her."

"So we're back at square one," Ryan said testily.

"It's worse than that," Jessie pointed out. "Whoever is doing this could be someone we haven't even thought of, in which case we're spinning our wheels for no reason. All while losing time on this double murder case. You hear anything new since we last spoke?"

"Our Beverly Hills detective friends called," Ryan muttered. "They have Gregg Dozier, Caroline Gidley's ex-fiancé, down at the station. They asked if we wanted to sit in on his interrogation. I told them we'd get there as soon as we could."

"It's worth a shot, I guess," Jessie said. "I don't hold out much hope that it's him though. Like I said, I think it's a stretch for him to have gone after all these women as a cover so he could kill his ex."

"It's great that your intuition is so honed," Ryan replied snarkily.

Jessie looked over at him, surprised at the sharpness of his tone.

"What's wrong with you?" she asked.

"What do you mean? Nothing."

"Then why so snippy?" she asked. "You've been poking at me since we came out here."

He looked like he was about to say something, then stopped himself.

"What is it, Ryan?" she pressed. "There's obviously something eating at you. If you don't spit it out, you're going to be miserable all day."

He didn't look any less pained but she could tell he'd decided to come clean.

"I didn't want to bring this up but we've reached the point where I think I have to. Are you sure this whole reputation-destroying vendetta thing is real?"

She stared at him, unsure how to respond.

"What?"

He pulled something from his pocket and held it out to her. It was a Ziploc bag filled with pills.

"I found these in my car on the floor next to the passenger seat when I dropped you off yesterday."

"What are they?"

"Anti-psychotic medications," he said, "Strong ones."

"They aren't mine," she insisted.

"It wouldn't be anything to be ashamed of if they are," he replied gently. "You've been through a lot lately. If you asked Dr. Lemmon to prescribe them because you were struggling, it would be understandable."

"Ryan," she said, speaking slowly to keep from losing it, "we basically live together. You see me every day. Have I been acting psychotic?"

"I'm no doctor," he answered unimpressively.

"Okay, I'll try not to take offense at that weak tea. Even if I was, do you think I'd hide it from you? Do you think I'd walk around with a bunch of pills in a plastic baggie? Does any of this make sense to you?"

"No," he told her. "But what also doesn't make sense is how your life went from seemingly normal to something out of a conspiracy thriller in a matter of days."

"What are you talking about?"

Again he looked reluctant to respond.

"You're in too deep to back out now," she reminded him sharply.

"Okay, fine. Your tires get slashed on a quiet street but there's no suspect. Your Facebook account suddenly starts spewing racist crap. You get a visit from Social Services. Those don't all have to be conspiracies against you."

Jessie looked around the courtyard, half expecting a crew to jump out and tell her she was being punked. When it didn't happen, she looked back at Ryan.

"What do *you* think happened?" she asked.

"Maybe it really *was* kids playing hooky who slashed your tires. Maybe someone *did* hear an argument between you and Hannah and called DPSS out of an abundance of caution."

Sensing that she was about to lose it, Jessie took a deep breath and counted to three before responding.

"Even if I bought that, it doesn't explain the racist posts," she pointed out.

"Maybe something else is going on."

"That's pretty cryptic, Ryan," she said acidly. "Maybe you care to spell it out."

"You're not going to like this…" he began.

"Compared to how I've loved what you said so far?"

Ryan sighed and tried again.

"I don't want you to take offense," he began, sounding uncomfortably like Jessie realized she must have when she'd asked Hannah if she'd made the anonymous phone call to Social Services. "But have you considered that if you are having some kind of…psychological incident, it could explain a lot of this?"

"Like what?" she demanded.

"Like maybe you slashed your own tires. Maybe you did write those posts yourself."

"You said we were in a meeting when some of them were posted," she reminded him.

"I was covering for you because it seemed ridiculous. But those things can be prewritten and set to post at specific times."

"So you think I snapped and forgot about writing a bunch of hate-filled comments. What else?"

He hesitated briefly but then plowed ahead.

"Maybe Hannah called DPSS in a moment of spite that she now regrets, or because something happened that you don't remember."

"I cannot believe we are having this conversation," she said softly.

"Neither can I," he said.

They were both quiet for a moment before she had a thought.

"But you said yourself, everything's been going well lately. Why would I all of a sudden have some kind of mental break?"

"Maybe that's why, Jessie. You've had trauma in your life for so long that maybe you've gotten used to it. And when it wasn't there for a little while, your mind created it for you."

Jessie shook her head in disgust.

"Is that what you really believe?"

"I don't know," he said.

"But you think it's just as likely that I did all this as it is that someone slashed my tires, hacked my accounts, called DPSS anonymously, and planted those pills?"

"Do you hear how wild that sounds?" he asked her.

"Did it ever occur to you that whoever's doing this to me *wants* to make everyone question me? That it's part of the plan to undermine my credibility and destroy my life?"

Ryan looked at her sadly but didn't respond. She continued.

"You've known me for a few years now, and pretty intimately for the last several months. The fact that you think this is even a possibility cuts me so deeply that I don't even have words for it."

"I'm sorry," he replied quietly. "I'm not trying to hurt you."

She nodded, standing up and looking away briefly before turning back to face him.

"I think you should meet up with the Beverly Hills detectives yourself. I'm going back to Brenda Ferguson's place to see if she recognizes the man in the hospital footage."

"We can do both together," he said pleadingly, standing up himself now. "I don't want to do this on separate tracks."

Ryan," she said as she got up to leave, "I think you better start getting used to separate tracks."

She walked off without another word.

CHAPTER TWENTY SEVEN

Jessie couldn't even go outside for air.

She was just about to exit the station lobby onto the street in front when she saw the protesters. There were about twenty people marching in a circle on the sidewalk in front of the station. They were chanting something and several of them held signs. Just before she dodged out of sight, she saw one that read "We all know that Hunt must go!"

It wasn't the most creative phrasing she'd ever heard, but Jessie chose not to engage on the matter. Instead, she decided to skip the fresh air and just go straight to Brenda Ferguson's. She got her car from the garage and pulled out onto the side street, which was devoid of angry picketers for now.

As she drove down Sixth Street, she saw Garland Moses walking leisurely down the sidewalk, apparently on the way to an early lunch at his favorite haunt, the Nickel Diner. Even though the diner was only a block away, she pulled over into the bike lane and called out the window.

"Need a ride, old man?"

He glanced up and smiled, unable to hide his amusement.

"I'm worried that you at the wheel might constitute elder abuse," he said.

"I'm an excellent driver," she said, winking.

"Even though I'm not a pop culture savant, I'll accept the offer," he said, getting in.

"You know, Garland," she said, pulling away once he'd shut the door, "the fact that you say you're not a pop culture savant is proof that you got the reference."

"Always profiling, this one," he said as if he was talking to an imaginary third person in the car.

"You laid that one out on a platter for me," she replied.

They continued quietly for a few moments before Garland spoke again.

"So you seem to be having quite a week."

"That is the understatement of the decade," she agreed. "And you don't know the half of it."

"Care to update me?" he asked.

"We're here," Jessie said, pulling up in front of the diner.

"My stomach's not grumbling too bad yet," he said. "Fill me in."

"Should I include the murder case I can't seem to catch a break on? Or the fact that I'm not on speaking terms with my sister, my best friend and, as of ten minutes ago, my boyfriend?"

"I'm assuming that's the usual 'rough week' stuff," he said. "Maybe skip to the unusual stuff."

"Okay," she said, overlooking the fact that Garland Moses apparently thought it was "usual" for all her personal relationships to be in tatters. "Here's the CliffsNotes version. Assuming you don't buy the theory that I'm having a psychotic break, which apparently isn't a certainty these days, someone is trying to destroy my life. It started with my tires—all of them—getting slashed. Then in quick succession, my social media was hacked and racist rants were posted. You seem to know about that one."

"Everyone does," Garland confirmed.

"Super," she said, then continued. "After that a witch from Social Services came to my place to investigate an anonymous allegation that I'm abusing Hannah. And I just found out someone planted anti-psychotic meds that have Ryan wondering if I'm in need of institutionalization. And that's on top of finding out that my murderous ex-husband is probably going to be released from prison on a technicality."

"Is that related?" Garland asked, showing an impressive ability to keep a straight face.

"Probably not. It sounds like he charmed a drug cartel into threatening the prosecutor in his case to confess to hiding evidence. I bet he promised to launder their money if he got out. But who knows at this point?"

"Do you have any likely suspects in the life-destroying plan?' he asked.

As she was about to reply, her phone rang. It was Delia Armbruster. She held up the screen for Garland to see.

"The Social Services witch," she said.

"Do you want to answer it?" he asked. "I can step outside."

"No. It's not going to be good news so I think I'll procrastinate in facing it," she said, sending the call to voicemail. "Where were we?"

"Suspects," he reminded her.

"Oh, right," she recalled. "Other than the aforementioned ex-husband, there's the corrupt cop awaiting trial because of me and the sociopathic society gal in a psychiatric prison because of me. We think we can eliminate two other folks that I helped put away. But I could easily be forgetting someone else I helped catch. Or it could just be some unhinged suspect we ultimately let go who was offended by my interrogation style. The list is endless."

"No it's not."

She looked at him sideways, unsure if he was joking. His serious expression suggested he wasn't.

"What do you mean?"

"Assuming you're not having a psychotic break," he said mildly, "and I'm willing to give you the benefit of the doubt for now, then the list of possible perpetrators is actually quite small. Whoever is doing this to you is not someone you simply slighted in an interview. This is someone who believes you destroyed their life and is meticulously trying to return the favor."

"Are you sure?"

"I am," he said. "And if you weren't so close to it, you'd be sure too. The person responsible for this clearly has access to you, either on their own or through a surrogate. They got close enough to slash your tires and plant medication. But they didn't try to kill you. Instead they tried to unsettle you. The person has access to resources that allowed them to hack your social media. They were creative enough to get authorities to investigate you for impropriety with someone in your care and to have someone you work with question your stability. Your torturer, and that's what he or she is, is very intelligent and has enormous patience. The person doing this wants your world to crumble around you slowly so they can enjoy it. This is personal."

Jessie sat with that for a moment, letting it settle in. Garland was right. There were only so many people who had the intelligence, means, persistence, ability to deceive, and true loathing to undertake something of this magnitude.

Some of them, like Sergeant Hank Costabile, her ex-husband Kyle Voss, and Andy Robinson, couldn't be removed from the short list. But there was one more name she realized she had to add, someone who knew her well, had easy, regular access to her, was dangerously intelligent, and had shown a troubling ability to mask the darkness that lurked inside. The one trait this person lacked was a loathing for Jessie. Or at least that's what she had assumed.

She looked over at Garland, wondering if she should say the name aloud. But doing that would make it real in a way that she wasn't sure she was ready for. Still, there were only two people in the world she felt comfortable asking this question of and one of them was sitting across from her now.

"Garland," she asked, not sure if she'd be able to get the words past her lips. "Is there any chance it could be Hannah?"

Garland Moses gazed back at her with an enigmatic expression. After a while, his face softened into something close to compassion. Finally he answered.

"I just don't know."

CHAPTER TWENTY EIGHT

Jessie's right hand throbbed.

It was her own fault. She should have known better than to listen to Delia Armbruster's voicemail while driving to meet a woman in peril after having her mentor admit he wasn't sure her own sister wasn't the one trying to reduce her world to rubble.

But she did listen to the voicemail. And she did subsequently punch the dashboard. And it did hurt so bad she wondered if she might have broken a few fingers.

By the time she got to Brenda Ferguson's house, she had regained the use of all her digits. But the pain lingered, as did the sense of humiliation that came from her inability to control her emotions. She had to get a grip before meeting with Brenda, who needed to deal with a competent professional, not someone whose life was obviously spiraling out of control.

She played back Armbruster's message again, hoping that hearing it a second time, she could focus on the content and not just the fury the message engendered.

"Ms. Hunt, as I mentioned when we met in person, I have recommended that the investigation of the allegations against you proceed. We have scheduled a formal interview for you at our downtown office tomorrow at ten a.m. In addition to myself, there will be a member of our investigative team asking you questions. You are free to bring counsel if you deem it appropriate and to access documentation in connection to the allegations. Please confirm that you got this notice. Your absence from the interview will be taken into consideration when making a determination on the allegations in question. Good day."

Even on a second listen, Jessie didn't know what to do with the call. It sounded like not showing up would hurt her irreparably. But she didn't even know a lawyer who could serve as counsel, much less have one.

But there was one silver lining she'd missed earlier. Apparently she could access the documents from the case. If she could look at them and get her hands on a transcript of that anonymous call, maybe she could discern something about the caller. It was better than nothing.

Rather than calling Armbruster back, she texted confirmation of her attendance and requested all records associated with the file, specifically the transcript and recording of the original complaint call. Feeling like she was making some forward progress, Jessie got out of the car and walked to the Fergusons with something approximating a good attitude.

When she got to the door, she was greeted by a uniformed officer standing guard.

"Can I help you, ma'am?" he asked politely.

"Yes, Officer…Tanner," she said, looking at his name tag. "Can you please let Brenda Ferguson know that Jessie Hunt is here to see her?"

She noticed his face twitched slightly when she said her name.

"Is she expecting you?" he asked.

"No. But she'll know what it's in reference to."

"Hold on, please," he said coldly before radioing the other officer inside.

Something about his manner was off-putting. The guy looked normal enough. He was in his late twenties with sun-bleached blond hair, a deep tan, and a skater tattoo she could see on his lower neck, despite the high shirt collar. But he gave off a frosty vibe. When he was done on the radio, she tried again.

"Also, can you please keep half an eye on my car while I'm inside?" Jessie asked. "Last time I was here, my tires got knifed."

"Of course," he said. "I'll keep watch for all the usual suspects."

Something about the way Officer Tanner said it felt false but Jessie tried to let it go. They waited silently for a moment before the officer said what had clearly been eating at him.

"Nice to be here in Brentwood where you don't have to deal with so many dark-skinned folks, huh, Ms. Hunt?" he said, smiling though his tone was cutting.

"Excuse me?"

"Oh nothing," Tanner said. "I'm just looking forward to seeing my wife tonight and telling her about meeting you in person. She's African-American, by the way. I know how you feel about the mixing of the races and all, but what are you gonna do, right?"

Before she could respond the door opened to reveal Ty Ferguson, who ushered her back to the living room where Brenda was waiting with a scowl on her face. A second officer named Kendrick was positioned in the corner of the room, where he stood silently.

"I almost told them not to let you in," Brenda said harshly. "But Ty said I couldn't let my personal disgust get in the way of my safety and I should hear what you have to say. So say it."

"Brenda…" Jessie began.

"Maybe we should go back to Mrs. Ferguson."

Jessie nodded and continued carefully.

"First, I didn't write those things. My accounts were hacked by someone who is trying to undermine my credibility. But we don't need to litigate that right now. I wanted to show you a few screen grabs of someone we think might be your abductor and see if you recognize him. Is that okay?"

Brenda nodded. Jessie walked over and sat down next to her on the couch. Her phone, which was on silent, began to buzz. She forced herself not to check who was calling and instead pulled up the screenshots from the hospital and held them in front of her. Brenda looked at each of them closely. Jessie could tell that something about them resonated. But she didn't speak. Instead she just frowned.

"What is it, Mrs. Ferguson?" she asked.

Brenda looked up.

"I'm hesitant to say this because I'm not one hundred percent sure. But he kind of looks like my old marriage counselor."

"You and Ty met with a counselor?"

"No," Brenda said. "I mean from my first marriage. I was with him for about three years. Things started to fall apart and we tried to salvage them by meeting with a counselor. He was actually a really pleasant man who did everything he could for us. It was just too much."

"What was?"

"Our issues. They were too much to overcome. I wasn't completely faithful. We couldn't move past it. But the counselor did his best."

"What was his name?" Jessie asked.

"Warren Fischer. This looks like him a bit, the hair and the glasses at least. And the clothes he wore before he changed into scrubs. But I haven't heard from him since the divorce and Warren never made me feel uncomfortable. Plus I know what his voice sounds like. This wasn't the same."

"Could he have altered it, knowing you'd recognize it?" Jessie asked.

Brenda looked over at her, clearly lost.

"I just don't know. I wouldn't have thought so. But I'm not sure of much of anything anymore."

"Okay," Jessie said, standing up. "That's all I need for now. I'll look into this. How do you feel having these officers around? Is it setting your mind at ease a little?"

"I guess. It's hard to feel at ease knowing two women were killed in the last few days by the man who took me. But having them here helps a little."

"Plus, you've got your panic room," Jessie reminded her, smiling wryly.

"Believe me, I haven't forgotten."

"Well, I'll let you get back to it. I'll let you know if I learn anything worthwhile."

"Thank you," Brenda said. "I appreciate you coming over. And I really hope what you're saying about being hacked turns out to be true. I don't like disliking you, Ms. Hunt."

"That's nice of you to say," Jessie replied. "And for the record, I'm still cool with you calling me Jessie, when you're comfortable with it."

She walked out without waiting for a response, passing Officer Kendrick, who looked at her like he wanted to hate her too but wasn't sure what to believe anymore. When she got to the front door, she saw that her tires seemed to have been untouched.

"Thanks for keeping an eye out," she said to Officer Tanner, who clearly hadn't been.

"You have yourself a great day, Ms. Hunt," he said with mock enthusiasm. "I hope everything turns out all white for you."

Jessie didn't reply. Rather, she pulled out her phone and texted Detective Trembley, asking him to get whatever he could on Warren Fischer. Then she checked the message she'd gotten while she was with Brenda. It was from Detective Ray Sands. Until this moment, she hadn't consciously thought about the fact that Sands was black. Despite her apprehension at what he might have to say about the posts attributed to her, she listened to his voicemail.

To her surprise, he made no mention of them. But he did tell her that he'd convinced Jayne Castillo, the third woman abducted, to meet with her. He gave her Castillo's address and wished her good luck. There wasn't an ounce of irony in his voice. It was a small thing, but considering everything else going on, his professionalism and lack of rancor was a breath of fresh air.

She got back in the car and punched in the address for Jayne Castillo. It was in the Mid-Wilshire district, a solid half-hour drive away. Jessie made good time and tried to keep her head clear by listening to some music. But an uncomfortable thought, one she'd managed to dismiss until now, kept creeping in.

Was there any chance that Ryan's concerns were legitimate? Could she have manufactured all these suspicious events herself because her brain needed to create imaginary crises when real ones didn't exist? Could she have blacked out and knifed her own tires? Could she have written those posts while in some kind of fugue state? Could she have wiped out a memory of abusing Hannah, verbally or otherwise? Might Dr. Lemmon have prescribed her some kind of medication that she forgot she was taking?

The idea was patently absurd. She had no lost time, at least that she was aware of. She'd been in close proximity to both Hannah and Ryan without either of them saying a word of concern prior to this week. And as for creating drama when her life was going well, that didn't jibe.

Despite her traumatic childhood and the recurring nightmares it provoked for decades afterward, she had led a fairly normal life from when she was adopted at the age of seven until her husband started gaslighting her at the end of their marriage, when he tried to make her think she'd killed his mistress. At no point during that two-decade-plus stretch did she ever have a psychotic break. And she doubted she was having one now.

All the same, she gave Dr. Lemmon a call. She wasn't in but Jessie left what she suspected would be the therapist's weirdest message of the day, even by Lemmon's standards.

"Hi, Dr. Lemmon. It's Jessie Hunt. This might seem like a strange question but I'm going to ask it anyway. Is there any chance that I've had some kind of breakdown recently that I don't recall, maybe one for which you prescribed hardcore anti-psychotic mediation? I've had a series of unfortunate events in the last few days that make me think someone is seriously messing with me. But it's been suggested that I might be making it all up and not aware of it. I tend to think that's a load of crap. But I wanted a second opinion. So if you could get back to me when you have a chance, I'd appreciate it. Sorry for the weird message. Hope you're having a nice day."

After she hung up, it occurred to her that even if Dr. Lemmon didn't think she was bananas before, that message just might change her mind.

CHAPTER TWENTY NINE

Jessie caught a break.

It seemed that Jayne Castillo didn't watch the local news religiously. So she apparently hadn't heard anything about the posts that had recently made Jessie infamous. After the officers guarding her small but charming 1950s-built home let her inside, Castillo led her back to the breakfast nook, where she offered coffee.

"I'm good, thanks," Jessie assured her. "I don't intend to take up too much of your time. I've read your statement about the abduction and don't need you to revisit it. I was actually hoping to show you some video images and get your opinion on them."

Castillo sighed. Though Jessie had never met her before, she could tell that recent weeks had been hard on her. Compared to the photo in her case file, the woman, who was thirty-three, looked to have aged over a decade in less than fifteen days. Her hair, jet black in the photo, was now at least half gray. Her eyes were droopy and red, with dark bags underneath. Her movements were sloth-like.

"I was hoping to just put this all behind me," she said tiredly. "But it turns out that being held captive in a dumpster for three days isn't something you move past that easily. And Detective Sands convinced me I couldn't ever truly do it until this man was apprehended. He said you might be my best shot at making that happen. That's why I'm talking to you, even though I really would rather not."

"I appreciate it, Ms. Castillo," Jessie said. "And as I said, I'll be brief. Can you look at the man in these images and tell me if he looks familiar at all?"

She pulled up the same images she'd shown Brenda Ferguson and watched the woman closely as she scrolled through them. Her expression remained blank.

"He doesn't look familiar to me," Castillo said.

Jessie tried a different tack.

"You're married, right?" she asked.

"Yes, for two years."

"Did you and your husband ever get counseling, either before or afterward?"

"No," Castillo said, with a look that showed she considered the question extremely odd. "I don't think we've ever had an issue serious enough to require counseling."

Jessie nodded, trying to hide her frustration. She was just starting to get up when Jayne Castillo continued.

"Not like in my first marriage."

Jessie sat back down.

"You were married before?"

"Yeah," Castillo said. "I thought everything was in my file."

"I guess I missed it," Jessie said.

"It didn't last long, less than six months. I'm not proud of this, but I never stopped seeing my previous boyfriend, even after I started dating my ex-husband. We got engaged and married. But I kept sneaking off to see my old boyfriend. My husband found out. We briefly tried to work it out but the wounds were too deep. Eventually we got divorced. A few months later I married the original boyfriend. We've been together ever since."

Something about the comment jogged a memory for Jessie. The Beverly Hills detective named Oxford had mentioned that Caroline Gidley had been cheating on her fiancé too. She made a mental note to follow up and see if that was more than a coincidence.

"How are things with your ex?" she asked

"Non-existent," Castillo said. "We didn't have kids so there was no reason to keep in touch. We had a small dispute in the divorce about who would pay for the failed therapy. But ultimately I paid just to have a clean break."

Jessie nodded again.

"Can I ask what your therapist's name was?"

The woman scrunched up her face, trying to recall.

"I'm not sure," she said. "I think it might have been Walter something."

"Could it have been Warren?"

"Yes! That's it. Warren Fischer. Why?"

Jessie showed her the screen grabs again.

"Does this look like Warren Fischer to you?"

Castillo looked at them, actually tilting her head sideways at one point.

"I guess it could be. Warren had bushy black hair and glasses like that. But I never would have made the connection on my own. His face, at least what I can see of it, doesn't really look the same. Do you think he could have done this?"

"We're looking into it," Jessie said. "Does that surprise you?"

"Yes. Warren was a sweetie. I always felt like he was genuinely trying to help me. He didn't seem to have an angry bone in his body. I remember he even offered to waive the cost of our final session if it was causing upset in our divorce settlement. I refused, of course, but that's the kind of person he was. I just can't fathom that he's responsible for what happened to me."

Jayne Castillo seemed convinced but Jessie could fathom lots of things most people couldn't.

"Okay, thanks so much for your help," she said, getting up. "I know it wasn't easy."

"It's just nice to know that someone's still trying to solve this."

"Of course," Jessie said. "And please, follow the instructions of the officers here. Don't take any unnecessary risks. We're making every effort to catch this guy. But in the interim, your priority is to stay safe."

Castillo nodded and walked her to the door. Jessie was worried about her. The woman looked like she might pass out at any moment. More than Brenda Ferguson, who seemed more angry than fearful, Castillo had a fragility that made Jessie worry that the sheer anxiety of the situation might get her before the killer did.

She returned to her car and headed to her next destination, the office of family and marriage counselor Warren Fischer. She considered calling Ryan, if only for backup. But she was still too pissed at him. Besides, she had gotten combat and self-defense training from FBI instructors. She had a weapon. She could handle this on her own.

*

The True Avenger sat at his desk, reviewing his plan for that night.

He knew this would be his last, best opportunity to mete out justice. Everything had to go just right. If he didn't time everything properly, then the last two Reckonings wouldn't succeed.

If they didn't, then one or both of the remaining sinners would surely be placed in protective custody. That wouldn't make them untouchable. But getting to them would be much harder. So it was important that tonight's Reckoning was triumphant.

He re-checked his annotations. In his day job, he was expected to take meticulous notes and it had become second nature. According to his information, both women were now holed up in their homes, afraid to leave. Both had police security.

That part made him smile slightly. It gave him a slight rush to know that these adulteresses were operating under a false sense of security. It would make their eventual retribution all the more satisfying.

The True Avenger could not make up for all the men he knew of who'd been wronged by their treacherous partners. He hadn't even been able to do that for himself. But he could at least do it for these four victims.

He still regretted waiting so long to take action in his own life. After he got home early from work one day to find his wife, Sasha, in bed with one of her co-workers, he'd responded in a manner that seemed alien to him now.

He'd yelled, of course. And the man—he'd later learn his name was Derrick—left quickly, though not with the level of appropriate shame. After Derrick was gone, the True Avenger actually cried, pleading with his wife not to ever let such a thing happen again.

In retrospect, it wasn't a good look. It might have been that pitiable moment of weakness on his part, more than the affair itself, which made reconciliation impossible. He saw the mix of disappointment and disgust in her eyes through his own tear-stained ones and knew he'd lost her for good.

She left that night and moved in with Derrick. Within months, mere days after the divorce was official, Sasha married Derrick. The True Avenger spent most of the time leading up to that date drowning his sorrows in alcohol and porn.

But on the day of Sasha's wedding, something changed. He woke up that morning with a bad hangover, but forced himself to get dressed in a nice suit. He knew there was no way he could just walk in and attend Sasha's wedding. So he went to the church very early and hid in a back office.

Once the service was underway, he snuck out and watched from the back, where he went unnoticed. He considered shouting something when the minister asked if anyone had objections, but remained silent. The couple exchanged vows and kissed. By the time they were declared husband and wife, the True Avenger had left the church.

He devised his plan that very day. It was intricate, involving the abduction, torture, and eventual murder of Sasha. He also planned to frame Derrick for the crime. Within weeks, he had everything squared away—the location where Sasha would be held, how he would eventually kill her, the alibi he'd prepared for himself. The arrangements were complete.

But something held him back. For nearly a year after that he dawdled, making excuses for the delay. He was still noodling around the edges of the plan, needlessly tweaking at perfection, when he got the news.

Sasha and Derrick had died when a tire blew out on their car while they were driving back from wine country on a winding coastal road. The car had plunged over two hundred feet to the rocks below. Because of the fire that consumed the vehicle, dental records were required to identify the bodies.

The True Avenger was left with a feeling of emptiness. He basked briefly in the belief that their last moments were filled with fear and horror. But that wasn't enough. Even if it was true, their suffering would have been brief, nothing like what he'd had in store for them.

He came to realize that it was his own procrastination and deficit of righteous, insistent zeal that was as much at fault as that blown tire. He'd been given an opportunity to right the wrong done to him and squandered it. He would not make that mistake again.

So he came up with a new plan. Through his work, he had access to the intimate details of marital relationships and the indiscretions that undid them. He was able to discern the worst offenders, the most objectionable degenerates, and select them for sentencing.

He established a four-part system—Collection, Purification, Unraveling, and Reckoning—that would take each violator through a cleansing that would ultimately end in her final Deliverance. It was beautiful in its simplicity. And unlike his dawdling with Sasha, he'd gone from inspiration to implementation in less than three months.

Tonight would be the culmination of all those efforts. There was no more prep to be done. Everything from this point forward would occur as designed as long as he kept his wits about him and didn't allow his fury to overcome his sense of righteousness.

His thoughts were interrupted by a beep from his computer calendar. He glanced at it and saw that he had a meeting in five minutes. Very carefully, he packed up his plans for the evening and slid them into the hidden section of his desk drawer. Then he stood up to stretch before re-engaging with the world.

CHAPTER THIRTY

Jessie knew better than to just walk in without preparation.

The last time she'd gone into the office of a medical professional, she'd been far too blasé about it. Even with Ryan at her side, they'd been taken by surprise and barely escaped with their lives.

That time, they were interviewing Dr. Richard Kallas, the plastic surgeon who they ultimately learned had killed porn actress Michaela "Missy Mack" Penn. They hadn't expected him to turn off the lights and come at them with a large surgical knife.

It was that unexpected ferocity that had temporarily put Kallas on the list of suspects in the attempt to undermine Jessie's reputation. And it was the memory of Kallas's fierceness that had Jessie on guard now as she entered Warren Fischer's counseling office.

She'd checked both her regulation sidearm and the extra one in her ankle holster before arriving. She also had Mace in one jacket pocket and a Taser in the other. Finally, she'd called Captain Decker on the way over to let him know what she was doing. She couldn't bring herself to reach out to Ryan but she wasn't so obstinate as to walk in without any potential backup.

Fischer's office wasn't too far from Jayne Castillo's place. It was located in a nice but unassuming office building on the Miracle Mile stretch of Wilshire Boulevard. She rode up the elevator to the sixth floor and walked down the thickly carpeted hallway. The door was unlocked. He didn't have a receptionist, just a small waiting room. She pushed the buzzer on the wall and waited. It only took a few seconds for him to pop his head out.

She saw immediately why Brenda Ferguson thought the man in the screen grabs might be Fischer. The counselor had a thick shock of bushy hair that seemed to defeat any attempt to control it. He wore gold wire-rimmed glasses. The shape of his jaw line didn't seem quite like a match for the man in the images. But because the hospital footage never provided a clear shot of his face, there was no way to draw any definitive conclusions.

"Jessie Hunt?" he asked hopefully.

"Yes," she said. "Thanks for fitting me in on such short notice."

"Not a problem," he assured her. "It worked out perfectly because I had a late cancellation. Come on back."

He held the door open for her but she didn't step forward.

"You lead the way," she said.

"Okay," he replied, pushing the heavy door open and starting down the short hallway to his open office.

Jessie tried to match his gait to the man in the video. But it was impossible to be sure. The killer had moved quickly and purposefully. Warren Fischer had a relaxed, languorous walking style. Either of those could have been tweaked by design. Fischer also seemed pudgier than the man in the video. But the quality of the hospital footage wasn't great and it was all shot from above, making certainty unattainable. Fischer looked back at her and continued.

"I should warn you that if you think this is going to run longer than about forty-five minutes, we may have to schedule a second meeting. I don't have any more appointments this afternoon but I am supposed to speak at a symposium later today."

"I don't think it will take that long," Jessie said as she warily crossed the threshold into the office. "You mind if we leave the door open? I tend to get claustrophobic."

"Of course not," he said, chuckling. "It's not my area but I could recommend someone if you'd like to talk about that issue."

The room was warm and welcoming. The walls were a mix of nature scene photos and paintings of seventeenth-century rustic life, including log cabins and women in bonnets milking cows. The furniture, including a desk at the far end of the room, was all dark brown, which contrasted gently with the beige walls. Everything about the office was designed to exude comfort.

He sat down in a high-backed leather chair and motioned for Jessie to take a seat on either the matching one or the adjoining loveseat. She chose the chair, which created more distance between them.

"So," Fischer said once they'd both settled in. "You mentioned on the phone that this was a pressing matter concerning some of my former patients. I assume it's related to the recent abductions and murders?"

"What makes you say that?" Jessie asked.

He smiled gently as if to suggest he understood she had to play this game but he would not.

"Several things, Ms. Hunt," he replied. "First, I've never had a criminal profiler call me for any reason before today. Second, I counseled three of the abducted women and one of the ones that were killed."

"You knew three of them?" Jessie repeated, trying to hide her shock at the fact and his casual revelation of it. "Who?"

"Brenda Ferguson, Morgan Remar, and Jayne Castillo. The only one I didn't know was the last one taken, Ms. Gidley. Frankly, I'm surprised that you're surprised. I told all this to the police already."

"You reported this to the police?" Jessie asked, surprised.

"Yes."

"When?"

"After Morgan Remar was kidnapped," he said, looking troubled that she didn't seem to already know this information. "I heard about Brenda Ferguson, of course. I thought it was terrible and I was so happy when she got away. But it wasn't until I heard about Morgan that I thought 'this is truly strange.' So I called the hotline and told them about the connection."

"And no one ever got back to you?" Jessie pressed.

"No. It was a recording so I left a message but I never heard back. I tried again after Jayne Castillo was taken because I thought it was simply impossible that this could all be a coincidence—still nothing. I assumed they must have it all in hand or they surely would have gotten back to me. But then, after Morgan died, I tried again. That time, I was vociferous in my message. I assumed that you were here because someone had finally listened to them."

"No," Jessie replied. "I never heard about them. You never tried to reach a live person?"

"Of course I did, multiple times. I got stuck in endless phone trees. I even went down to the Mid-Wilshire station—it's not too far from here—and submitted a statement. I explicitly told the desk clerk about the odd connection and asked to speak to a detective. To be honest, he blew me off, said someone would be in touch. But I could tell he wasn't impressed. I walked out of there pretty frustrated. Is that standard—to just dismiss leads out of hand?"

"No," Jessie assured him. "I don't know what happened there. I'm sure there were hundreds, maybe even thousands of hotline tips.

But between that and your station visit, you should have heard back."

Fischer shook his head in exasperation.

"I even considered calling Brenda or Jayne directly. I thought maybe someone would listen if it came straight from them. But I knew they'd suffered such trauma and I didn't want to insert myself into their lives, so I held off. I was actually reconsidering that decision today when I got your call."

Jessie studied the man closely. His entire demeanor conveyed mild-mannered empathy. He wore a rumpled sport jacket over a shirt and vest, along with wrinkled beige Dockers and brown loafers. His voice was soothing but direct and he was diligent about making eye contact. There was no overt deception coming from him, which suggested one of two things. Either he was being honest or he was a master at concealing his deception.

Jessie determined that she wasn't going to glean anything revelatory about the man if she let him continue to dictate the terms of the conversation. So she decided to try to shake him out of his comfort zone a bit.

"You said you didn't know Caroline Gidley?"

"No," he said. "She was the one who was taken last and just died, correct?"

Jessie nodded.

"That's right. Never heard of her?"

"No," he said confidently. "In fact, after I learned of her abduction, I went back and checked my files. I was actually surprised there was no connection, considering that I knew the first three women. Of course, I've had hundreds of couples visit me over the years and many of the women have changed names, so I thought it could just be me forgetting. But my files didn't turn up anything and when I saw her photo on the news, she didn't look familiar."

Jessie hedged, debating whether to be aggressive or hold off a little longer. She decided to wait.

"Was there anything similar about the three women you knew, something that connected them beyond simply coming to you for couples' therapy?"

Fischer smiled, clearly pleased that he'd get to address this issue.

"I wondered the same thing. I went back through my files and did a little amateur detective work. Obviously each relationship is different but I did find that they all had one thing in common."

Jessie waited but he didn't continue so she prompted him.

"What was that?" she asked.

"Normally, confidentiality would prevent me from sharing this. The only reason I feel comfortable telling you this is because I went back to review the paperwork when the divorce papers were filed with the courts. What I'm about to tell you is in the public record so I don't consider it an ethical violation."

"I appreciate your professionalism," Jessie said, trying not to sound impatient. "What did you find?"

"All three women had engaged in extramarital affairs. It wasn't the only reason for the breakup in every case. Their files are thick. But it was a factor in each. All three of them eventually married the man they were cheating with. Other than smaller things—all were college-educated, all were at least middle class—that was the one thing that jumped out at me."

Jessie tried not to visibly react. But internally, she sensed the pieces clicking into place. Fischer's words reinforced the growing suspicion she'd had while talking to Jayne Castillo earlier.

"How did you feel about their cheating?" she asked, posing a personal question for the first time.

Again, he gave her his gentle smile, the one that indicated he knew what she was doing and wouldn't be baited by it.

"I didn't feel anything, Ms. Hunt," he said calmly. "That's not my job. I was there to help these couples work through how they felt about what happened and see if they could find a path forward together. Other than abuse, I don't insert myself into the moral quagmire of the relationships. I've found it's not very constructive."

"You never got offended on behalf of the wronged party?" she pushed.

He paused for a long time before replying.

"Thank you," he finally said.

"For what?"

"For taking all this seriously," he told her. "I was initially worried that my concerns were being dismissed when I never heard back from anyone. And then I feared that you might just be doing this interview out of obligation. But the fact that you're poking at me tells me there's at least one person taking this seriously, who thinks the man who counseled three of the abducted women might be worth at least looking into."

"That's very flattering, Mr. Fischer," she said. "But I noticed you didn't answer my question."

"Of course. Sorry to get sidetracked. The answer is that I don't get offended on behalf of either party. And viewing one or the other as 'wronged' doesn't help them repair the relationship. I do try to put myself in the shoes of both people so that I get a sense of their perspective. But I don't view anyone as wrong so much as self-interested. We all do what we can to make ourselves happy. Sometimes we misjudge what that is. Sometimes we neglect others' needs in the service of our own. But I don't think most people do these things out of malice as much as out of selfishness."

"That hasn't been my experience," Jessie countered.

"Are you speaking professionally or personally, Ms. Hunt?"

"Are you trying to practice a little off-the-books therapy right now, Mr. Fischer?" she shot back.

"I'm sorry," he said, smiling sheepishly. "Occupational hazard, I suppose. I'm always on duty. But I sense that you're not just talking about the people you profile when you reference your experience. Am I right?"

Jessie relented slightly, admittedly only partly because she thought revealing something personal might make him vulnerable.

"In my work, I find that malice is actually a pretty powerful motivator."

"And in your personal life?" he asked.

Jessie thought about the man she'd been with for a decade, who tried to kill her and who might imminently be out of prison.

"There too," she said, glancing down at her feet.

"Should we be scheduling a session?" he asked, only half-joking.

Jessie decided now was the moment to pounce. She looked him in the eyes again.

"Where were you yesterday mid-afternoon?"

He looked appropriately startled.

"I believe I was here all day," he said after a moment.

"Conducting sessions?"

"I don't recall. I can check my schedule."

"That'd be great," she said, before moving on quickly. "What about the night before, Tuesday, around eleven p.m.?"

"I think I was at home," he said, increasingly flustered. "I'd have to check on that too."

"Are you married? Is there anyone who can confirm your location?"

For the first time, he looked a genuinely apprehensive.

"I live alone. I'm divorced."

"*You're* divorced? A couples' therapist? What broke you up—selfishness?"

"There was that," he admitted. "It took the form of infidelity."

"On whose part?" she demanded.

Fischer found his soft smile again. When he spoke it was with resignation.

"My wife cheated on me, Ms. Hunt. Does that make me look bad?"

She was quiet for a moment before replying.

"It doesn't help," she conceded. "I'd like to make a proposal, Mr. Fischer."

"Why do I have a pit in my stomach all of a sudden?" he asked.

"I couldn't answer that," she said, sliding her hand into the jacket pocket with the Taser. "Would you be willing to come back to my station to resolve some of the confusion regarding your alibi? Maybe you'd consent to let us review the files of the women in question? I'd like to rule you out as a suspect and the more accommodating you are, the faster we can do that. What do you say?"

He sat silently in his high-backed chair, his own forearms resting on the chair's arms. His long-sleeved shirt extended past his wrists, making it impossible to see if he had a bandage on underneath the right sleeve. He seemed to be doing some quick metal deliberations. Jessie gripped the Taser tightly.

"I'm amenable to that," he said reluctantly. "Do I need to bring an attorney?"

"We're just trying to clear a few things up," Jessie answered indirectly. "But that's entirely up to you."

"I guess I can come in on my own. Should I stop by after my symposium?"

"Actually, I was thinking more like right now."

"And miss my talk entirely?" he asked incredulously.

"Two women are dead, Mr. Fischer," she reminded him. "But you do what you feel is right."

CHAPTER THIRTY ONE

Jessie stared at Warren Fischer through the interrogation room mirror.

He had followed her back to the station and willingly handed off his files before walking into the interrogation room, where he'd been sitting patiently for a half hour. Captain Decker had insisted Jessie wait for Ryan to arrive back from helping the Beverly Hills detectives question Gregg Dozier, Caroline Gidley's aggrieved ex-fiancé. Not wanting to hint at any conflict between them, she agreed.

In the interim, she reviewed the files Fischer had given her. It was clear that despite his claims to the contrary, he did take a dim view of each woman's infidelity, though it was couched in therapy-speak. To be fair, he was also critical of their husbands' refusal to move past the indiscretions. Still, she couldn't tell whether he added those latter comments sincerely or out of professional obligation.

Her phone buzzed and she looked down to see a text message from Dr. Lemmon. It had only three words: "Load of crap."

It took her a few seconds to comprehend what that meant. Then she remembered that her rambling voicemail to her therapist had included the question of whether she was possibly in the middle of a mental breakdown or if that notion was a load of crap. This seemed to be the doctor's professional opinion on the matter. Jessie couldn't help but smile.

Just then, Ryan stepped into the observation room. He looked at her anxiously.

"How's it going?" he asked, keeping the question open-ended.

"Okay. We've got a possible suspect there," she said, pointing at Fischer. "How'd it go with Dozier?"

"Not great," Ryan said. "It turns out that while Caroline Gidley was being murdered he was in a two-hour meeting. The whole thing was recorded. I watched him closely to see if he was antsy, maybe wondering if some guy he'd hired was getting the job done at that moment. But there was nothing like that. In fact, at one point it looked like he nodded off for a few seconds."

"Did he have any connection to Morgan Remar?"

"None that we could discern," Ryan said. "And he had an alibi for that night too. He was home with his new girlfriend, who vouched for him. The BHPD guys are following up but he seemed like a guy who had moved on more than one nursing a grudge."

Jessie nodded without speaking.

"I appreciate that," he said quietly.

"What?"

"You not rubbing in the fact that you thought he was a long shot from the start."

Jessie shrugged.

"It had to be checked out," she said.

"How's it going otherwise?' he asked, hinting at their earlier argument.

"How do you think it's going?" she asked, keeping her eyes on Fischer.

"Probably not great," he said, his shoulders sagging. He looked around the observation room to make sure they were alone before continuing. "Listen, on the way back from Beverly Hills, I got to thinking and came to a startling realization."

"What's that?" Jessie asked, though she wasn't especially interested in the answer.

"I realized that I'm an asshole," he said.

She looked at him, stunned.

"What?"

"Yeah," he said, his eyes now on the floor. "The more I thought about it, the more it became clear to me that maybe suggesting the woman I love was having a psychotic episode wasn't the way to go."

"No?" she asked, only able to get out one word at a time.

"No. I realized that I can choose to believe one of two things. Either you're a paranoid nut job who slashed your own tires, abused your sister, turned into a racist overnight, and conveniently 'left' hardcore anti-psychotic drugs in my car. Or someone really is attempting to ruin your life and tried to co-opt me into that by getting me to buy into the allegations against you."

"Which way are you leaning?" she asked quietly.

"I'm leaning toward believing the person I've entrusted my life to on multiple occasions, the woman who makes me smile when I think of her face, the person I care most about in the world."

Jessie tried to fight off a smile.

"You're *leaning* that way?"

"I may already be there. Do you forgive me?"

She looked at him hard and realized that she wasn't entirely sure.

"You really hurt me, Ryan," she said quietly. "You made me doubt myself. I haven't felt that way in a long time. I didn't think it would ever happen with you."

"I know. I'm sorry."

The dark room was silent.

"Look," she finally said. "I accept your apology. But I'm not sure I'm ready to just jump back into things the way they were. I know I can count on you at work. You've always had my back. But I need to know I can count on you the rest of the time. I thought I could. But that confidence is a little shaken. I think we need to ease back into things on the personal front."

"Okay," he said, though he didn't look like he thought it was. "I understand. And that's fair. You let me know when you're ready and I'll be here."

"Thank you," she said, and then, forcing herself to climb out of the emotional well she was in, added, "In the meantime, we've got a suspect to talk to. You in?"

"I am," Ryan said, taking her cue and returning his focus to the professional. "Decker gave me the basics on my drive back. It sounds like this guy has some promise."

"Maybe," Jessie said, making sure he didn't get too excited. "On paper he's a real contender. He admits to knowing three of the four women. No definitive alibi for either murder yet. He's critical of their marital indiscretions in his notes. And he looks roughly like the guy in the video."

"You don't sound convinced," Ryan noted.

"I'm not," she granted. "For one thing, he reached out to the tip hotline multiple times. I checked and his calls are in the system but they were either overlooked or dismissed."

"Ray Sands told me they've gotten over thirteen thousand tips and have barely had a chance to work through half of them."

"Maybe that explains it," Jessie replied.

"Right," Ryan said. "Plus, he might have called in to cover his tracks for when we discovered the connection. If he didn't call, he'd look especially guilty."

"That's true," Jessie allowed. "But that's not what's making me question whether it's him."

"What is?"

"He doesn't seem to have any connection to Caroline Gidley. He said he didn't know her and he allowed our tech crew to look through his computer files. There's no record of her."

"Could he have deleted it?" Ryan wondered.

"I suppose, though I bet our people would be able to uncover that. Besides, if it's him, why delete her records and not the others? I feel like there's another connection among these women that we're missing and once we find it, it will break everything open."

Neither spoke for a moment. Jessie's phone rang suddenly, making both of them jump. The call was from the front desk.

"Hunt here," she said.

"Ms. Hunt," the desk clerk said. "There's a Katherine Gentry here to see you. She said it's urgent. What should I tell her?"

Jessie looked at Ryan, whose eyebrows were raised.

"She's as pissed at me as I was at you," she told him. "If she's here, it must be something important."

"Go ahead," Ryan said. "I'll get started on questioning Fischer. You've laid the groundwork. I'll play dumb, make him walk me through everything again and see if he makes a mistake."

"Thanks," she said, before replying to the desk clerk, "Tell her I'll be right there."

CHAPTER THIRTY TWO

Jessie's mouth was dry.

As she approached the station reception, she noted that she was more nervous about talking to Kat than she was before most interrogations. Though she still felt raw about her friend saying she had Caroline Gidley's blood on her hands, she understood Kat hadn't really meant it.

And she could even sympathize. Kat was frustrated. Jessie had asked for her help on numerous occasions when it served her purposes. It wasn't crazy to ask why she couldn't have reached out to ask Kat to look in on the women who'd been abducted, especially when she was already intimately involved in the case.

True, she'd been exhausted at the time and not thinking clearly. But she had to admit that some part of her just didn't want to farm out such an important job to a person whose potential screw-up might reflect badly on Jessie. It was selfishness.

Hey, maybe Warren Fischer does have a point.

She stepped out into reception where she saw Kat leaning against a pillar, scrolling through her phone. In her jeans and leather jacket, she looked less like an investigative professional than a regular civilian. But maybe that was the point—she wanted to blend in. It was just a different style than Jessie was used to. It didn't mean it was wrong.

"Hey," she said as she walked over. Kat looked up. Her eyes had the same nervousness that Jessie felt.

"Hi," she replied. "Sorry to bother you at work. I know you're busy. But I have news and I didn't want to share it over the phone."

"What is it?" Jessie asked, intrigued and concerned at the same time.

"Nothing good," Kat said. "Can we go outside?"

"Yeah, but we'll have to go out the side exit. Those protesters out front would lose it if they saw me."

Kat nodded in understanding and followed Jessie through a maze of hallways until they reached a side exit of the building in the alley.

They could still hear the chanting protesters but no one was in sight. Kat launched in.

"I got a message a little while ago from a woman named Delia Armbruster. She said DPSS was conducting an investigation of your guardianship of Hannah and needed me to come in for an interview tomorrow afternoon. She asked me to call back to confirm. But considering I had no idea what the hell was going on, I thought I'd check with you first."

Jessie sighed.

"I don't want to bore you with all the details," she said heavily.

"I have a feeling I won't be bored," Kat said.

"Okay," Jessie said. "The short version is that someone—I'm not sure who yet—is trying to ruin my life. I mentioned it in passing the last time we…spoke. They hacked my social media to make me look racist. They planted anti-psychotic drugs that made Ryan think I was having a breakdown. They slashed my tires. And they anonymously called DPSS to say I was abusing Hannah. The call you got was related to that last bit of fun."

"Jeez. Should I go in?"

"I don't even know how they got your name but I don't think you have a choice," Jessie said. "I have an interview tomorrow too, in the morning. They said I could bring counsel. Of course, I don't have one. The last attorney I dealt with was my divorce lawyer."

"I might be able to recommend someone," Kat said. "When I got fired and the psychiatric prison started blaming me after Bolton Crutchfield escaped from the place, I hired a bulldog who shut them down. The threats stopped within a week of bringing him on. He specializes in representing individuals going up against large companies or bureaucracies. This sounds right up his alley. Want his info?"

"Yes," Jessie said, surprised at the relief in her own voice. "Thank you."

"Sure," Kat replied before they fell into an uncomfortable silence.

"I'm glad you called," Jessie finally said. "I was meaning to reach out to you. I wanted to tell you something."

"Okay."

"I screwed up. I'm sorry. I should have asked for your help watching the abductees. I just…no, that's it. I'm sorry."

Kat squinted at her as if the sun was in her eyes.

"Thank you," she said. "I know that wasn't easy to say, especially considering everything you're dealing with right now."

"No excuses," Jessie told her. "I should have reached out. I didn't. You deserved better than that from a friend."

Kat leaned against the brick wall of the station and shook her head slightly.

"I might have been a little hard on you," she replied. "Saying you were responsible for Caroline Gidley's death wasn't fair. The truth is, even if you had asked me to look in on one of those women, she would have been my last choice. I just assumed that in the hospital, she'd be the safest one of the group."

Jessie shook her head far more vigorously than Kat had.

"Don't let me off the hook. I should have asked you to look in on one of them. I should have pushed Decker harder."

"Jessie," Kat said softly. "I have to let you off the hook because I know you won't let yourself off. I know you tried to get the powers that be to protect them and they didn't listen. I was just mad because I made a promise to Morgan Remar and her family. I felt like I betrayed them. But that's not on you."

"I'm not so sure," Jessie muttered.

"You know what?" Kat said, forcing an upbeat tone. "We both feel like failures. Let's think about what we can do about that. How are things going with the investigation? Is there any way I can help?"

Jessie thought for a moment.

"I'm not sure. Ryan's in there right now questioning a couples' counselor. I found out the guy had seen all three married victims."

"That sounds promising," Kat offered.

"Maybe," Jessie allowed. "But I'm not totally convinced. We don't have anything tying him to Caroline Gidley. As you know, she wasn't married."

"No, but she was engaged," Kat reminded her. "He didn't see her at any point?"

"It doesn't look that way. The counselor turned over all his files and our tech crew has been going through his digital files. There doesn't seem to be anything."

"I'm surprised he wouldn't fight giving you all that stuff," Kat said. "Aren't there privacy rules for that sort of thing?"

"There are, but he said that since it was all in the public record because of the divorce proceedings, he could release the info. That's why he was also willing to tell me that all three women cheated."

"That makes sense," Kat said. "I suppose he would have said the same thing about Caroline too if she'd been one of his patients."

Jessie looked at her, confused.

"Wait. What do you mean?" she asked. "What difference would it make if she was unfaithful? There wouldn't be any legal paperwork for her if she was only engaged, right?"

Now Kat was the one who looked confused.

"There is," she said. "But not because of the cheating, because of the ring."

"What are you talking about?" Jessie asked.

"Gregg Dozier sued her to get his engagement ring back."

Jessie stood there for a moment, allowing the fireworks that had just started exploding in her brain to subside. Kat stared at her with concern.

"Either you have an idea or you're having a stroke," she said. "Please tell me it's the former."

Jessie smiled at her.

"Do you have all your case files with you?" she asked.

"They're in my car," Kat replied.

"I think we should go for a ride."

CHAPTER THIRTY THREE

They barely made it in time.

The law offices of Brendon, Hannigan & Gellar officially closed to visitors at 5 p.m. But the place was full of staffers well into the evening. So when Jessie and Kat arrived at 4:57, demanding to speak to the office manager, the receptionist's lame assertion that they'd have to come back tomorrow didn't go over well.

"Please tell your manager that if she doesn't speak with us now, we'll be returning tomorrow with a phalanx of LAPD officers in tow," Jessie said firmly.

The receptionist nodded submissively and darted to the back.

"You're sure Ryan's cool with this?" Kat asked for the third time.

"Don't worry about it," Jessie assured her again. "He's still questioning Warren Fischer, fruitlessly, it sounds like. He said as long as you didn't question anyone and just helped out with research, it shouldn't be an issue. Just keep a low profile."

"Don't I always?" Kat asked, winking.

A moment later, the receptionist returned with a fifty-something woman who looked like she could cut glass with her cheekbones. In fact, everything about her was sharp-edged, including her tone.

"Threatening staffers probably isn't the ideal way to endear yourself to me," the woman said piercingly as she walked over. "You almost made Miranda here cry."

Jessie decided to go with honey unless vinegar was needed.

"I'm so sorry, Miranda," she said to the receptionist before turning her attention to her boss. "We're just in a serious time crunch. Who are you, may I ask?"

"I'm the Team Lead for Firm Strategies and Facilities. My name is Moira Halperin. What do you want?"

Jessie smiled to herself. It was apparent that Moira had insisted on that title, though it was clear to everyone that she was the firm's officer manager. The woman was proud but insecure, a combination that was susceptible to manipulation.

"Moira, I'm Jessie Hunt with the LAPD. This is my associate, Katherine Gentry. We're investigating a series of murders and we believe you can help."

"I know who you are, Ms. Hunt," Moira said in nasally huff. "I watch the news. And frankly, I don't cotton to your views."

Kat started to respond but Jessie shot her a look that shut her up before she spoke herself.

"Be that as it may," she replied, "you have information here that could be relevant to our investigation. Nothing we need from you is outside the public record. We could get it from the court. Unfortunately, they're closed for the day and you're not so here we are."

"Technically, we *are* closed," Moira said snippily.

Jessie could sense that Moira wasn't going to back down in front of someone she supervised so she tried to deescalate things. She saw an empty conference room off to the left and pointed to it.

"May we speak privately for a minute?" she asked.

Moira glanced at the room, then at the very curious Miranda, who seemed nowhere near tears, and nodded. Once they were inside with the door closed, Jessie laid out the facts.

"Moira, I'm going to level with you. We think the person who murdered two women in the last two days is going to try to kill a third tonight. And we believe that information in some of your files could help us find the perpetrator. Both women were involved in legal disputes in which your firm represented the other party. Two other women we believe are at risk also had cases in which your firm was involved."

"Are you asserting that Brendon, Hannigan & Gellar is somehow involved in this?" Moira asked, truly aghast.

"Absolutely not," Jessie lied. "Would we be coming to you for help if we thought the firm was in any way responsible? We just know there's a connection. It's not a coincidence that two dead women and two women facing that fate had legal interactions with your firm. All we want to do is look at the public filings and see what that connection might be."

"Couldn't you just review the documents digitally?" Moira asked. "Surely the police department has access to the LA Court database?"

"We do," Jessie said. "But neither my associate nor I are experts at navigating the database and time is short. The first victim was murdered in late evening. The last one was killed yesterday afternoon. We're in the window where it might happen. Looking at the hard copies will save us time. And your assistance will reflect well on the firm, a clear sign that you have nothing to hide."

Moira pondered the idea. Jessie remained silent, allowing the woman to draw her own conclusions. While it was true that Jessie was no expert in the database, she could muddle through. Kat was more adept. But the real reason they were there was that Jessie did indeed suspect Brendon, Hannigan & Gellar, or at least one of their lawyers, of ill intent.

As Jessie had guessed when Kat mentioned the lawsuit over the wedding ring outside the station earlier, the firm representing Caroline Gidley's former fiancé was the same one they were at now, the same one that represented all three of the married women's ex-husbands.

Not coincidentally, as Kat discovered on the drive over, according to the documents Scott Fellows had sent Jessie, the firm also represented Construction Associates, which meant any lawyer here could access information about legal disputes that might force various construction sites to shut down temporarily.

And while Jessie was hopeful that something in the legal paperwork would reveal the killer's identity, she also just wanted to get into the offices and look at the lawyers to see if any of them matched the man in the hospital video footage.

"I suppose you can look at the files," Moira finally said. "Assuming you take nothing and are gone in an hour. Can you abide by those terms?"

"We can," Jessie promised.

"Very well then," Moira said. "Give me the case numbers and I'll have one of the girls bring you copies."

"Thanks so much," Jessie said, managing not to smirk until Moira had left the room.

*

It only took about twenty minutes for Jessie's enthusiasm to turn to desperation.

Things looked promising at first. All three divorce cases referenced the counseling sessions with Warren Fischer, which meant that someone reading the files could have easily researched him in order to frame him. But the Caroline Gidley ring dispute had no connection to Fischer.

Furthermore, it became clear within minutes that none of the same lawyers had handled all of the cases. Brendon, Hannigan & Gellar was a mega-firm that operated throughout California. Their Los Angeles office had fifty-nine attorneys. Only one had handled even two of the cases. But it was a woman named Jessaline Pordoux, who had moved with her French husband to Paris last year.

After that disappointing revelation, Jessie had been reduced to "getting lost" on the way to the ladies' room. As she walked through the halls of the firm, she held her phone at her side, recording as she slowly walked past every door, hoping to stumble across the man who was a perfect match for the hospital video.

She saw lots of men, but most were hunched over computer screens and none jumped out at her as obvious candidates. Besides, if the killer did work here and was planning to attack again tonight, it was quite possible that he'd already left for the day.

"What now?" Kat asked when Jessie returned. She was clearly frustrated that her contribution, which had led them here, seemed to be another dead end.

Jessie rubbed her temples, hoping to get another fireworks spark, but nothing came. She looked up.

"I'm out of ideas," she said, unable to keep the defeated tone out of her voice. "I think all we can do now is circle the wagons."

"What does that mean exactly?" Kat asked.

Jessie turned to her and did her best to smile.

"You up for a stakeout?"

CHAPTER THIRTY FOUR

Jessie wasn't worried about slashed tires tonight.

For the third time this week she was parked outside Brenda Ferguson's house. But unlike the previous two visits, this time she hadn't left the car. She and Kat found a spot a half block down the street, where they could eat burgers and sip coffee while they kept an eye out.

"Should we be eating salads?" Kat asked after a big bite. "I feel like we're a stereotype right now."

"I think we'd be a stereotype if we ate salads too," Jessie pointed out. "There's no way to win that one, so I'm going to eat what I want. I doubt Ryan and Trembley are questioning their stakeout dining choice right now."

Whatever they were eating, those detectives were doing it outside Jayne Castillo's house. After consultation with Captain Decker, they'd all agreed that having extra support for the uniformed officers on guard was a good idea. They had also agreed that, while the officers on duty were made aware of their presence, the families would not be. No need to freak them out more than they already were.

Jessie had volunteered to go to the Fergusons'. She didn't admit it out loud, but part of the reason was that Brenda had kids. The death of either woman would be a tragedy but Jessie couldn't bear the thought of those children losing their mother. So she and Kat were here.

Ryan didn't seem to care where he was sent and Detective Alan Trembley was just happy to be around for the ride. As the low man on the totem pole, he rarely got his pick of assignments. But spending the evening with the celebrated Detective Ryan Hernandez was one he happily jumped at. Trembley made up for his lack of experience with an enthusiasm that often bordered on giddiness.

As they sat in the car, Kat chomped down a few fries before moving on altogether from discussing dining habits.

"So Ryan ended up thinking Warren Fischer wasn't the guy either?" she asked.

"By the time he finished the interrogation, he was as skeptical as me," Jessie answered. "But he still had a tail put on him just in case. Someone will be following the guy all night."

"Speaking of all night, is Hannah going to be okay if this thing runs into the wee hours?"

"She's been on her own through the night often enough that she's used to it by now. But I haven't been able to reach her to tell her what's going on. I think she's screening my calls."

"Use my phone," Kat suggested. "She loves me."

"First of all, it makes me feel *great* to know she'd answer your call but not one from her own sister. Second, that's a fantastic idea. Give me your phone."

"Wait," Kat scolded. "Let me call her. I'll chat her up for a moment, and then hand it over. She'll be less likely to hang up after talking to me than if she picked up a call from me and you answered. Delay the trickery."

"That is another great idea," Jessie admired. "You are getting better at being sneaky every day."

"Thank you," Kat said as she called, putting the phone on speaker.

"No," Jessie said. "Take it off speaker. I don't want her to think I'm monitoring her every word."

Kat switched it back just as Hannah picked up. Jessie could still hear her slightly but forced herself not to strain to catch every word. The two of them talked for a minute before Kat pulled the rug out.

"Hey, girl," she said. "I have someone here who wants to say hi. Hold on a second."

She handed Jessie the phone, who spoke more hesitantly than she would have liked.

"Hey, it's Jessie."

After a long pause that made her briefly think her sister had hung up, Hannah replied.

"Hi. Is this what you've been reduced to—putting your friends up to calling me?"

"Something like that," Jessie said, deciding there was no point in defending herself. "I needed to get a hold of you somehow to let you know I might not be home tonight."

"What a shocker."

"I also wanted to apologize."

Another long silence.

"For what?" Hannah finally asked.

"For suggesting you might have called Social Services," Jessie said. "I was upset and grasping at straws. I should have never said that."

She didn't mention the fact that she still wasn't certain it didn't happen. But telling Hannah that at this moment seemed like an unwise move.

"I can't believe you would ever think that," Hannah said quietly.

Jessie tried to answer without lying.

"I can't explain everything that was going on in my head at that moment. And even if I could, it wouldn't justify what I said. But I had a moment of weakness. After a major lack of sleep and the sense that I was being targeted by powerful forces I couldn't even identify, much less stop, I lashed out at the person in front of me. I'm not proud of it. I'm hoping that we can work through it and that, if I can professionally survive this investigation, you'll want to stick around."

"Maybe if you get me a new pair of AirPods, I could put in a good word…"

"What?" Jessie asked.

"I'm just kidding," Hannah said after a long, cruel pause. "Of course I want to stick around. You're not perfect but you're better than my other options by a long way."

"Thanks?"

"It's a compliment," Hannah assured her. "Anyway, I plan to testify myself. We'll get through this. That is, assuming you don't kill me with your scones before I talk to these people."

"Hey!" Jessie said, feigning hurt feelings, before conceding. "Actually that seems fair. Maybe you could make me some of *your* scones. It might give me something to look forward to after I get through this night."

"Sure," Hannah said, her voice hinting at something more.

"What's wrong?" Jessie asked.

Hannah's indecision was almost audible. Finally she replied.

"It's just, maybe I can do more than bake scones to help. Remember, some of the things I told you about girls I knew at school helped when you were investigating that porn actress who was murdered. Maybe I could offer a different perspective on this case."

"Is that how you want to spend your evening?" Jessie asked incredulously. "Listening to details about a murder investigation?"

"It's either that or binging more episodes of *Top Chef*. And those are all reruns."

Jessie looked over at Kat, who had clearly been listening in. She gave a "why not?" shrug. It wasn't a crazy idea. Maybe reviewing what they knew would allow them to come up with an angle they'd missed so far.

So as they finished their burgers, she walked her sister through the details of the case, from the first abduction of Brenda Ferguson a month ago to their visit to the law firm earlier this evening. Hannah asked occasional questions. Many were thoughtful but none of them sparked any sudden revelations.

When Jessie concluded by telling her that the visit to the law office had been a dead end, Hannah spoke.

"What about the paralegals?"

"What?" Jessie said, not following.

"You said none of the lawyers worked on all four cases, but what about the paralegals? Remember, my adoptive dad was a lawyer. I remember he used to always say that he'd never have won a single case if not for his paralegals. Sometimes they would be handling a dozen cases for multiple lawyers all at once. He used to give them huge gifts at the holidays because he said they were the lifeblood of his firm. Did any of them work on all the cases?"

Jessie and Kat exchanged embarrassed looks.

"I have no idea," Jessie admitted.

"They'd be referenced in the footnotes of the firm's copies of each document they prepared, even if it was never filed with the court," Kat said. "Good thing I took photos of every page I looked at while we were there."

Jessie looked at the phone in her hand, realizing the answer to their questions might be there.

"Hey, Hannah, mind if we let you go for a bit?" she asked. "We need to see if you maybe just solved our case."

"Okay," Hannah replied. "But if I did, I definitely deserve those AirPods."

CHAPTER THIRTY FIVE

His name was Joseph Setts.

It hadn't taken long to determine that. Once they knew where to look, it was obvious. Though his name didn't appear on any documents filed with the court, it was visible in the footnotes of work product related to all four cases. He'd worked on each case, sometimes for months at a time.

Once they'd learned that, Jessie pulled up his employee page on the firm website. It didn't offer any personal details. But there was a photo, which she used as she went back through the video she'd secretly taken when walking the firm's halls.

She found him ninety seconds in, sitting at a desk in a paralegal office. He was the only one there, his attention focused intently on the screen in front of him. As he typed, Jessie thought she saw a bandage poking out under his right sleeve at the wrist.

She thought of the hospital footage in which the killer had the bandage on his right forearm. Then she flashed back to the mental image of Morgan Remar, lying dead on the floor of her kitchen with a butcher knife clutched in her hand. None of it felt coincidental.

Jessie studied him on the screen as she called Ryan and Decker, conferencing them in.

"Our guy's name is Joseph Setts," she said without preamble. "I'm sending you images of him now."

He looked to be in his early thirties with short brown hair, brown eyes, and a pleasant, unremarkable face. Nothing about him screamed serial kidnapper and murderer. But in Jessie's experience, a person's motives were rarely discernible based on looks alone.

More immediately, despite the bandage, there was no way to tell for certain if the guy at the desk or in the employee photo was the same man from the hospital footage. The wig, glasses, and graininess of the video were too limiting. But even without that visual proof, there was more than enough to think this was their guy.

She filled both men in on the details as she sent them everything she had. Decker sprang into action.

"Get to that law firm, Reid," he ordered while he kept the rest of them on speaker. "Have Pete Clark lead a unit to Setts's home. I want experienced officers on that assignment. Tell Camille Guadino to get authorization to track the guy's phone and car location data and to put out an APB, including facial recognition."

When she was done barking, he returned his attention to the stakeout teams.

"You all stay put," he ordered. "At this point, knowing who he is doesn't help unless we know *where* he is. And since it's reasonable to suspect that he's headed to where one of you two is anyway, there's no reason to change what you're doing."

"What if he's *not* headed our way?" Trembley asked on Ryan's phone.

"If that's not his plan for the night, we'll find him," Decker said. "But better to assume he's coming to you and be wrong than the alternative. Stay alert, people."

*

Detective Ryan Hernandez wasn't worried about Alan Trembley staying alert. The guy was nearly bouncing off the walls already.

"Trembley," he said to the overexcited detective in the passenger seat, "just stay cool. It's only just getting dark. We might have a long night ahead of us. You're so pumped that, at this rate, you're going to burn out before midnight."

"Sorry," Trembley said, taking a series of too-fast deep breaths. "I've been on stakeouts before. I'm not sure why I'm so amped for this one."

"Maybe it's the three cups of coffee you've had," Ryan chided mildly.

"I just don't want to drift off, you know? That's my fear—falling asleep and having something terrible happen."

"Don't worry," Ryan promised. "If you fall asleep, I'll give you a solid punch in the gut to wake you up."

Trembley looked at him, unsure if he was being messed with. Ryan let him wonder as he retreated into his own thoughts.

It had been a rough few days. Until their recent break in the case, he'd felt like he'd been spinning his wheels. Add that to pissing off his girlfriend by essentially accusing her of being a whack job and he could be having a better week.

He hoped that if they could resolve this case, he'd have a little down time to square things away with Jessie. Everything just felt too unsettled right now. He wasn't sure where he was sleeping most nights. And on the nights he was at her place, there was a teenage girl there who, despite being shockingly well-adjusted all things considered, was still a constant threat to erupt like a hormonal, trauma-ridden volcano. It was intense. Something had to change to make it less so.

He was weighing his options on that front when he saw it. There was movement on the roof of the house next door to the Castillos. Though it wasn't completely dark out yet, the light was too low to see clearly.

He grabbed his binoculars with one hand and whacked Trembley with the other to get his attention. The other detective followed his gaze and grabbed his own set of binoculars. As Ryan focused in, he saw what looked like a male with short brown hair exiting a second floor, street-facing window and scurrying across the roof to the adjoining roof of the Castillos. He looked like he was about to leap from one to the other.

"This is Hernandez," he said into his radio, using the frequency designated for the officers on guard. "Be advised. I have a white male on the roof of the home just south of the Castillo residence. He seems to be planning to jump across. No visible weapons but proceed with caution. Do not engage until we are on scene. We are leaving our vehicle now and approaching from the southeast."

He hooked the binocular strap around his neck, nodded at Trembley, and got out. The two of them hurried across the street. The officer standing on the front doorstep moved onto the lawn so he could get a better view. By the time they got to the Castillo front yard, the suspect was mid-leap.

Unfortunately for him, he misjudged the distance. His torso landed on the roof but his legs fell short, slamming into the exterior wall of the house. The man grabbed at the roof gutter, trying to keep from falling. But within a few seconds, his grip failed and he dropped to the ground. The hedges broke his fall slightly before he thudded down, his back slamming hard against the grass below.

The uniformed officer joined Ryan and Trembley at the side of the house. The other two men had their weapons drawn. Ryan had pulled out his flashlight, which he shined into the man's eyes.

But it wasn't a man at all. The person lying on the ground with his legs snagged helplessly in the hedges was a teenage boy who looked to be about sixteen. When he saw three men standing over him, two with guns pointed at him, his eyes went wide with panic.

"Care to explain yourself?" Ryan asked.

"What's going on?" the kid asked, half-hysterical.

"That's what I'd like to know," Ryan said. "And please be honest up front. As you can see, my friends here aren't in the most understanding mood."

"I was just leaving my girlfriend's house," he blurted out, his eyes beginning to water. "Her mom came up to check on her and I was sneaking out. I swear that's all it was."

Ryan sighed in frustration.

"Show me some ID, kid," he said before turning to Trembley and the other officer. "You guys can probably put your guns away."

He turned off his flashlight and pulled out his phone. Before calling Jessie and Decker to let them know about the false alarm, he gave Trembley one more instruction.

"Take this kid to the front door and see if the family knows him. If he's legit, don't rat him out."

Trembley nodded and began to help the boy extricate himself from the hedge. Ryan hoped that letting the kid go without shaming him would get him some good karma on the case and in his own life.

He could use it.

CHAPTER THIRTY SIX

"It was just a kid."

Jessie was filling Kat in on the situation and the disappointing outcome. Both of them had held out brief hope that this nightmare was over. Now they had to force themselves back into high alert mode.

Jessie was studying the roofs of the houses on either side of the Fergusons' in case Joseph Setts was considering the same maneuver. But it quickly became apparent that the distance between these extravagant Brentwood lots would make even an Olympic long jumper hesitate.

Just then, her phone rang. It was Decker. She picked up immediately.

"Yes, Captain?" she said excitedly.

"Don't get your hopes up," he warned. "I have an update for you but it's not on this case."

"Go ahead," she said, though she wasn't sure she wanted him to.

"I just got a call from the assistant warden at the Twin Towers Correctional Facility. Andrea Robinson tried to kill herself."

"What!"

Kat, who couldn't hear, looked at her with shock. Jessie put the call on speaker, her finger shaking slightly.

"Apparently she'd been hoarding her medication somehow," Decker said. "They found her in her cell, unconscious. She's been stabilized and transported to the nearest hospital."

"Is she conscious now?" Jessie asked. "Did she say anything?"

"She's not awake," Decker told her. "But she did leave a message for you. Considering the week you've had, I thought about not calling tonight. But I don't need you pissed at me for holding out."

"Good call, Captain," she replied. "What was the message?"

"It said 'tell Jessie this is all part of the plan.' Also, she wrote it on the wall of her cell in blood."

"Also?" Jessie said incredulously.

"Like I said, it's a lot."

"What does that mean?" Jessie demanded, trying to stay focused on the content of the message rather than the delivery system. "All part of what plan?"

"I was hoping it would make sense to you," Decker said. "One possibility is that we were right to suspect her of trying to ruin you. This could be the final step, to pin the blame for her suicide on you somehow."

"Maybe," Jessie said. "But of the three people we most suspected of doing this, I would have pegged her as the least likely. Both Costabile and Kyle probably have ways of reaching people on the outside. I checked her file. She's held in isolation most of the day. She's under constant observation. And she's heavily medicated."

"It seems she's not as medicated as we thought if she was hoarding enough pills to overdose," Decker noted.

"Fair point," Jessie agreed. "Still, I assume the guards there are on alert in case she's somehow faking or wakes up early. She's not the sort of person who should be underestimated."

"They doubled the guard contingent for her transport to the hospital. Everyone's aware of who they're dealing with."

"Great," Jessie said, relieved. "I guess we need to do a more detailed deep dive tomorrow."

"I've already got people rechecking her visitor logs and call records again," Decker assured her. "We should have something for you to review tomorrow."

"Thanks Captain," Jessie said, impressed that all her concerns were being preemptively addressed. "Will you update me if her condition changes?"

"I'll do my best," he said. "But I want you to stay focused on the task at hand. There's nothing you can do about Andrea Robinson tonight. You *can* make a difference in this case."

"Yes sir," Jessie said, hanging up and looking over at Kat, who wore a skeptical expression. "What?"

"I don't want to bring you down," her friend said. "But something about this just doesn't feel right to me."

"Just one thing?" Jessie said. "I have a list of about ten. What's yours?"

Kat didn't respond at first, as if she was deciding how best to phrase her concern.

"If Andy Robinson is out to get you," she began at last, "this doesn't seem like the most effective way to get to you. Yes, doing this might give you an undeserved pang of guilt. But unlike the other things that have been done to you, this doesn't seem like it could hurt your career or relationships that much. I don't see how it advances the ball. Maybe the 'plan' she mentioned has nothing to do with what's happening to you."

Jessie considered the point. It was a good one. If this was part of Andy's grand plan to destroy Jessie's reputation, then it wasn't clear how it fit. Of course, the woman was a brilliant sociopath who almost got away with murder, so sometimes her plans were hard to decipher.

"You could be right," she finally admitted, though she wasn't convinced.

She was about to put up her phone when she noticed a text she'd missed while talking to Decker. It was from Delia Armbruster. She looked at it and a slight gasp escaped her lips.

"What is it?" Kat asked.

"A message from Armbruster. She says she just e-mailed all the files on the case they've opened on me, including the recording and transcript of the anonymous call that started this whole investigation."

"That shouldn't be surprising," Kat said. "I think she's required to give you everything. The rules are pretty strict."

"I guess I figured she'd find some way to keep them from me," Jessie said, opening her e-mail, forwarding it to Camille in tech in the hope she could ID the caller, and then downloading the relevant files. "I've got the call here. Want to hear it?"

Kat nodded. Jessie hit "play" and a bland, unmemorable male voice began to speak.

"Hi. I live near Jessie Hunt, the police profiler. I hate to get involved in people's personal business. But I've been hearing some terrible things coming out of her place. She has a younger girl living with her and Jessie screams at her all the time, saying terrible, vicious things. I can't repeat them. I've also heard what sounds like…hitting. And I've heard the younger girl crying. I've seen the girl limping sometimes. Jessie didn't seem to care. She just told her to buck up. Please, help this girl."

That was the end of it. Kat looked like she was about to speak but Jessie held up her hand. Something about that line at the end regarding bucking up stirred a vague memory in her mind but she couldn't quite place it. No matter how hard she concentrated, she couldn't remember where she knew it from.

"What were you going to say?" she finally asked Kat.

"It can wait. It looked like you were on to something."

"One of the things he said sounded familiar," Jessie explained. "But I don't know why. It'll come to me. What were you thinking?"

"Just how non-specific everything was. He lives 'near' you and has heard terrible things coming from your 'place,' not your condo or apartment? It's like he doesn't know what your living situation is and doesn't want to screw up by being too detailed. If this was really someone who lived on the same floor as you, or even in your building, he'd have been more specific about all of that. He'd have given an address at least."

"Maybe he figured with the news covering my racist posts, it would be obvious," Jessie said bitterly.

"That's a major 'maybe,'" Kat countered. "Did you recognize the voice?"

"No. It didn't ring a bell," she acknowledged, frustrated.

They sat in silence for a minute before Jessie's phone rang. It was Camille.

"You're popular tonight," Kat teased.

"That depends on who you talk to," Jessie said, answering the phone.

"Jessie?" the tech said. It was clear from her voice that she was excited.

"What's up, Camille?"

"I found something," she said, talking a mile a minute. "I'm not sure how big a deal it is but it's more than we had before."

"Okay, that's great. Just calm down and tell me. And remember, I'm not a tech genius."

"Right. So I looked at the information you sent me from DPSS and it included the number the anonymous call came from. It's a burner phone, which is no surprise. That's part of why it's anonymous. But we were able to get some information. This phone was one of a batch that was stolen from a long haul truck en route to Los Angeles six weeks ago."

"Okay," Jessie said. "How does that help? If the phone was stolen, we can't even check the video footage from the point of purchase."

"That's true," Camille conceded. "But that's not what's interesting. I checked the point of origin of the truck shipment. When I saw it, on a hunch, I tried another trace on the protected IP address used for your recent social media 'posts,' But this time I used an algorithm that allowed me to check probabilities of possible origin and destination points."

"I literally have no idea what you're talking about," Jessie said. "Remember the 'not a tech genius' thing?"

"Sorry. Long story short, I'm ninety percent sure the hack and the call came from the same place."

"Where?" Jessie asked anxiously.

"Monterrey," Camille said.

Something in Jessie's brain exploded.

"The town south of San Francisco?" Kat asked, confused.

"No," Jessie told her before Camille could reply. "Mexico."

"That's right," Camille said. "We haven't nailed down anything more specific than that. But it's a start."

"That's great work," Jessie said, trying to stay cool. "Maybe check with the drug task force. Give them what you found and mention the Monzon cartel. See if they can help you out. I've got to go."

She hung up and stared at Kat, who could tell she'd had an epiphany.

"What?" her friend demanded.

"I remembered why the line from the anonymous call to DPSS about bucking up was so familiar. It was something my mother used to say to me when I was little—'buck up or you'll muck it up.'"

"How is that possible?" Kat asked, stunned. "It can't be a coincidence, right?"

"It's not. It was intentional. And it means I know who's been setting me up this whole time."

"Who?" Kat asked.

But before Jessie could reply, the sky lit up a bright orange. A fraction of a second later, they heard the explosion.

And then they felt it.

CHAPTER THIRTY SEVEN

When Jessie came to, the sky was still ablaze.

She looked over to see that Kat was slumped in the passenger seat, knocked out. A crack in the window told her that her friend's skull must have been smashed against it. Kat was breathing but when Jessie tried to shake her awake, she was unresponsive.

She opened her door and stumbled out, looking for the source of the explosion. It was no surprise to see it had come from the Ferguson house. From this vantage point, it looked like the blast had originated somewhere in the back of the second floor. A thick swirl of smoke curled upward from the spot.

Jessie grabbed the police radio and called in the incident. Then she rushed over to the house, unholstering her weapon as she moved. She scanned the area with blurry eyes, looking for any sign of Joseph Setts. She didn't see him but did come across a uniformed officer sprawled on the ground at the foot of the front door. It was Tanner, the same one from earlier who'd chided her for the online posts and mentioned his interracial marriage.

He was conscious but clearly out of it. Though he didn't have any obvious injuries, he looked confused and was having trouble sitting up. She bent down next to him.

"Officer Tanner, it's Jessie Hunt. Can you hear me?"

He nodded.

"There's been an explosion in the house. It looks like it came from the second floor. We need to check on the family. Are you able to stand up?"

He nodded again and she helped him to his feet.

"Where in the house was your partner?" she asked.

"Family room," he said, breathing heavily, "with the parents. Just put kids to bed."

"Okay, we're going in now," she said, looking in his eyes to see just how clear-headed he was. It was hard to tell. "We need to find Brenda and Ty, the kids, and Officer Kendrick. Are you up for this? I can't have you inadvertently shooting a civilian."

That seemed to shake him out of his malaise.

"I'm good," he said convincingly. "Let's go."

The front door was locked but Tanner had a key and opened it. As soon as the door swung open, a gust of billowing smoke blew out. The officer led the way to the living room, which was empty.

"Upstairs?" he asked, looking back at her.

She nodded and looked up. The stairs were accessible but hard to see clearly as waves of smoke cascaded down from the second floor. As they rushed up the stairs, Jessie felt the temperature rise dramatically. She could hear the crackle of flames in the distance. The acrid smell of burning paint filled her nostrils.

Once they got to the second-floor landing, they found Officer Kendrick lying face down in the middle of the hallway. Blood from somewhere on the front of his body was seeping onto the carpet. Tanner knelt down beside him and gingerly rolled him over. He was alive, moaning softly. Jessie saw that the blood was coming from multiple stab wounds on the side of his abdomen. It reminded her of what was done to Caroline Gidley.

"He's here," she whispered. "Setts is here. We'll come back for Kendrick but we need to find the Fergusons."

Tanner looked conflicted about leaving his partner but nodded. The back of the hall, where she knew Ty Ferguson's study was located, no longer existed. She could see clear into the backyard. That was obviously where the explosion had originated.

Where there had once been a back wall, there was now only a gaping hole surrounded by flames that quickly danced toward her. The entire study was already consumed and the fire was creeping forward along the hallway walls. Another, smaller explosion made her stumble and almost fall to the floor.

"We have to move fast," she said. "This whole house is going to be one big inferno in minutes."

She pointed for Tanner to look in one of the three bedrooms while she took another. It turned out to be the master, which she moved through quickly. It was empty. She checked the bathroom, where the plastic shower curtain seemed to be melting. There was no one inside. When she stepped back into the hall, Tanner was waiting for her.

"The boy's room is empty," he said in a hushed voice.

They both looked at the one remaining bedroom. The door was slightly ajar. Jessie counted down from three and pushed it open.

Tanner stepped in with gun in hand. She quickly followed. Though it was dark, she could tell it was the little girl's room. It looked empty too. Then they heard a soft voice from the closet.

The sliding door opened to reveal Ty Ferguson, holding his three-year-old daughter in his arms. His five-year-old son was next to him, clutching his waist.

Jessie moved toward them as Tanner covered her.

"Where's Brenda?" she asked quietly.

"I don't know," he said in a panicky whisper. "We ran up the stairs together. I grabbed Coy. When I came back into the hall, Officer Kendrick was on the ground and Brenda was gone. I hurried in here, grabbed Cady, and we've been hiding in the closet ever since. I wanted to look for her but couldn't risk leaving the kids alone."

"You made the right decision," Jessie assured him. "We're getting you all out now and we'll find Brenda."

"Is it the guy?" Ty asked.

Jessie nodded. Before she could say anything, a shadow appeared in the doorway. She spun in that direction, aiming her gun. She had just heard Tanner's safety click off when she saw who it was.

"Hold your fire," she ordered. "She's with us."

It was Kat. She was holding a gun in one hand and a flashlight in the other. Blood dripped down the right side of her face from the gash on her forehead.

"Setts is here," Jessie said without introduction. "And Brenda Ferguson is missing. We need to get these kids out and then find her."

Kat nodded. Her face was set in grim determination. Jessie imagined this was how she had looked on the battlefields of Afghanistan.

"You take lead," she barked at Tanner. "Then the family. I'll be behind them, carrying the other officer out. Jessie, you take the rear and cover us all from the back. Got it?"

Everyone nodded, even little Coy and Cady.

"Let's move out," Kat ordered. "The fire is spreading fast."

Tanner led the way down the stairs. Ty was next, with Cady hugging him tight, her face buried in his chest. Coy was beside him, holding his hand. Kat holstered her gun and swooped up Officer Kendrick like he was a sack of potatoes. She did her best to position him so that the side with the knife wounds wasn't being squeezed. Jessie came last, swiveling back and forth as she followed, flinching at every flame-heightened, flickering shadow as she desperately wiped the sweat away from her eyes

When they got to the bottom of the stairs, she looked back up. The entire second floor was now consumed in flames. The fire was already licking at the top of the banister. Paint peeled off the stairwell walls. She turned back around to see that the others were already to the front door. She rushed to catch up.

"Go all the way out to the street," Kat yelled as they stepped over the threshold and out into the comparatively clear night air.

Jessie had just stepped onto the lawn when she had a flash of recognition. The Fergusons hadn't left this house in weeks. That meant that whatever explosive had been used to blow up Ty's study had been planted a long time ago.

And if Setts had planned that far in advance, he'd almost certainly done other things to the house. He would have probably set up cameras and listening devices so he could enjoy hearing Brenda's suffering in the weeks following her escape. That meant he would have known about all the security procedures the family had added after she "escaped," including the panic room.

"Kat," she called out to her friend, who was doing her best to haul the 200-pound police officer across the expansive front lawn to the street.

"What?" Kat asked, glancing back over her shoulder but not turning around.

"I know where Setts is," she said. "I know where he took Brenda Ferguson."

"Where?"

"To their panic room," she told her. "I'm sure of it. The explosion was just a distraction so he could grab her."

"Okay," Kat said. "Let's get these people to safety and then you can show me where the room is."

Jessie looked back at the house. The entire second floor was alight. Much of the first floor was too. Soon she wouldn't be able to get through the front door. She could hear sirens in the distance but knew the fire trucks would arrive too late to help.

"There isn't time," she yelled back. "I'm going back in."

CHAPTER THIRTY EIGHT

She couldn't see a thing.

For the first few seconds after returning to the house, everything was acrid blackness. Then Jessie dropped to her knees and found that lower to the ground, she could see a bit better.

She crawled down the hallway in the direction of the bookcase that served as the hidden door to the panic room. It was hard to be sure where she was and she thought she might have gone too far when her shoulder slammed into the edge of the bookcase.

Taking a moment to gather herself, she tried to ignore the stifling heat and sucked in three quick breaths of stinging, ashen air. Then she held her breath and stood up, fumbling around in search of the red book that would open the door. She was just starting to feel the burn on her lungs when she found it. She pulled it and stepped back as it snapped forward and back, all the while pointing her gun at the space beyond the retracting bookshelf.

The fluorescent light was already on. In front of her was Brenda Ferguson. She was seated in one of the room's two chairs. Her hands were tied behind her back. Next to her, with a knife in his right hand, was Joseph Setts. The blade was about six inches long and gleamed when the light above flickered. Setts stared at Jessie with a mix of surprise and amusement.

"I know you," he said, sounding unexpectedly casual, considering the situation. "You're the racist profiler lady I saw on the news. You should be ashamed of yourself."

As stunned as she was, Jessie preferred this to the alternative. At least Setts was engaging with her rather than plunging the knife into Brenda. She decided to respond in kind.

"You're calling me out?" Jessie said disbelievingly. "The guy who kidnaps and kills innocent women for kicks?"

Setts looked much as he had in his law firm photo, with the same brown hair and eyes. But now the hair was sweaty and plastered to his forehead. His eyes had a wild, frenzied look. He was of average size, maybe slightly shorter than Jessie with only about twenty pounds on her. In an unarmed, close combat situation, she thought she could hold her own. But the man was only about two feet from Brenda and he was *not* unarmed.

"Innocent?" he repeated, disgusted. "These women aren't innocent. They've all committed the sin of faithlessness. They're as guilty as you say I am."

Jessie tried to ignore the flames in the hallway behind her, lapping at her back and making her skin swelter. She needed to keep the man's attention focused on anything other than killing Brenda, at least until she could think of a plan. She knew she had to come up with one quick, as the smoke from the hall was fast permeating the panic room too.

"Are they really as guilty as you?" she asked, trying to keep the urgency out of her voice. "Because it seems like we're talking apples and watermelons here."

Setts re-gripped the knife and almost spat as he spoke.

"I'm not surprised that you would mock my mission. You're probably a betrayer too. You all are."

Though her heart was pounding, Jessie forced herself to project calm.

"Actually," she told him, "I was betrayed. My husband cheated on me with a cheap, dime-store slut."

She saw his eyes widen in astonishment. Before she could say anything else, there was a loud crash. She glanced over her shoulder to see that a large section of the second floor had collapsed in the hall behind her. Sparks flew into the panic room along with waves of smoke.

"It looks like we're not getting out that way," she said jadedly. "If you don't mind, I'm just going to close the bookshelf door before we roast. It would be a shame if we all burned to death before we cleared this mess up."

She stepped over to the wall and pushed the button Brenda had used the first time Jessie visited the house. The bookshelf door swung closed, creating a barrier from the hallway but trapping in the enormous cloud of dark smoke. She could barely see Setts or Brenda now. She also observed that even with the door closed, a thin carpet of smoke was snaking in underneath the bookshelf. Soon the entire room would be consumed by it. She pretended not to notice.

"So you see, betrayal takes lots of forms," she continued. "But I didn't kill my husband. I divorced him. And there are other paths for you too."

"It's too late for that," he replied, coughing as he spoke. "You've seen me now. I have to finish the job I started. If I don't take out all four sinners, I've failed in my mission and I'm not the True Avenger."

Jessie set aside the absurd title he'd given himself to focus on the sentence prior to that.

"What do you mean, all four?' she asked. "If you're here, then you can't get to Jayne Castillo."

Setts smiled cruelly at her.

"You think this is the only bomb I set? Don't insult me. I had to have an insurance policy in case I didn't get out of here. Looks like it was a smart move, don't you think?"

Only then did Jessie comprehend that Jayne and her husband, along with the cops guarding them, were also in immediate danger. And if Ryan decided to check up on them…she refused to consider the thought. Instead she refocused on the threat in front of her.

The smoke was now so thick that the overhead light could barely penetrate it. If she waited any longer, she wouldn't even be able to see if the man attacked Brenda, much less do anything about it.

I need to shake things up somehow.

"Here's what I think…" she started but he cut her off.

"Enough talk. Like you said, it would be a shame to burn up before getting the job done."

Jessie realized she was out of time. She had to act now.

"That's not exactly what I said, Joseph."

Even in the murky gloom of the room, she saw his head pop up at that last word. His eyes were wide with shock. Just then, she saw movement to his left. Brenda shoved him. Somehow she must have extricated herself from her bindings. Setts stumbled backward for a moment before regrouping and lunging toward her.

Jessie fired, hoping she was at least close to her target. She heard a thud and raced across the room to find both Setts and Brenda on the ground.

Oh no! What have I done?

But a second later, Brenda looked up and Jessie realized she hadn't been hit, but had simply tumbled off her chair. Setts however, remained still. She saw blood leaking onto the floor from some unseen wound on his body.

"Hurry," Jessie said, pulling the woman to her feet.

"There's nowhere to go," Brenda exclaimed plaintively.

"Sure there is," Jessie replied pointing to the Nirvana poster on the wall.

Just then, there was aloud groan. Jessie looked over at Joseph Setts but he wasn't moving. It hadn't come from him. There was a second groan and she looked up to see the roof above them buckling. It looked like it might give out at any moment.

She ripped the poster off the wall, revealing the narrow tunnel behind it. It was lit every few feet by a dull light embedded into the tunnel wall.

"You first," she said to Brenda, just before all the lights cut out.

CHAPTER THIRTY NINE

Jessie kept bumping her head.

Even crawling on her hands and knees, she seemed too tall for the tunnel and kept banging the top of her head on the metal walls. Because it was completely dark, she had no way of gauging how high it was or how far they had to go. In addition, she feared that once the roof in the panic room collapsed, it would send a fireball after them down the tunnel, which would suddenly become a human-sized oven.

As she scurried along the tube, she felt something hard bang against the side of the metal wall and realized what it was.

"Hold on, Brenda," she said. "I have a small flashlight in my pocket. I'm going to hand it ahead to you. Reach back."

"Okay," Brenda said.

With the tight quarters, it took more time than Jessie would have liked to get the light out and pass it forward. When Brenda turned it on, Jessie half-regretted the decision. Until that moment, they'd been blind to but ignorant of their surroundings.

Now they saw just how narrow the tunnel was and just how far they still had to go to get to the ladder in the distance. Jessie estimated it to be at least another forty feet. And she noticed something else she'd somehow blocked out. The tunnel was fast filling up with the smoke from the panic room that had nowhere else to go.

She felt herself start to hyperventilate. Though she'd been in many tough situations, something about being burned alive in a thin metal tube evoked an extra level of dread. She did her best to force the feeling down, trying to focus only on Brenda's bare feet moving slowly forward.

They were about twenty feet from the end of the tunnel when she heard it. Behind here, there was a noise that sounded like a combination of grunting and scraping. Though she couldn't look back, she didn't need to. There was only one explanation. Joseph Setts was in the tunnel.

He must have regained consciousness and managed to climb in. Jessie didn't know where she'd shot him, but based on the pace of his crawling, it sounded like he wasn't that badly injured.

Just in front of her, Brenda suddenly stopped.

"What is it?" Jessie asked in a hushed voice.

"He's back there, isn't he?" Her voice quivered with fear.

"I think so," Jessie said. "But it doesn't change anything. We have to keep moving."

"I can't."

"What do you mean?" Jessie demanded. "Just keep doing what you've been doing. You were fine."

"I can't," Brenda whimpered. "My body won't move."

The scraping and groaning behind them was getting closer, fast. Jessie felt the sudden urge to scream at the woman. But she stifled it, partly because she knew it wouldn't help but also because, with all the smoke, she'd probably just end up coughing.

"Brenda," she said, her voice calmer and firmer than she expected. "You *can* do this. You escaped from this man once before, when you were all alone. You're not alone now. I'm with you. And your family is at the top of that ladder, along with a bunch of cops who will protect you. You just have to get to them. Your children need you, Brenda. You've been so strong. Stay strong for them."

"How?" Brenda begged.

"Just move your right arm and leg forward and then do the same with your left."

Brenda did it.

"Good," Jessie said encouragingly. "Not do the same thing again. And again. Keep it up. We're getting close. Almost there."

The truth was that Brenda was moving unfathomably slow. But Jessie feared anything but positive reinforcement would make her freeze up again. She pretended not to hear the grunts from Setts, who had used their lull to make up lots of distance. He was close now. She thought she could smell him, though that seemed impossible with her nose full of smoke and ash and her own seared flesh.

And then they were there. Brenda was no longer crouched in front of her but was upright, climbing up the short ladder. Jessie could only see her from the waist down and for now she was stuck waiting. She couldn't go any further forward until Brenda was up the ladder. She heard the woman bang on what sounded like a metal hatch.

"Let us out," she screamed.

"Brenda," Jessie called out, ignoring the mumbling, incomprehensible voice that sounded less than a dozen feet behind her. "There has to be a way to open the hatch from the inside. Is there a button or a lever?"

After a second of unresponsiveness, Brenda answered.

"There's a release lever," she shouted. "I'm pulling it now."

A moment later there was a loud click, followed by a whoosh as a pressure seal was released. Suddenly Jessie heard all kinds of noise above her—sirens, voices, and a loud crackling that she suspected was the burning house.

"It's open," Brenda called down to her. "I'm climbing out."

"Please hurry!"

And then the legs were gone. The ladder steps were unoccupied. She scooted forward and had just let go of her gun and grabbed the metal ladder rail when she felt a hand grip her ankle. Before she knew what was happening, she was being yanked backward into the tunnel.

Only her hands clinging to the ladder prevented him from pulling her all the way back to him. A twisted, hoarse voice growled one word at her.

"Reckoning."

Suddenly she felt a searing pain in her left calf. She knew immediately that he'd stabbed her with his knife. The pain sent a shot of adrenaline through her exhausted body. She re-gripped the ladder rail and jerked herself forward.

The force of her action pulled her all the way into the small opening at the base of ladder. She heard her gun tumble somewhere nearby but couldn't guess where. Rolling onto her back, she saw that Setts was right behind her. He had a large lump on his forehead where he must have collapsed when she shot him. But he seemed oblivious. In a matter of seconds, he would be out of the tunnel and on her.

She glanced up the ladder. Beyond the open hatch she could see the night sky. Brenda was repeatedly screaming the words "over here." But no one would make it to them before Setts was on her. She'd have to do this herself.

Bracing her left leg on the ground, the one with the knife jutting out of the back of it, she reared back with her right leg and kicked forward. The bottom of her foot made solid contact with Setts's face, slamming squarely into his nose. The move seemed to stun the man as much as injure him as he lost his balance and plopped hard onto the bottom of the metal tunnel.

Jessie didn't wait to see what he'd do next. Grabbing the highest ladder rail she could reach, she heaved herself to an upright position and turned around to start climbing. For a fraction of a second, she considered reaching down for her gun but decided it wasn't worth it.

She stepped up with her right leg. But when she pushed off with her left, the agony that shot through her calf made her foot slip off the rail. She started to lose her balance and felt herself dropping back down. But she'd only fallen a few inches when she felt a hand firmly grasp her left forearm and hold her steady. She looked up to see Kat right above her.

"I won't let go," her friend told her.

Before Jessie knew what was happening, she was being hauled upward, her feet completely leaving the ladder. A moment later she was lying on her stomach on the Fergusons' front lawn. She'd barely had time to catch her breath when she heard a plaintive voice call out from below.

"Help!"

She pushed off the ground, scrambled over to the hatch door, and looked down. Joseph Setts was at the bottom of the ladder. Blood poured from what was clearly a broken nose. She could see that his pants were also covered in blood that seemed to be coming from his right thigh, where she assumed she'd shot him before.

"I can't get up," he pleaded. "Help me please."

"Leave him," she heard Kat say from beside her.

Jessie looked over at her friend, who stared back at her with cold conviction. Brenda lay on the ground beside her, too wiped out to even sit up. Behind her, Officer Tanner was running over in their direction.

"Do we really need this guy out in the world?" Kat continued. "Even if he's sent away for life, these women will always be afraid he might get out. Just leave him, Jessie. Close the damn hatch before that cop comes over. Let him boil down there."

Jessie was tempted. But before she could act on it, there was another massive explosion, twice as large as the first one. It knocked her to the ground hard. When she looked up, she saw that the entire Ferguson home had collapsed onto itself. It only took a second for her to process what that meant.

She leapt back toward the hatch.

"Give me your hand," she shouted down to Setts. "There's going to be a massive fireball headed down that tunnel any second."

Setts reached up and grasped her wrist and she clamped down on his left forearm and tugged. As she pulled, she saw that he was smiling. Something was wrong. It took her a moment to discern what it was. He was hiding his right hand behind his back.

But if the knife was in her leg, what could he be holding? Then it hit her. He had her gun.

CHAPTER FORTY

Everything happened at once. Joseph Setts pulled his hand from behind his back to reveal her own weapon in it. As he raised it in her direction, she saw the tunnel behind him start to glow orange. The fireball was coming. She looked Setts in the eye and, as she released her grip on his forearm, saw the madness there.

Even as he lost his grip on her wrist and fell backward, his expression didn't change. He still looked at her with crazed determination. He was just hitting the floor when Jessie felt her whole body torn back from the mouth of the hatch.

As she hit the ground, flames consumed the spot where she'd just been, shooting fifteen feet into the air. She thought she could hear screams from inside the hatch below but couldn't be sure. After about ten seconds, the flames subsided and were replaced by thick smoke, which churned out of the hatch without end. She also smelled something: charred flesh.

Jessie glanced around. Next to her on the ground were Kat and Officer Tanner, who had obviously both yanked her away from certain death. A short distance away, Brenda was locked in a group embrace with her husband and kids.

Fire trucks were on the scene and were just pulling their hoses across the lawn, though there seemed little point now. Two ambulances were parked nearby. Multiple squad cars were pulling up. The sight of them jogged Jessie's memory and she pulled out her phone, dialing Ryan's number. He picked up right away.

"Are you all right?" he asked.

"Where are you?" she demanded.

"I'm on my way to you," he said, surprised by the question. "Are you okay, Jessie?"

"I will be but you need to call the officers guarding Jayne Castillo right now. Setts told me he set a bomb at her place. I think it's on a timer. They all need to get out of there right away."

"I'll call now," he said, hanging up before she could say another word.

She slid her phone back into her pocket and sighed deeply. She wanted to lie down but wasn't sure she had the energy.

"Jessie," Kat said. "Hold still okay?"

"Why?"

"Because you've got a knife in your leg," she replied. "It's bleeding pretty badly."

Jessie noticed that Officer Tanner had run over to an EMT from one of the ambulances and was pointing in her direction. Just beyond that, she saw Officer Kendrick on a stretcher in the back of the second ambulance.

"Is Kendrick okay?" she asked.

"They stabilized him," Kat said. "They sounded optimistic. I think he'll recover. Let's focus on you."

"I think I need to lie down," Jessie said, suddenly feeling slightly faint.

Kat grimaced.

"I'm not sure that's a great idea. You've got some ugly burns on your back. And I think we both suffered concussions when we were in the car for that first explosion. You should probably try to stay conscious."

"Now that you mention it," Jessie said, "my back really does sting. And my leg is throbbing. And my head hurts."

"I'm not surprised," Kat said soothingly. "But the EMTs are on their way over. They'll take care of all that and give you something for the pain."

Jessie smiled up at her friend for a second before a better look at her head wound made her frown.

"Have them look at your forehead too," she insisted. "It looks like you might have glass in there."

"Don't worry about me," Kat said. "It's just another scar to add to the list."

Jessie wanted to tell her not to be so blasé but couldn't seem to find the words. She noticed that a sudden clamminess had overtaken pain as her primary sensation. And then her vision started to fade in and out. The last thing she remembered was falling forward as two hands reached out for her.

*

Jessie saw a white light in the distance.

She had to blink a few times to realize it was the light coming in from her hospital room window. She lay there quietly for several minutes in the otherwise darkened room, trying to do a self-evaluation.

She knew she must be on some quality pain medication because the sting in her back and the throbbing in her leg were both dull. She glanced over to the tray beside her bed and saw a cup with a straw. She tried to reach out for it but her arm felt weak and wobbly. She was about to push the call button when the door opened and someone in scrubs backed in pulling a cart.

Despite the medication and her weakened state, she felt a surge of anxiety. She couldn't see the person's face but it was clearly a male with thick black hair. She slammed down on hard on the call button with her closed fist just as he turned around.

But it wasn't Joseph Setts. The man was much younger and Latino. He smiled gently at her.

"Looks like we had perfect timing," he said mildly. "You called just as I was bringing you lunch. I'm Daniel, your nurse. I'll let the doctor know you're awake. Do you need some help with that water?'

Jessie nodded, unable to speak yet. Daniel raised her bed a bit and propped an extra pillow behind her neck so she could sit upright. He held out the cup for her but when she fumbled with it, he simply moved the straw to her lips. She was sucking down water when the doctor came in.

"Hi, Ms. Hunt," he said. "I'm Dr. Bright. Your friends and co-workers are anxious to see you but I've asked them to wait outside for a moment so I can let you know where you stand privately. Do you think you're up for that?"

Jessie unattached her lips from the straw and managed to give him a throaty "yes."

"Good. So the very short version is you're going to be okay. The slightly longer version is that you suffered a number of injuries. You have several second-degree burns on your back and the back of your legs. No grafting is required but you'll be going through a lot of ointments and dressings over the next few weeks."

"Leg?" Jessie managed to croak.

"Ah yes. You were lucky when it comes to your calf. The knife didn't penetrate to its full six inches and it missed any major arteries. We stitched you up and with a little physical therapy, the muscle should recover nicely. Still, you're going to be sore for a while as a result of that and the burns so we've prescribed some strong medication. You should remain housebound as much as possible because your level of alertness may be a little dulled. For those reasons, you'll be out of commission for a couple of weeks, first here at the hospital for a few days, then at home. After that, if you're feeling up to it, you can work—desk duty only—for a couple more weeks. Then, we'll reevaluate. If you feel okay, a full return might be possible at that point. I've told your captain all this so please don't try to accelerate the process."

Jessie nodded, deciding there was no point in arguing when she'd only been conscious for a few minutes. Dr. Bright continued.

"You also have a mild concussion which may cause some lingering headaches, though nothing as dramatic as your friend outside itching to see you."

"How bad is she?" she asked.

"I can't get into details on another patient. But as her friend, you might want to keep an eye on her. She's quite stubborn and insists she's fine. But sometimes we're not the best judge of how we're doing."

Jessie nodded in understanding.

"Can I see them now?" she asked.

"Yes. Just please keep the visit as short as you can. I understand there's a lot of catching up to do but you need your rest."

He motioned for them to enter and Ryan, Kat, and Captain Decker all streamed in as Dr. Bright and Daniel stepped out. Kat had a bandage wrapped around her head. She saw Jessie's eyes grow wide and immediately beat her to the question.

"Don't worry. I've had far worse."

Jessie decided not to press the matter for now.

"Where's Hannah?" she asked, concerned.

"She's outside with Dr. Lemmon and Garland," Ryan said. "We asked her to wait until we could update you. We figured you'd be itching to get caught up."

"You figured right," Jessie said.

"First, how are *you* doing?" he asked.

"I'll be doing a lot better once you catch me up, Hernandez," she said impatiently.

"Okay," he replied. "Good to know you're feeling better. What do you want to know first?"

"Is Jayne Castillo okay?"

"Yes. We got her and her husband out right away. The bomb squad came and found a device. It had seven minutes left on the timer when they disabled it."

Jessie breathed a sigh of relief.

"What about Setts?" she asked.

"He's dead," Kat said, not unhappily. "Burned to a crisp. He was still clutching your gun when they found him. You may want to put in for a new one."

"We'll take care of that when the time is right," Decker promised. "Right now you should take it easy."

"How long have I already been in here taking it easy?" Jessie asked.

"Just since last night," Decker said. "You've been here about twelve hours."

A rush of awareness came over Jessie.

"I know who's been trying to destroy my life," she said suddenly. "You have to reach out to Dolan right away and tell him Kyle did it."

Decker gave her an odd look she didn't understand.

"You're saying that your ex-husband, Kyle Voss, has been behind all the recent incidents?"

"Yes. I figured it out last night just before the explosion. Kat and I were able to listen to the recording of the anonymous call to DPSS. The caller said he heard me tell Hannah to 'buck up.' The line sounded familiar. I couldn't place it at first but later I remembered that when I was little, before my mom died, she would always say 'buck up or you'll muck it up.' The only person I ever told that to was Kyle."

Decker exchanged troubled looks with both Ryan and Kat. Sensing they didn't believe her, she pressed on.

"That's not all. Camille from tech was able to back trace the phone used to make the call. It was stolen from a shipment that originated in Monterrey, Mexico. She determined that my social media was hacked from an IP address that also originated in Monterrey. The gang that Kyle was hooked up with in prison is associated with the Monzon drug cartel, which is headquartered in Monterrey. You can't think all that's a coincidence."

"We don't," Ryan assured her.

"Then why the surprised looks all around?"

"We're not surprised, "Kat said delicately. "It's just that we've got some bad news for you."

"What?"

They all looked at each other apprehensively. Captain Decker finally answered.

"Kyle Voss was released from prison about an hour ago."

CHAPTER FORTY ONE

Jessie's head was swimming.

The idea that the man who'd tried to murder her, the husband she'd slept next to for years, unaware that he was a sociopathic killer-in-training, was now walking free, made her feel like she was sinking into the mattress. At some point she realized Decker was still talking.

"Agent Dolan called to give us a heads-up before it happened. He was trying to reach you but didn't know you were here."

"Are you sure?" Jessie asked even though she knew it was true.

"Yeah," Ryan said. "It happened just as he predicted. The prosecutor formally confessed to misconduct, specifically withholding evidence. Dolan's sure his family was threatened by the Monzons but he can't prove it. Regardless, the judge threw out the conviction. He was livid, even apologized to Voss on behalf of the court. He wished him all the best and sent him on his merry way."

"He wasn't at all suspicious?" Jessie asked.

"Suspiciously, no," Kat interjected. "Your boy really laid it on thick too. Apparently he was a real altar boy in the courtroom. He said this was a chance for him to turn over a new leaf; to redeem himself. He held a press conference afterwards on the courthouse steps in which he pledged to donate half of his money to various charities supporting innocence projects around the country. The media fawned all over him. He's a full-on cause célèbre now."

"It's not all bad," Decker said. "Dolan told me the FBI is going to be tracking Voss closely. Even if they can't prove the cartel threatened the prosecutor, they know the Monzons did it. And those folks aren't in the habit of just helping out some random guy for no reason. They know your ex-husband was a major player at a wealth management firm before he was imprisoned. They're going to expect him to pay them back somehow, maybe as their latest money launderer."

Jessie sat with that theory for a moment before replying.

"Whatever they want from him, he's way too smart to get caught. He'll know he's being watched like a hawk. He won't make any mistakes, just like he didn't make any when he did all this to me."

"What do you mean?" Kat asked. "We know he did it."

"Yeah. But there's no way to prove it," Jessie reminded her. "He had that anonymous caller say 'buck up' to let me know it was him. But I can't do anything about it. It's not *that* unusual a phrase. Besides, only I, my mom, and he knew anything about it. And as far as the cartel goes, now that the FBI's informant was killed, there's no way to definitively connect Kyle to them."

"There must be footage of them hanging out in the prison yard or something," Kat said.

"I'm sure there is," Jessie agreed. "But that's not enough to convict him of anything. And after what happened with the last prosecutor, the bar is going to be extra high to bring Kyle in for anything. It's too bad that informant couldn't wear a wire. If a judge heard Kyle telling his buddies that he'd like to gut me and bathe in my warm blood, maybe it'd be a different story."

"So he just gets away with it?" Kat asked incredulously.

"For now," Jessie conceded.

"At least we know it wasn't Sergeant Costabile who was messing with you," Ryan said, trying to find the bright side.

"That's true," Captain Decker agreed. "But it's exactly the sort of thing he would do. And now that he's heard how effective it was, how vulnerable you are, I wouldn't put it past him to try to join in the fun."

"You know she's just recovering from a near-death experience," Kat said disapprovingly. "Maybe you don't have to throw every unpleasant tidbit at her all at once."

"It wasn't meant to be unpleasant," Decker replied. "I was going to add that we're now carefully monitoring all his prison communications for that very reason. If he tries anything, we'll be on top of it."

"Thanks, Captain," Jessie said, trying to sound positive, though she didn't really feel it.

"There are some other positive developments," Decker added with uncharacteristic enthusiasm.

"What's that?" Jessie asked, happy for any.

"With what Camille uncovered about the anonymous phone call and the hacked posts, your job should be safe and the DPSS investigation should dry up."

"Are you sure?" Jessie pressed. "I already missed my meeting about Hannah."

"You were unconscious," Kat noted. "I think they'll let it slide this one time."

"I'll start work on both as soon as I leave you here," he promised. "Of course, just because all that's been disproven doesn't mean everyone will believe it. There will still be some people who assume it's a conspiracy to protect you from what they think you've done. But for now at least, those people aren't in charge."

"I'll take whatever good news I can get," Jessie said.

"In that case, I have a little more for you," Kat said. "Your bestie is all better."

"What?" she asked, confused.

"Andy Robinson, your bosom buddy," she prodded. "She woke up a few hours ago."

"How is that good news?" Jessie asked.

"I know you were feeling a little guilty," Kat reminded her. "Like maybe reaching out to her pushed her over the edge. But it sounds like she's going to be okay, at least physically."

"What does that mean?" Jessie asked.

Kat looked over at Decker, who was once again tasked with being the bearer of the bad news.

"My understanding is that when she woke up, the first thing she asked was whether you had gotten her message."

"The hits just keep on coming," Jessie said, shaking her head in disbelief.

"You know what?" Ryan said. "I think you deserve some actual good news."

"I'm afraid to ask," Jessie said.

"I think you'll be okay with this. There's someone waiting outside who really wants to see you. Mind if I let her in?"

Jessie nodded. He walked over to the door and motioned for someone to enter. A second later Hannah popped her head in.

"I think I'll leave you all alone for a bit," Decker said, heading out.

As he left, Hannah stepped inside, a shy smile on her face. She was holding a small tray with aluminum foil over the top.

"Whatcha got there?" Jessie asked.

"I figured you might want something a little better than hospital Jell-O," she said, pulling off the foil to reveal a stack of cranberry orange scones.

"You figured correctly," Jessie said. "I may have to wait to eat them until I can swallow water without my throat burning. But after that, I'm all over these."

Hannah put the tray down, then looked at her sister with slightly wet eyes.

"How are you?" she asked softly.

"Better, now that you're here."

"Can I give you a hug?" Hannah asked tentatively.

"Maybe a kiss on the cheek for now," Jessie suggested. "Everything else kind of aches."

Hannah leaned in and grazed her sister's cheek with her lips, then stepped back, wiping away a tear.

"I wanted to thank you," Jessie said.

"For what?"

"Your paralegal idea," she said. "The guy we were after *was* one. If you hadn't suggested it, we never would have known who he was."

"Glad to help," Hannah said. "You can mail my fee to…you know the address."

"We'll see," Jessie said. "I hear AirPods are popular these days."

Hannah smiled but seemed muted.

"What's wrong?"

"What about the investigation?" Hannah asked. "I know you'll get a pass for the interview today, what with being hospitalized and all, but they're going to make you come in again at some point."

"Maybe not," Jessie said. "I don't want to get your hopes up. But we think we can show the anonymous call was a fake. Captain Decker's working on it."

Hannah smiled more broadly.

"I'm glad," she said. "I kind of like hating living with you."

Jessie leaned over as far as she could and Hannah leaned in to meet her.

"I won't tell anyone," Jessie whispered loudly.

In that moment, she couldn't help but wonder if all her concerns about Hannah lacking an empathy gene were just paranoia. The girl in front of her looked like a damaged but hopeful teenager, not a serial-killer-in-training. And yet, to her dismay, a kernel of doubt lingered.

There was a long silence interrupted by the occasional sniffle. Kat finally broke it.

"I was thinking of seeing what the vending machine had to offer. Anyone in?"

"I'll go," Hannah said, wiping her cheek with the back of her hand.

"I was going to stay another minute," Ryan said. "Then you can get some more rest. Do you mind?"

Jessie shook her head and Kat and Hannah started to file out. Before they left, Kat turned back around.

"Thanks for sticking by me when the chips were down, Jessie," she said, with heartfelt emotion.

"Same to you," Jessie said quietly.

When they were gone, Ryan sat on the edge of the bed.

"Hi," he said.

"Hi back."

"So I was thinking," he began. "You're going to need some extra care and feeding while you recover, right?"

"That's what the doctor told me."

"I thought that maybe, if we lived together, it might make that process a little easier."

Jessie stared at him, speechless.

"To be clear," he said, "that was my quippy, beat-around-the-bush way of asking you to move in with me."

"It was pretty clear," she assured him.

"So what do you think?' he asked, his brow furrowed in nervousness.

"That's a pretty big step, Hernandez. Are you sure you're up for it?"

He gazed into her eyes.

"Well, I love you and want to be with you as much as possible. So yeah, I think I am."

Jessie gazed back at him for a long time without speaking.

"You're kind of leaving me hanging here," he finally said.

"I love you too," she said. "But…"

"Uh-oh."

"But I have two conditions. One, you would need to move in with *me*. I live closer to work and Hannah's already registered at a good school for next year."

"This is so romantic," Ryan cracked.

"And two," Jessie continued, "I'd have to check with Hannah to see if she's cool with it. She's my top priority right now."

"I understand that," he said, "which is why I already asked her if she had a problem with it."

"You did? And what did she say?"

"She said that if we could come to some agreement on AirPods, she was open to it."

"Seriously?" Jessie asked.

"No, not seriously," he answered, smiling. "She said she wants you to be happy and if that does the trick, she's all for it."

Jessie smiled.

"Then I guess that's a yes," she said.

"I guess so," he agreed, leaning in to give her a long, soft kiss.

They were interrupted by Daniel, who came in carrying a large bouquet of flowers.

"Oh," he said, his face turning red. "I'm so sorry. I should have knocked but I was excited to give you these. They just arrived. Should I put them on the dresser?"

"Sure," Jessie said. "Who are they from?"

Daniel looked through the flowers and pulled out a small envelope. He got a delighted smile on his face.

"It says 'To Jessie, from Anonymous.'"

Despite the pain medication Jessie was on, she felt a sudden twinge in her gut. She looked over at Ryan, who wore a concerned expression.

"Can I see it?" she asked seriously.

Daniel brought the card over, confused at the reaction. She opened the envelope and read the note on the card. It was brief.

"Buck up. Be seeing you. Soon."

NOW AVAILABLE!

THE PERFECT NEIGHBOR
(A Jessie Hunt Psychological Suspense Thriller—Book Nine)

"A masterpiece of thriller and mystery. Blake Pierce did a magnificent job developing characters with a psychological side so well described that we feel inside their minds, follow their fears and cheer for their success. Full of twists, this book will keep you awake until the turn of the last page."
--Books and Movie Reviews, Roberto Mattos (re *Once Gone*)

THE PERFECT NEIGHBOR is book #9 in a new psychological suspense series by bestselling author Blake Pierce, which begins with *The Perfect Wife*, a #1 bestseller (and free download) with nearly 500 five-star reviews.

In an exclusive and wealthy neighborhood in Manhattan Beach, a new neighbor moves into a luxury home—only to be found dead soon thereafter. The case brings Jessie into another wealthy beach town, evoking bad memories of her marriage and forcing her to confront her own demons—while trying to unmask the lies of this seemingly perfect town.

Was the murder connected to an exclusive party for the elite?

Or is there an even more nefarious motive at stake?

Making matters worse, Jessie's husband is now out of prison—and a potential threat to her once more.

A fast-paced psychological suspense thriller with unforgettable characters and heart-pounding suspense, THE PERFECT NEIGHBOR is book #9 in a riveting new series that will leave you turning pages late into the night.

Book #10—THE PERFECT DISGUISE—is also available!

Did you know that I've written multiple novels in the mystery genre? If you haven't read all my series, download a series starter!

Blake Pierce

Blake Pierce is the USA Today bestselling author of the RILEY PAGE mystery series, which includes seventeen books. Blake Pierce is also the author of the MACKENZIE WHITE mystery series, comprising fourteen books; of the AVERY BLACK mystery series, comprising six books; of the KERI LOCKE mystery series, comprising five books; of the MAKING OF RILEY PAIGE mystery series, comprising six books; of the KATE WISE mystery series, comprising seven books; of the CHLOE FINE psychological suspense mystery, comprising six books; of the JESSE HUNT psychological suspense thriller series, comprising eight books (and counting); of the AU PAIR psychological suspense thriller series, comprising three books; of the ZOE PRIME mystery series, comprising four books (and counting); of the new ADELE SHARP mystery series; and of the new EUROPEAN VOYAGE cozy mystery series.

An avid reader and lifelong fan of the mystery and thriller genres, Blake loves to hear from you, so please feel free to visit www.blakepierceauthor.com to learn more and stay in touch.

BOOKS BY BLAKE PIERCE

EUROPEAN VOYAGE COZY MYSTERY SERIES
MURDER (AND BAKLAVA) (Book #1)
DEATH (AND APPLE STRUDEL) (Book #2)
CRIME (AND LAGER) (Book #3)

ADELE SHARP MYSTERY SERIES
LEFT TO DIE (Book #1)
LEFT TO RUN (Book #2)
LEFT TO HIDE (Book #3)
LEFT TO KILL (Book #4)
LEFT TO MURDER (Book #5)
LEFT TO ENVY (Book #6)
LEFT TO LAPSE (Book #7)

THE AU PAIR SERIES
ALMOST GONE (Book#1)
ALMOST LOST (Book #2)
ALMOST DEAD (Book #3)

ZOE PRIME MYSTERY SERIES
FACE OF DEATH (Book#1)
FACE OF MURDER (Book #2)
FACE OF FEAR (Book #3)
FACE OF MADNESS (Book #4)
FACE OF FURY (Book #5)
FACE OF DARKNESS (Book #6)

A JESSIE HUNT PSYCHOLOGICAL SUSPENSE SERIES
THE PERFECT WIFE (Book #1)
THE PERFECT BLOCK (Book #2)
THE PERFECT HOUSE (Book #3)
THE PERFECT SMILE (Book #4)
THE PERFECT LIE (Book #5)
THE PERFECT LOOK (Book #6)
THE PERFECT AFFAIR (Book #7)
THE PERFECT ALIBI (Book #8)
THE PERFECT NEIGHBOR (Book #9)

CHLOE FINE PSYCHOLOGICAL SUSPENSE SERIES
NEXT DOOR (Book #1)
A NEIGHBOR'S LIE (Book #2)
CUL DE SAC (Book #3)
SILENT NEIGHBOR (Book #4)
HOMECOMING (Book #5)
TINTED WINDOWS (Book #6)

KATE WISE MYSTERY SERIES
IF SHE KNEW (Book #1)
IF SHE SAW (Book #2)
IF SHE RAN (Book #3)
IF SHE HID (Book #4)
IF SHE FLED (Book #5)
IF SHE FEARED (Book #6)
IF SHE HEARD (Book #7)

THE MAKING OF RILEY PAIGE SERIES
WATCHING (Book #1)
WAITING (Book #2)
LURING (Book #3)
TAKING (Book #4)
STALKING (Book #5)
KILLING (Book #6)

RILEY PAIGE MYSTERY SERIES
ONCE GONE (Book #1)
ONCE TAKEN (Book #2)
ONCE CRAVED (Book #3)
ONCE LURED (Book #4)
ONCE HUNTED (Book #5)
ONCE PINED (Book #6)
ONCE FORSAKEN (Book #7)
ONCE COLD (Book #8)
ONCE STALKED (Book #9)
ONCE LOST (Book #10)
ONCE BURIED (Book #11)
ONCE BOUND (Book #12)
ONCE TRAPPED (Book #13)
ONCE DORMANT (Book #14)

ONCE SHUNNED (Book #15)
ONCE MISSED (Book #16)
ONCE CHOSEN (Book #17)

MACKENZIE WHITE MYSTERY SERIES
BEFORE HE KILLS (Book #1)
BEFORE HE SEES (Book #2)
BEFORE HE COVETS (Book #3)
BEFORE HE TAKES (Book #4)
BEFORE HE NEEDS (Book #5)
BEFORE HE FEELS (Book #6)
BEFORE HE SINS (Book #7)
BEFORE HE HUNTS (Book #8)
BEFORE HE PREYS (Book #9)
BEFORE HE LONGS (Book #10)
BEFORE HE LAPSES (Book #11)
BEFORE HE ENVIES (Book #12)
BEFORE HE STALKS (Book #13)
BEFORE HE HARMS (Book #14)

AVERY BLACK MYSTERY SERIES
CAUSE TO KILL (Book #1)
CAUSE TO RUN (Book #2)
CAUSE TO HIDE (Book #3)
CAUSE TO FEAR (Book #4)
CAUSE TO SAVE (Book #5)
CAUSE TO DREAD (Book #6)

KERI LOCKE MYSTERY SERIES
A TRACE OF DEATH (Book #1)
A TRACE OF MUDER (Book #2)
A TRACE OF VICE (Book #3)
A TRACE OF CRIME (Book #4)
A TRACE OF HOPE (Book #5)

www.ingramcontent.com/pod-product-compliance
Lightning Source LLC
Chambersburg PA
CBHW030618310726
48979CB00003B/768

* 9 7 8 1 0 9 4 3 8 9 9 7 4 *